BLOOD VENGEANCE

(MATT DRAKE #7)

BY

DAVID LEADBEATER

For my family.

Other Books by David Leadbeater:

The Bones of Odin (Matt Drake #1)
The Blood King Conspiracy (Matt Drake #2)
The Gates of Hell (Matt Drake 3)
The Tomb of the Gods (Matt Drake #4)
Brothers in Arms (Matt Drake #5)
Swords of Babylon (Matt Drake #6)

Chosen (The Chosen Few trilogy #1)

The Razor's Edge (Disavowed #1)

Walking with Ghosts (A short story)
A Whispering of Ghosts (A short story)

Connect with David on Twitter - dleadbeater2011
Visit David's NEW website – **davidleadbeater.com**
Follow David's Blog -
http://davidleadbeaternovels.blogspot.co.uk/

All helpful, genuine comments are welcome. I would love to hear from you.

davidleadbeater2011@hotmail.co.uk

BLOOD VENGEANCE

CHAPTER ONE

"They call me depraved and deceitful, the most dangerous man in the world. But I'm just a man. I live and breathe and bleed just like they do. They call me inhuman, but I was born in blood, in battle. What do they expect? I am the Blood King. I am the nightmare made flesh, the terrorist they really should be scared of. And I . . ."

Dmitry Kovalenko stared through the bars of his cell, speaking to the stale air, to the heavy silence that marked the passage of time.

". . . I am coming. Right into your homes."

The message fell on deaf ears. The cells around him were empty, the guards occupied elsewhere. The maximum security prison, a research facility according to the sparse signage scattered around the lonely desert approach, sat baking in the Nevada heat. In the ancient silence of Death Valley there was no one to hear a prisoner scream.

Kovalenko waited. The appointed hour was almost here. Finally. The last few months of incarceration had passed quickly for him, so caught up was he in the formulation of his greatest plan. Countless hours had passed whilst he studied the filthy ceiling, tracking the nightly movements of spiders and other bugs, fine-tuning ideas that he would then run past his new trusted lieutenants, Mordant and Gabriel. They were his now. Loyal to a fault and deadlier than VX gas, in a perverse way Kovalenko was glad to have been incarcerated with them. It was only with their terrible, invaluable help that he would see his violent, outrageous plan brought to fruition.

No good deed goes unpunished. His thoughts turned briefly to other matters, to the smug team that had put him in here and their various key figures. They would all experience the deepest devastation before the coming week was out.

The distant sounds and movements started as they always did when the guards prepared to release a group of prisoners from their cells to get breakfast. The guards worked their routines efficiently and carefully, but, by necessity, the schedule never varied. The Blood King shuffled forward, hampered by ankle chains, holding the gaze of every guard he passed, as he always did, demonstrating the unbending iron will of a man who was prepared to blow up the entire world just to get his way if he had to.

Quickly, the short line of prisoners passed along the cell block and down a ramp. A group of men, the first bunch, were just finishing up. Kovalenko saw Mordant, the big, well-muscled albino, and Gabriel, the powerful, wiry African, among them, and knew the time was at hand.

And, although he had never seen the outside of this prison, he knew exactly what would be happening up there.

It didn't take many capable and determined men to organize the kind of assault designed to throw a previously undisturbed facility into total chaos. Around two dozen soldiers would be operating up top, some choppered in from the surrounding desert, others driving tourist SUVs from nearby Las Vegas by way of Pahrump. They would be pounding the fences, striking what they could reach of the main facility and its communications room. And the guards would react, some leaving the mess hall as orders were barked at them by their superiors . . .

Never realizing that the real attack was about to strike like a hammer blow from within.

Mordant and Gabriel rose fast, emanating such a sense of terror they might have been rampaging demons, and took hold of the nearest guard. These two men were truly frightening, they were ex-Special Forces soldiers from an insanely proficient covert unit, mercenaries from hell, men who got into it for the battle and the bloodshed and never looked back. They could have dispatched the guard in less than a second, but instead took their time, holding him and making him scream so that every guard in the room focused on them.

Weapons swung around.

The sudden sound of gunfire caromed off the walls, lead slugs zinging and crisscrossing paths. Kovalenko didn't flinch. Instead, he watched the guards themselves convulse, targeted by one of their own. The single man he had been able to buy.

Dom Sullivan's face twitched manically as he aimed and fired his weapon. His new friends 'up top' had carefully introduced him to the finest things that wealth and privilege had to offer these past few months after understanding early that an escape could not be properly facilitated without the help of a guard. Now he proved just how far he would go to partake of his nefarious dreams, shattering apart the men he worked with. The ones he couldn't take down—the guards protected by their wall-mounted bulletproof cages—he left for the time being, to be dealt with momentarily.

Kovalenko watched as Sullivan crossed over to a control panel, input a code, and released all the other prisoners. The riot would start down here, the prison to be left under the control of the inmates. It was all just a smoke screen though, every act facilitating and masking the escape of the Blood King.

Mordant was at his side, but Kovalenko didn't acknowledge him at first, he was too interested in watching the guards hidden behind their cages get their just desserts. Never again would they stare hatefully into his eyes. Some of the inmates used a mixture of detergent and chemicals found in a key-coded cleaning cupboard, which Sullivan had unlocked, to start a small localized fire underneath the cages. The Blood King settled back to watch. It would take some time, but the guards would either have to come out to face the prisoners or die of smoke inhalation if they weren't rescued. Kovalenko saw every one of them scream into their radio headsets.

It reminded him of Mordant's presence. "Time to go?"

Mordant's deep voice was emotionless. "It's now or never."

"Lead the way."

Kovalenko followed the bald albino across the mess hall and into a small square unadorned room, one of many on the lower floor of this facility. Behind a gray metal door at one end stood the familiar oblong glass panel signifying a lift shaft entrance.

Kovalenko frowned. "Is this right?"

Gabriel spoke from behind, guttural tones practically making the air cringe around him. "It's smoke and mirrors. Dey'll see you on camera." The African loped forward like a puma chasing a gazelle, pressed a button to open the doors, and deposited a churning bowl of liquid inside. "Confusion is our friend."

"The battle up top should be raging by now." Mordant swung Kovalenko toward another door. "Let's go."

His voice was intentionally loud, signaling all those who had been chosen to escape. Sullivan joined them, along with half a dozen inmates who had agreed to offer themselves as cover just for the chance of breaking free. It was almost certainly the only chance they would ever get.

Mordant waited for Sullivan to input the code, then threw open the door and raced up the concrete steps. In addition to the code, two guards' thumbprints would be needed to exit at the top level, so Gabriel had thoughtfully brought along the severed appendage of one of Sullivan's colleagues. The stream of men leaped upward two steps at a time, heads down, expecting no resistance and getting none. Bare peeling walls passed them by. The dizzying turnaround at every mini-level made Kovalenko feel light-headed by the time they reached the final platform.

Before them stood the exit door.

Sullivan immediately stepped forward, holding his weapon low, and input the code, finishing by pressing his thumb to the small scanner lock. Gabriel followed suit and every man held their breath and then sighed as the little security device flashed red.

"Can't have initiated lockdown yet," Mordant said confidently. "It takes warden approval and *he's* back home, all in pieces. These clowns are still sittin' with their thumbs up their asses, waiting for him to get in. Try it again."

Sullivan and Gabriel stepped up again, and this time, after a short delay, the lights flashed green. The sound of the door unlocking was more soothing to Kovalenko's ears than the trickle of Southern Cross vodka into a frozen shot glass.

Something else he would be enjoying come evening.

Mordant stepped cautiously out into the corridor beyond, a steel-walled rat run with no doors, no windows and another security scanner at its far end. Hopefully by now the men downstairs were taking out the security cameras—they had been left with half a dozen rifles, not to mention tasers and other more makeshift weapons. Kovalenko thought it would be interesting to monitor the evolving situation below, to see who came out on top, who failed, who lived and died and who bled the most, but this time his own plans were far more appealing.

Maybe another time, another place.

Sullivan stepped up and shot out the caged CCTV camera. Kovalenko mused on the fact that the success of this mission would be subject to more than one fortunate situation, but it was the only chance he would get, and he had made sure all the best players were on his side. Mordant beckoned Sullivan and Gabriel forward again, skull shining under the bright lights. The dome-shaped head looked unnatural, adding to the man's ferocious appearance. If any man could be said to be born with one foot already in the Devil's door, Mordant the albino was that unfortunate man.

The door clicked open and Mordant pushed his way through. The chaotic scene beyond provided a soothing balm for the Blood King's aggravated mind. Through a set of thick iron bars lay a large open-plan office. Cluttered desks and partly concealed cubicles took up the floor space. To a man, the prisoners fanned out and stared at the long row of windows beyond, seeing daylight for the first time in a long while. A hubbub of cursing, shouting and harsh exclamations imbued into the office a desperate atmosphere. Most of the assembled guards and administrators were assembled in front of the expanse of windows, staring out and shaking their heads. Others were shouting into a phone, gazing at their colleagues as if they might see through them to the tumult beyond. Even from where he stood, Kovalenko could hear the gunfire and see the rising smoke outside the window. Many of the phones rang incessantly, ignored. Gabriel and Sullivan opened the inner door in less time than it took for Mordant to say the words, and it was only then that one of the men saw the escaping prisoners.

His shouts were lost in the bedlam. The only time his fellow colleagues noticed was when his blood sprayed across the windows, soon followed by their own. The glass shattered instantly, showering down to the ground as an encouraging message to the attackers, and a howl of desert wind whipped into the room. Some of the men did manage to get shots off, but their efforts were in vain as both Mordant and Gabriel skipped through the carnage of bodies, desks and chairs to scoop up discarded guns. Both men fell to one knee and took out the last of the guards, a dead-center head shot at a time.

Kovalenko strode toward the bank of windows. Below, he saw a small parking lot bordered by a high fence. The fence would be high-security, but the problem with presenting a secret facility to the world was that it couldn't appear to be heavily guarded. At least on the outside.

Its designers had trusted in the abilities and morals of the men who worked there. But it only took one rotten apple to spoil the barrel.

Part of the fence was leaning inward, the result of a rogue unmanned vehicle with a plank of wood jammed against its accelerator pedal. Two helicopters were waiting outside the prison, painted with the logo and colors of a local Grand Canyon tour operator. Fire splashed up against the high fence time and again as homemade bombs were lobbed at it. Gunfire rattled off the uprights and smashed into the cars standing in the parking lot. Many of the guards must have been staring, bemused, wondering just what the hell the attackers were trying to achieve, maybe even hoping to re-educate their misbegotten asses at length in the near future, when Kovalenko and his men bust out.

Never dreaming it was a mere distraction. 'Smoke and mirrors', as Gabriel had said.

Now they lay in pools of blood, dead.

Mordant headed unerringly toward the facilities entrance, no doubt following a blueprint he had committed to memory. They weren't out of here yet. Gabriel turned as one of their fellow prisoners rifled the guards' lifeless bodies.

"What de fook you doing, man?"

"Cell phones. Cash. Jewelry. We're gonna need it on the outside. Maybe we should take their clothes, too."

Gabriel stepped up to him. “Fookin white ape. Dey jus’ trace you with dat shit. Follow me twin brother o’er dere. He get y’out.”

Mordant grinned back at him. The two men—known inside as The Twins—were equally as good or as bad as each other, matched in every way, never defeated or even close to being challenged, the worst of the worst made doubly strong by their union.

“No dawdling now,” the albino said. “Their response time ain’t too shabby. No army bases around, but both Nellis and Fallon are close. Unless they send a team from Area 51.” He grinned.

“Look out. Dey hav’ dem fooking ray guns.” Gabriel shot back.

“Who *would* respond to a prison break?” Kovalenko was confident Mordant knew his business.

“Locals. Feds. Whoever’s available. SWAT, most likely. But this is one of the notorious US black sites. The confusion and official ass-covering might add hours to their response time.”

“Black sites?”

“An unacknowledged project. Secret prisons, that kind of thing. The mid-US has several.”

Mordant studied the doors, which had been locked from the inside the moment the assault began. To his right stood a sturdy functional desk bearing a computer screen. With a single bound he cleared the desk and found the hidden keypad that controlled the doors. He glared at Sullivan.

“Code.”

“One, one, nine, four, one. But it could be on lockdown protocol.”

“Ya tink?” Gabriel pushed him aside and aimed a rifle at the locking mechanism. “Try it, bro.”

Mordant input the code. Machinery clicked, but nothing happened. The albino rose to his feet. “Override time.”

Gabriel opened fire, destroying the lock instantly. Both doors sagged outward, held up only by broken hinges. The African pushed the twisted frames and held them open, motioning Kovalenko forward.

“You are free.”

The Blood King stared up and sighed as sunlight struck his face for the first time in months. It was good to be free. Not since the latter days of his childhood had he felt so constrained, so in need of breaking out and making a statement. It had worked back then—the young Dmitry Kovalenko had seized the day and piled victory upon victory, eventually becoming the world’s most notorious criminal—but he had not killed a man in over twelve weeks. Around the world, his reputation would already be weakening.

So the statement should be big. And for a man born in blood, there could be none bigger than the one he was planning.

The escapees strolled out of the prison entrance and into the parking lot. Mordant spied one of the prison guards hiding in the back of his car and laughed. “Looks like someone was late for work.”

Gabriel brayed. “De chance for some sport.”

“We have no time,” Mordant said reluctantly. “Hey, Sullivan.” He turned to their pet guard. “Go light your friend up, and make sure he knows we’ve left his prison in the hands of the inmates.” His white face showed no expression. “No comms. Just anarchy. I almost wish I was there to play king of the hill.”

They strode toward the waiting choppers, hearing nothing above the constant clatter of the rotor blades. Kovalenko scanned the skies but saw only the bright desert glare. "Today," he said. "Is a good day. The start of something special."

"All's ready to go in DC, and the flight's prepped," Mordant told him as they negotiated the busted fence. "What about the other matter?"

"Yes." Kovalenko flashed the grin of a predator assured of his primary kill of the day. "First things first. Restart the Blood Vendetta. Drake and his friends and family will know no respite, no happiness, and no safety from this moment until the day I die."

CHAPTER TWO

Ben Blake slammed the rear door of the three-year-old Ford Transit and stretched his aching back. Being the lead singer in a band did have its advantages, but sitting on a cushion with your back up against the van's ribbed steel wall, jarred by every bump and pothole, crowded by the band's haphazardly stowed gear, whilst the carefree driver took ninety minutes to negotiate his way back from an unwilling Manchester crowd was not one of them. Still, his new girl, Stacey, was by his side and full of smiles. One look at those big doe eyes and all his troubles melted away.

"Laters."

He slapped the side door twice and watched the vehicle drive away. None of the guys waved. It wasn't that kind of night. Stacey snuggled in.

"C'mon, let's get upstairs."

Ben headed for the communal door that led, via a dusty old set of barely carpeted stairs, to their second floor flat. He checked his watch and couldn't believe it was after 0200 hours. The street was quiet, despite its close vicinity to the center of York. At this time of night most but the hardiest of party animals would either be at home or whiling the time away inside one of the city's nightclubs or new entertainment venues such as Popworld.

"Lie in tomorrow," he muttered.

"What else is there to do on a Saturday morning?"

Ben fished out his key. "Bugger all, I'm sure."

He paused as his mobile phone sang a little text-message tune. "Who the—"

"Not your dad is it?" Stacey's tone was only mildly mocking. She knew how close Ben was to his family. She was lucky enough to have a tight-knit family of her own.

"No. It's bloody Karin. Over in the States. Says she's okay and that they saved the world again four days ago."

"She texted you that?" Stacey leaned over his shoulder.

Ben tapped out a quick reply. "It's probably true."

"Do you miss them all?"

"Sometimes." Ben pocketed the phone and played with the loose lock. "Getting into this place is a work of art," he grumbled. "We'll have to ask Mike to—"

"Here," Stacey grabbed his arm. "Step aside, geek. Let me help. Us district nurses can do more than save lives you know."

Ben playfully fought her off, silently reflecting that this was the kind of tussle he could handle. The experiences of the 'Odin thing', and subsequent adventures had scarred him deeply, leaving him more of a timid, amicable guy than he had been before, much to his surprise. But there was no doubt getting out had been the right move. At least once every night he woke up soaked in sweat, the tatters of a nightmare still entangled with his brain, the blood of a dying soldier stained into and soaking right through the palms of his hands.

Stacey had questioned it at first, but he had mumbled something about a childhood trauma and she hadn't said anything since. He didn't know if she believed him, but didn't care. Some things he would never share. And Stacey was too nice a girl to bring it up again.

Ben heard the lock click. Stacey stepped back. He turned to her with a smile on his face. "There, see—"

The man standing behind her materialized out of nowhere. He was big, with a crew cut and a scar stretching all the way across his forehead that almost matched his mouth, which was grinning from ear to ear.

"The Blood King sends his regards," the man growled.

Stacey jerked, her eyes wide, and blood flew from her wide-open mouth. The blade of a knife burst through her chest. Ben stared, staggered, and fell to his knees. Drops of red spattered his face.

"Wha—"

The scarred man threw Stacey's body to the ground and stepped across her. The red pool was already flowing toward him. He felt the hair on his head pulled hard and looked up into the cold eyes of a killer.

"Don't worry, sissy boy, you'll be meeting your parents soon enough. They're next."

The knife came down fast, but then suddenly clattered away as a shot rang out. A curse split the night's odd silence. Ben felt his head released as a creeping coldness started to soak through the knees of his jeans.

Stacey?

Something hit the killer head on: another body. The sound of men struggling tore through Ben's malaise as he realized one of those men was trying to save his life. He rose on shaking legs. Stacey's body lay still before him. Beyond that, the killer groaned as a broad-shouldered figure straddled him and began to pound.

"Sam?"

"Ben!"

The shout came from around the corner of the house. Ben whirled to see Jo, another of Drake's old SAS pals, beckoning him over. "Hurry."

Ben stared at his girlfriend's dead body. He couldn't just leave her there, sprawled and lonely and broken. He fell to his knees, and it was only the pain of striking the ground that jerked his mind back to what the killer had said.

My parents are next.

Another shot rang out. Ben screamed as a body dropped next to him, almost knocking him over: a second killer. Another knife clattered across the driveway. Then Jo was at his side.

"Need to get outta here, kid."

"He said my parents are next," Ben said as he was pulled away. "What's happening? And why are you here?"

"Your lucky day. We've been around, on and off, for weeks. Never could be sure the vendetta was lifted. You, being the isolated one of the team, were the one to watch."

Ben tried to get his head around it. "You were using me? Us?" His head swiveled inexorably back toward Stacey.

"Don't be a little fool." Jo swung Ben around as two more men approached. Both wore black leather jackets and had an East European hardness to their features. They came at Jo without hesitation. An underhand knife thrust tore through his jacket, but snagged the arm long enough for Jo to break his attacker's windpipe with stiffened fingers. The second man struck a second later. Jo rolled with the blow, coming around and hefting the big man over his shoulders with ease. A shrug, and the knifeman landed neck first.

Sam ran up. "C'mon. Quick."

The two army men led Ben down the darkened street. Lights were blazing in windows up and down the quiet neighborhood. Curtains twitched. Sam pointed out a blue Mercedes A Class.

"In there."

"What about my parents?" Ben knew he sounded like a whiny child, and his thoughts should probably be more centered around his own situation and Stacey's, but his parents meant the world to him.

Sam opened the door wide. "Get in."

As Jo cracked open the back door, two dark figures climbed out of a car opposite, dropping instantly to a firing stance. Jo threw Ben to the pavement and leaned across the Mercedes' roof, gun in hand. Three shots crashed loudly through the night, returned twice by the attackers. The closest of them twisted and screamed before curling into a ball and trying to jam his body underneath his own car for cover. Sam scrambled around the back of the Mercedes as Jo laid down covering fire.

The other car shuddered as its windows smashed and holes appeared in its front wing and engine compartment. Ben imagined the local York residents on their mobiles, calling the police. He crouched by a back tire, protected, eyes again drawn toward the front door of his flat. The darkness huddled there was the dead body of Stacey Fielding. *What am I going to tell her parents?*

At last the firing stopped, and Jo was back, flinging open the door and all but throwing him inside the car. The seats fit snugly around his body, the suddenly operational satnav screen a blinding light. Sam rammed in the key and peeled away from the curb.

Jo laid low in the back, already on the phone, shouting orders at some unfortunate operator. It took a code word and five minutes of cursing, but Jo got his message across in the end.

"Firearms officers and ARVs are on the way to your parents' place in Leeds. ETA five minutes."

"ARVs?" Ben fought to focus.

"Armed Response Vehicles. Each one is equipped with a safe that's armed to the teeth. Those guys don't fuck about, mate. Your folks will be secured in a jiffy."

"Take me there," Ben said, and Sam nodded.

"We're already on the way, mate."

CHAPTER THREE

President Coburn rose to take the podium amidst thunderous applause. Taking a moment to compose and fine-tune the words in his head, he gazed across the faces of the audience. Many of the people out there were friends, acquaintances and staunch supporters he could rely on. A goodly amount were critics, and a select few currently straddled the fence. The Correspondents' Dinner was always an astute affair, it had to be. His speech was riddled with incisive wit and insider jokes that would be the envy of any stand-up comedian, mostly based around current issues and some even poking a bit of gentle fun at the President himself.

Coburn glanced to his right where the First Lady was seated several positions down. Tonight, she positively glowed. Her hair had been styled by the owner of a local popular salon that sported the kind of name Coburn could never get his head around. Her silky sparkling midnight-black gown was the product of another odd name, a loaner for the night. No way in this, or any, economy could they justify spending thousands of dollars on a scrap of material she would only wear once. It wasn't as though they were movie stars.

Coburn put these thoughts away for the night, allowing himself one brief incredulous moment when he thought about how far he had come. From a boy on the streets to an army officer. To hard, harsh battle, then to military rank and beyond—the inner circle. Was it luck, providence, or plan? He still didn't know. Then to the rosewood-clad rooms and the nights and days of the campaign trail. To the Oval Office . . .

Where would it end? Certainly not here at the Hotel Dillion, at the Correspondents' Dinner in the heart of DC.

At last, the applause began to subside. Coburn smiled and gave the audience a once over. "I want to start tonight by thanking everyone here for the outstanding work they do on behalf of our country. And Bob," he looked to the man on his right, "my staff, and the extraordinary First Lady." He continued as more applause broke out, "And in particular the men and women who wear uniform and protect our way of life day after day, wherever they may be."

The ovation swelled, every person in the room adding voice to the acknowledgement.

Coburn studied faces again, letting each man and woman see that he noticed them. "So, time passes. We all get a little grayer, a little larger—" He glanced at Bob slyly to a few guffaws. "My military days . . . they ain't coming back. I may have lost a step and, despite appearances," he lowered his voice, "have even been known to make the odd mistake."

He put a finger to his lips. "Shh. Don't tell anyone."

Fresh laughter rang out, fuelled by the free champagne. "This job can indeed take its toll." He raised his voice. "Just ask the men and women of the White House Press Corps."

Someone choked with laughter in the front row. A few others made unhappy noises. That was the purpose of Coburn's speech tonight. To take a little and give a little back. *The TV stations not so much*, he thought. MSNBC and Fox News were in the firing line tonight. Maybe next year it would be CNN.

"The media highway changes so rapidly these days, don't you think? Former advisors taking the wrong turn—" He referred to a recent scandal. "Every day a new government conspiracy. Ah," he laughed, "They just don't know us at all."

"But we have all seen the darkness." He launched immediately into a fresh tack, buoyed by his own beliefs. "We have touched it. It has blighted all our lives. But in darkness, good can be allowed to shine. And yes, we have all seen it shine. First responders leaping through flames to save those who can't save themselves, civilians rushing into danger to help each other." He paused. "We have all seen the good sparkle in the dark."

A tumultuous applause broke out. Coburn swept the crowd with his eyes. Even the people on the fringes were clapping, the wandering staff stilled, rapt with concentration. Even the presidential aides, usually vying for attention, for recognition, barely moved a muscle.

But there was one select group of men who remained far above the captivations of a presidential speech. These men would never be beguiled. They were the best of the best. The Secret Service knew every inch of this hotel like the backs of their hands. They had memorized every square foot of the twelve floors, the three hundred and thirty nine rooms, the forty one suites all the way down to the kitchens, the basement and the sub-basement underneath with its tunnels, which also existed as a blueprint in every one of the forty shrewd minds that formed the President's protective detail. They had swept for bugs close to the stage and behind it, using a Digital Spectrum Analyser; every one of them was acquainted with the EER – the primary Emergency Escape Route drawn up around the hotel.

Now one of them spoke into his wrist mic, then stepped forward unexpectedly, leaning toward the President's ear. "We need to leave, sir."

Coburn didn't argue. He knew these men and their utter professionalism. With a quick glance at Marie, the First Lady, he ducked his head and fell into line. Under his breath he whispered, "What's going on?"

"Trouble across the street, sir. We aren't taking any chances."

Coburn paused. "With Jonathan? The Secretary of Defense?"

In answer, an agent encircled his waist with an iron-like arm, making him realize he'd slowed down. Several others crowded around him, herding him away from the stage and through a network of passages. Other black-suited men manned entry points and fell in as they passed, calling all-clears and prepared for every single outcome.

Coburn heard the chatter alongside him. "Eagle One is on the way. Prepare for evac." And more, "Report on exterior needed now. Is the route clear?"

"Don't worry, sir," He recognized the voice of Marnich close to his left ear. "We're only two blocks from the White House."

Coburn said nothing. He hadn't even thought about his own safety. His only thoughts were for Jonathan Gates and Marie, his wife. She would be undergoing a similar evac, through another route. Thank God the kids weren't here.

"Maybe you should give me a gun," he finally said. It was a one-liner that regularly passed between Marnich and himself, born of yearnings for his simpler fighting days that would never return. Marnich was one of the agents who truly understood the urge.

"Only when we get you back to the White House, sir."

In other circumstances, Coburn would have laughed. Tonight, he didn't think he would ever laugh again. He slowed as they entered the parking structure. "I want two of you to go over there with the Secretary," he said firmly. "And I want reports. Regularly."

"Sir, that can't—"

"It will happen." Coburn read the lead agent's mind. "And now. Send two of your best men, Jeff. Send them now."

The agent immediately ordered two men away, speaking through his military-grade communications device. The line was unhackable; the GPRS coordinates masked beyond anyone's ability to crack.

"A short hop to the White House," Marnich said as they approached one of three identical black Escalades. The President would choose the vehicle at random before Jeff Franks would order the convoy to form an equally random procession and speed back to the White House. Coburn climbed into the back of one of the cars as Franks spoke constantly through his comms.

"All secure. Eagle One is ready. Once we're clear of the hotel, all personnel back home. Check in."

Every Secret Service agent checked back in the correct order and using the right code words, signaling their understanding that they should all immediately vacate the hotel and head back to the White House as per protocol, and that no one had been compromised. Franks climbed into the car.

"Go."

The Escalade roared. Coburn hung on as the powerful vehicle tore across the empty first subfloor of the hotel's parking garage and hit an up-ramp, passing another check point. Marnich sat to one side of him, Franks to the other. Fleetwood drove with Tyler in the passenger seat.

Safely in the car, Marnich filled him in on the dreadful events of the night. It didn't sound right, didn't seem plausible. Coburn, struggling with the news, tried to peer around Marnich's bulk as they bounded out of the garage and onto the open street, but the man didn't stand on ceremony. He blocked the President's view of the scene across the street, at the same time blocking anyone else's view of him—not that the Escalade didn't have black-out windows and rocket-proof cladding, but the Secret Service could never be too careful.

"God, Jonathan," Coburn whispered.

Marnich checked his watch and glanced over at Franks. "We ready?"

Franks tapped the driver's seat. "Green lights all the way. Hit it."

Coburn peered ahead, gazing at the slightly undulating concrete roadway that led all the way to the great, wide, blockaded expanse of Pennsylvania Avenue bordering the back of the White House, amazed to see every set of stoplights suddenly turn green. The Escalade's driver punched the accelerator, sending the car spurting forward. Coburn fell back, momentum driving him into his seat. The first set of green lights flashed by, marked on both sides by the bland façades of buildings whose windows literally blazed with light, government buildings, shops, restaurants and hotels. The heart of DC would not rest tonight.

The driver let out a loud curse. Coburn forced his body forward, staring amazed as the few remaining sets of stoplights ahead suddenly changed, all hitting red in less than a second. The driver slammed on the brakes as Franks shouted, "Don't stop!"

"How the hell did that happen?" Marnich cried.

Cars popped out across the intersections ahead. The Escalade's driver had no choice but to slow down. Then the growing streams of cars began to swerve and plunge into one another as the stoplight sequences went crazy. Fender benders littered the road. The sound of screeching metal vied with squealing rubber as a nightmare pile up of vehicles began to block the road ahead.

"Shit."

Franks thought fast and hard.

"Sorry, Mr. President, but this is no fucking coincidence."

CHAPTER FOUR

The restaurant was truly unique, and Jonathan Gates' favorite haunt these days. The inner decor was the perfect mix of blond woods, intimate tables and intricately carved ceiling scrolls. Gates certainly did not surprise himself when he chose it as the place to take Sarah Moxley on their first date. It was a comfortable retreat for him, a home from home, an office away from work, only a few minutes from his workplace and the White House itself. Gates had organized more than one power lunch here, partaking of politics and fried green tomatoes, the food good enough to distract even the most resilient of campaigners and lobbyists.

As Sarah Moxley took the seat opposite, he knew there would be no shop talk tonight. Despite her position as a reporter for the Washington Post, she had never once prodded him for information or brought up a story she was working on. It was one of the many good reasons that had brought them to this point.

"You look lovely tonight," Gates said, once his four DoD bodyguards had retreated to a respectful distance.

"I do like the 'no tie' look," Sarah replied. "I take it that means you're 'off duty'?"

Gates poured the wine. "President Coburn is directly across the street, giving a rousing after-dinner speech. What do you think?"

"That you would rather be here." Sarah clinked glasses and tasted the Burgundy. "Wonderful."

Gates signaled the waiter. "Let's take a look at the menu. The Perlau is superb here, by the way."

"With head-on shrimp?" Sarah winced as she read the menu. "Maybe not."

"Well, I'm sure the chef would . . ." Gates made a slicing motion with his knife. "You know."

"Still." Sarah hid provocatively behind her menu. "Black-eyed pea cake for me please."

Gates nodded, feeling a sudden bloom of affection for this woman which he carefully concealed. Despite his position, the US Secretary of Defense was a vulnerable man, even if only on an intimate level. Slow and steady was the right way to go with any potential affair of the heart.

He made a quick decision, one of honesty. "In truth, Sarah, I must say I'm not entirely yours tonight. A situation developed this morning about which they are keeping me fully briefed at all times." He paused. "A group of particularly dangerous inmates took over a prison earlier today and continue to hold the authorities at bay even now."

"Really? It wasn't on the news." Her eyes twinkled.

Gates raised his eyebrows. "And never will be. I mention it only to explain if I start acting . . ." he shrugged, "Odd."

Sarah laughed out loud, then covered her mouth with the back of her hand. "I'll be sure to watch out for that."

The appetizers were served, followed by entrees. The quiet atmospheric buzz of the restaurant and the absorbing company he kept, not to mention the wine, began to put Gates at his ease more than at any time since his wife had died. He enjoyed the mix of clientele, the sight of the passing businessman alongside the idling congressman, the intimate couple. And of course the tourist crowd. Gates found himself posing for more than one passing photo, and not once did any of his guards have to step forward.

"Is there always another crisis?" Sarah asked as she finished off her entree.

Gates nodded, wiping his mouth with a napkin. “Everything is always in crisis,” he said. “The country wouldn’t run right otherwise.”

“I understand,” she said, and Gates knew that she really did. Out of chaos, and out of the sharply challenged minds of men and women, came order.

Another couple stepped in through the front door of the restaurant, letting in a quick gust of cold air. Gates flicked a brief glance their way, more out of habit than curiosity, and didn’t immediately understand the plain fear written across both their faces. The scene held his attention as they entered the dining area.

Sarah frowned at his expression. “What’s wrong?”

“I’m not sure.” Gates half-turned toward his protective detail, but then the couple parted and a lone man stepped between them. He was dressed as a tourist: jeans, jacket, white training shoes, even the black rucksack slung across his back wasn’t unusual in the Capitol. But what might once have been a wool hat fitted over his head had now been pulled down so that it covered his face. Skull-like eye sockets glared straight ahead. The right hand held a big pistol, possibly a Magnum.

It was aimed at Jonathan Gates.

The Secretary of Defense stared in horror. He heard his bodyguards shout, sensed them move, even caught the *snick* as their weapons came free of their shoulder holsters. And then he heard the masked attacker’s words, “The Blood King sends his regards.”

All he could think about was Sarah. If Kovalenko had sent a man to kill Gates, he would surely have orders to kill Sarah too. She sat between him and the gunman, and Gates was damned if he was going to let another woman die because of him. He stood up fast, skirting the table, focusing the gunman’s attention, and no doubt getting in the way of his own bodyguards.

"Down!" one of them screamed, but Gates made himself as threatening as possible. The hard blue eyes regarding him from behind the homemade mask showed nothing other than cold implacability. The gun didn't waver. The man was a pro.

Shots rang out. The first hammered into the gunman's shoulder, sending him to one knee without a sound. The second, again from Gates' protective detail, flew through the space the gunman had just been occupying. The third came from the assassin, striking Gates' upper torso and driving him back.

At first he felt no pain, just fear for Sarah and regret that he would never accomplish most of the dreams he had already set in motion. He landed heavily on his knees, but still held the gunman's stare, still struggled to approach. All around, waitresses, officials and tourists were screaming, ducking for cover, or were just frozen in place, hands held across pure-white terrified faces. A second bullet struck the gunman, this one slamming into his gun hand, giving Gates a millisecond of hope. But the pro didn't hesitate, instantly picking up his weapon with his other hand and discharging it at the Secretary of Defense.

Gates shuddered under the hammer blows. Three bullets hit him, one glancing across his temple. As he collapsed, the world was already fading. Sarah's mouth was open; she was diving toward him and would no doubt beat his bodyguards. A third bullet hit the gunman, but his aim did not waver.

In a terrible split-second, three things happened. Jonathan Gates died, Sarah Moxley landed across his body in a desperate, selfless act of heroism, and the gunman fired his last round.

CHAPTER FIVE

Ben Blake felt his frustration build as Sam drove the Mercedes hard through the clinging, black night. The A64, the fastest road between York and Leeds, was all but empty at this hour, the perpetual set of roadworks along its length not even slowing them down. As they neared Leeds, the skies began to artificially brighten as thousands of street lights turned night into day.

"Can't you find out what's happening?" Ben asked Jo. It had already been fifteen minutes since the army officer had made the call.

"They won't keep us *civilians* in the loop. We're acting unofficially here, don't forget. Downside to that is it gives us no juice."

"Unofficially? What do you mean?"

"If things had been made official this op would have been cancelled weeks ago." Jo sighed. "Due to no credible threat. Drake didn't agree. Hence," another sigh, "you're alive."

"Drake? He sent you?"

"That he did, mate."

"Damn. He can still do that?"

Sam laughed at the lad's naivety. "Not a chance. But we've had some downtime coming for months."

"That being said," Jo added. "We're on our last two days."

Silence descended as Ben realized how close he had come. Grief struck him a moment later when he thought about Stacey lying in a pool of blood back there, dead because she had done nothing but go out with him. He choked and had to push a hand over his face to stem the sorrow.

A hand covered in dried blood.

Again. He flashed back to the soldier who had died during the battle of the Singen tomb. Was this his destiny? To always have fresh blood on his hands?

Man up, kid. Man up. It was way past time.

Sam tapped the silver-trimmed satnav. It showed the estimated time of arrival as being eight minutes from now. "Let's start prepping."

Jo made sounds in the back seat. Ben heard fresh magazines being inserted into two guns and the sound of clips being pulled back. He stared out the windscreen at the familiar streets. "Thought you said these special cops know what they're doing."

Jo leaned forward. "We're always prepared." He handed a fully loaded weapon to Sam and sat back.

"Stay in the car," Sam said as the secluded entrance to the street where Ben's parents lived came up on the right. The vehicle swung into the tree-lined road, stopping immediately as they saw two big police cars blocking their path.

"That's good," Sam said, noting Ben's panicked look. "Jo, c'mon."

The two men jumped out. Ben watched them go, but could not stand to stay alone. Twenty minutes ago he had spoken to his dad, voice trembling, running quickly through the details and begging his dad to get to safety. At first the older Blake had laughed, both Ben and Karin had always played down their role in world events, but when Ben explained what had happened to Stacey, the raw emotion which had thickened his voice had made all the difference.

"I hear the sirens," his dad had said. "I hear them, Ben."

Then the line had gone dead. Sam explained that the police sometimes used a cellular phone jammer and had also been known to sever landlines, though Sam didn't sound particularly convincing on the latter detail. The hardening of his features betrayed his concern.

Now Ben watched Sam and Jo approach the tree line surrounding his parents' house. They moved gracefully, in time, and with a modicum of energy expended. Their heads were in constant motion, surveying every angle and each other's backs. Their professionalism was unmatched.

But still . . . he couldn't just wait in the dark, hoping his parents would come running out surrounded by a gaggle of cops. Chances were the cops were interviewing them inside. They would want to know he was safe.

Ben cracked open the door and stepped out into the cool night. The tall, densely packed trees whispered their observations high above, stirred by a flurry of breezes. The blue Mercedes ticked in the sudden silence. From another street, a world away, a car alarm yelped out a warning. Ben crossed the road, following in the footsteps of Sam and Jo. He paused at the tree line, then made his way to the open gate. It swayed and creaked slightly, making Ben smile. His mother had hounded his father for years about that creaking gate. "All it would take is a blast of WD40," she used to moan. "Can's in the cupboard," he used to retort, smiling affectionately. They enjoyed many such friendly squabbles.

Now Ben made his way through the gate and up the driveway. The front door was open, but that could be for any number of reasons. Lights burned in the front room—a good sign. Sam and Jo were nowhere to be seen . . .

Ben strained his ears but heard no sound. Shadows scudded across the moon overhead, creating patterns of black and silver. A light rain began to fall, so gentle it was barely noticeable. At that moment, movement caught his attention from the back of the house. He crouched, feeling both foolish and scared, but soon recognized Sam's face.

"What did I tell you to do?"

Ben saw that the hardness molding the army man's features had deepened, if that was possible. The deep crags and inflexible lines had become chasms. Behind him, Jo pulled up, his face a mirror to Sam's.

"No." Ben whispered. "No . . ."

Sam rushed forward, lowering his weapon. "I'm sorry." He crushed Ben into his arms and held the lad as he struggled.

Ben tried to push Sam away. He might as well have tried to reason with an anaconda. Sam continued to apologize, then Jo was there too, laying a hand on his shoulder.

Ben felt the true horror of it all sink in. With legs turning to jelly, he managed to turn his head toward Jo. "The cops too?"

"All dead. This was a professional hit, carried out by world class pros." He shook his head. "They're long gone."

But that didn't make sense either. "It's me they want."

"They might not be in touch with the team sent to take you out. No strategic reason for them to be."

Ben allowed Sam to lower him to the ground. The sudden shock of it all set in and he began to shiver. "We should go," he heard Sam say. "We can call it in on the way. Drake needs to know too, if he doesn't already."

Through chattering teeth, Ben managed to say, "Why would he know?"

"This Blood King character," Jo said. "Clearly he's restarted his blood vendetta. I don't know why, but everyone needs to be aware. They could be hit at any minute."

Ben's mind flickered back to the moment they had captured Kovalenko. "We could have killed him, you know. Back then. We could have hurled his body into a fucking abyss."

Sam hauled him to his feet. "Stay close."

Ben refused to move, he just couldn't take his eyes off his parents' place. "Oh God, Dad. Are . . . are they in there?"

"Yes, Ben, but we—"

"My dad. My . . . *mum.* It's my fault."

"No. It's the desire of a psycho. Now come on, man. Other people's lives are at stake."

The last sentence penetrated the fog of despair that had incapacitated his brain. *Karin is still out there!*

Forcing his legs to move, Ben shuffled along with Sam. Jo led the way. The front part of the Mercedes was visible at the top of the driveway, headlights shining. As they approached, a horrific figure stepped out from the utter darkness of the nearby trees, a figure covered in concealing bits of shrubbery, and lobbed something underhand at them.

Jo stared in disbelief. "Fuck me it's a—"

"Grenade!" Sam screamed, gripping Ben's coat to drag him away.

But there was no time. The thrower had timed the grenade to explode on impact. Not even the reactions of a Special Forces unit were faster than an exploding bomb.

Fire and fragments of metal discharged in a wide radius, shredding and burning everything in the vicinity. Ben saw the flicker of fire blasting toward him, felt agony as tiny shards sliced his flesh, and then, mercifully, a split second later knew no more.

He was dead, and the two lifeless bodies of Matt Drake's army pals lay beside him.

CHAPTER SIX

Hayden Jaye faced Mano Kinimaka across the conference table that sat in the center of the third of three large rooms which formed the hub of the new HQ on Pennsylvania Avenue, opposite the Pennsylvania Mall. The big Hawaiian was showing her his newest collectible—a Hard Rock pin badge, newly acquired from the store that stood opposite the imposing, featureless FBI building on E Street. Business and pleasure had never been so closely situated for the Hawaiian before.

"That's . . . great."

"Say it like you mean it," Kinimaka urged. "Go on. And you might get lucky later."

Hayden flipped her hair. "I'll get lucky whenever I want to, thanks."

Kinimaka grinned and was about to retort when another voice spoke up from the doorway. "I'd believe her," Smyth, the newest member of their team, along with Romero, growled. "She's hotter than a rack of those Hooter's chicken wings, but still a little shy of the Mai Kitano level."

Hayden sent the ex-Delta commando an emotionless glare. "You're lucky we're off duty, soldier."

Smyth pulled a face. "I know that. I'm not stupid. Romero's the stupid one, you'll see."

"Did you actually need anything?" Hayden asked.

"Yeah. I just wondered how it is that when I come to Washington to join the team, friggin' Maggie flies off to Tokyo on her own."

"Personal business." Hayden thought about the meagre amount Mai and Drake had told her—that her old clan had made contact, still believing they had a right to her services, and how Mai had travelled east to disillusion them of that view. It all seemed kosher and above board to Hayden, apart from her desire to travel alone. Drake would surely never let her face such danger by herself.

Unless Mai had given him no alternative. Which meant her mission was far more than she had revealed. And imperative too, it seemed. Only four days had passed since the 'Babylon thing' had ended.

"Has she gotten tired of all the texts?" Kinimaka added slyly. "Did she block you yet?"

"What?" Smyth's natural irritability got the better of his brain. Quickly, he dug out his cell phone and checked the screen. "No she ain't. And she told you about those texts?"

Hayden and Kinimaka nodded as one.

"Shit. Hope she didn't tell Drake. It's the auto-correct feature on my smartphone that's the problem, you know? 'I'm ordering in a small pizza' becomes 'I'm ordering in a small penis'. 'I love this song' becomes 'I love this boner'. They really need to get that shit sorted."

Romero appeared behind his team mate. "You ready for the showers, bud?"

"Ready."

The two soldiers made to walk out of the room. Gates had plans to install a fully equipped gym on a higher floor, just one of the ways he was trying to offer his team all the luxuries of home. Both Smyth and Romero were pushing for it at every opportunity.

Hayden saw an opening for a little revenge. "You two enjoy the showers, do ya?"

Smyth turned quickly, grimacing. "I know how it sounded. Don't be a smart ass. Romero here, he's just an innocent."

"Oh yeah?"

"Stop it. You ain't funny. And I thought the boss of a secret agency would be more professional."

Hayden gave him a 'touché' gesture. "As should be the newest grunt."

"Fine." Smyth growled, beaten. "Whatever you say."

The two men started to leave the room together, but then Smyth grunted and lagged behind a little for appearance's sake.

When they were alone, Hayden came around the table to Kinimaka's side. "I do love you, Mano. You're the only person who's ever made me feel completely safe."

"Likewise." Kinimaka took her in his big arms. "We're there for each other. Always will be."

"Always."

Hayden stared through the darkness pressing against the window panes, across the street at the bright lights of offices and first floor shops. "I wonder what tomorrow will bring."

"Doesn't matter. We can beat anything."

Hayden pulled away. Her instinct had been to say, "Nothing lasts forever," but she saw no reason to tempt fate. Mano was good for her. His family were lovely, apart from his wayward sister—Kono. Hayden had made a surprise visit to Mano's parents only a few days ago and had been shocked to find how openly and completely they had welcomed her into their family. When the time had come to leave, she had been more than a little disappointed.

And shocked at the differences between *his* happy family life and what she remembered of her own pretty much ruled by her workaholic legendary father.

She led him back into the main ops room. To her and Kinimaka, the room was familiar—it closely resembled an old CIA layout with ultra-modern upgrades. But the upgrades were now largely hidden within the items of technology rather than upsetting the interior arrangement. Karin sat behind the largest desk, three computer consoles positioned around her within easy reach. Her fingers tapped at the keyboard, her eyes flicking between the computer screen and the big TV display that took up half a wall and was the main focus of the room.

Komodo stood behind her, watching her every move, a hand placed protectively on the back of her seat. The ex-Delta man had been excited to see Romero and Smyth joining the team, but made it clear he would only socialize with them once a week during downtime, preferring to spend the bulk of his free days with Karin.

The ribbing he had endured only strengthened his resolve. Yes, he enjoyed cooking for her. No, he wasn't about to sizzle Romero and Smyth up some smokehouse wings.

Hayden surveyed the big screen. "You're playing *Galaga?* Seriously, is nothing happening in the world?"

Karin motioned toward her other screens, in between shooting the enemy spacecraft. "Got everything set up. Nada on the agency feeds, the news links, the Web troll bots. Hey, it's only been four days. Don't worry, some highborn, arrogant ass will decide he wants to rule the world in the next day or two. Besides—" she nodded at the wall clock, "— shift's over. T-vor's going to show me his expertise around the kitchen."

Hayden had to admit she was right, and the prospect of spending a relaxed night with Mano did sound appealing. "Alright. We're heading out." She snaked an arm around her boyfriend's large, muscle-bound waist and pulled him toward the single lift that led down to the underground parking garage.

"Night," Karin called.

Hayden leaned in. "What's new at the movies?"

"There's this new film playing at Casa Kinimaka. It's called, *Here's to us.*"

Hayden hugged him harder. "Raise a glass . . . 'cause the last few weeks have kicked our ass?" she paraphrased. "I know the song." She reached out to press the lift's call button, surprised to see it was already lit.

"Must be Romero and Smyth on their way back up. Those boys would—"

The lift dinged and the doors slid open with a whoosh. The small space beyond was jam-packed with men, all wearing black bodysuits, adaptive goggles and carrying Heckler and Kochs. The leader, face as white as a sheet, shouted an order as he saw Hayden and Kinimaka, then the whole world went straight to hell.

Hayden sprang to the side, hitting the wall hard. Kinimaka rolled with her, keeping his immense body between her and the attacking force. Men poured out of the lift. Komodo appeared in the doorway behind, fantastically quick, gun in hand, and sized up the situation in less time than it takes to kill a man with a bullet. He fired at the crowd, sending men sprawling and scrambling for cover. Kinimaka started to drag Hayden back toward Komodo, but already half a dozen gun barrels were drawing a bead on them. They had no time.

The plaster wall beside them exploded outward. Two huge figures stepped into the corridor, Romero and Smyth, already firing. Only the leader stayed upright, maybe sensing that ducking for cover in this situation would get him nowhere and increase his risk. He reached in and calmly sent the lift back down to the parking garage.

Shit, Hayden thought. *Did they have more men down there?*

Romero grunted as a bullet struck his Kevlar vest. Two of the attackers fell back, painting the corridor walls with their blood. Two more folded over, also hit hard in their bulletproof armor. Kinimaka scrambled back as best he could, pushing Hayden behind him. She was the first to reach Komodo, and he knew her well enough to forget the rescue and hand her a gun.

"How the hell did they get in here?"

But Hayden knew, rather than be worrying about that just yet, Karin would be calling for back up. It should already be on its way—unless something bigger was going on in Washington tonight.

Why that thought crossed her mind, Hayden never knew. It probably had something to do with a sense of foreboding that crept down her spine on spidery feet, but more likely the result of the leader of the group removing his goggles and giving them a big grin.

"The Blood King sends his regards," he said, and fired at the same time as his men.

Hayden forced the terrifying sight of that crazy white albino face from her mind and tried to scurry away. Bullets whizzed above her head and around Kinimaka's frame. Romero and Smyth, clad in body armor, leaped in front, taking multiple hits, their bodies jerking like marionettes.

"No!" *Was that my own screaming voice?* she thought.

Showers of plaster blasted from the walls and cascaded all around. A bullet parted Kinimaka's hair, so close to killing him that Hayden saw the lock of hair that flew from his skull. It was only a matter of time.

She leaned around him even as he forced her further back, firing over Romero and Smyth, seeing at least two of the attackers convulse. The albino's hard, battle-worn face stared back at her so fiercely she had to look away. She forced Mano to the side and fired until her clip was empty.

Smyth scrambled on his elbows and back toward her, firing hard, groaning as Romero clambered across his legs. Komodo must have caught a weapon thrown by Karin for he suddenly reappeared, rifle in hand, and began to give their assailants some solid return fire.

Because of his position, Hayden pushed Kinimaka into the ops room first. Her brief view showed Karin on her knees, sliding a second rifle across the floor to the big man.

Fucking A. They had a chance here, a chance made out of nothing by a competent and clever team with crazy skills. Kinimaka spun and added his fire to Komodo's. Hayden slid through the doorway, Smyth and Romero staggering after her.

"What the fuck!" Smyth yelled.

"I thought you two had left." Hayden stooped to pick up another rifle.

"Nah. We hit the showers. But I gotta ask, what's the point of communal showers if there're no chicks around? Available chicks," he added.

"Shut it." Romero slammed Smyth's shoulder hard, wincing with pain. "Took one in the forearm. Listening to your caterwauling don't help it much."

"Shit, are you okay?" Smyth's tone changed instantly as he bent to examine his team mate's arm. "You're bleeding. Fuck!"

"Calm down. It just a bullshit flesh wound."

"Oh. Ya fuckin' pussy."

Komodo was last through the door. Karin rose as he crossed the threshold, relief apparent in her face. *The trouble with this team,* Hayden thought. *Is that we all love each other too fucking much.*

"Retreat," she breathed unnecessarily. They all knew what to do.

Komodo led the way, with Karin, Hayden, and then Kinimaka coming up behind him. Romero and Smyth brought up the rear. Before they had moved three steps, Hayden heard the lift ding again and the soft whispering of orders. Their attackers had just been reinforced.

"Someone planned this," she said as she walked. "Down to the last detail. But Kovalenko's still in prison . . ." she paused as something occurred to her. They all knew it was his prison that had suffered the riot much earlier that day, and no one in law enforcement had so far managed to get near the place. Could some inmates have escaped in the chaos? It didn't seem likely, but then this was Kovalenko they were dealing with; a man who for many years had convinced the world he was a mere myth.

In that case, *everyone* needed warning.

She ran harder. *Where's Gates?* she wondered. *And fuck, even more important than that, where's the man who signed the order to incarcerate Kovalenko—the President?*

CHAPTER SEVEN

Through the ops room they dashed, Karin pulling down a large lever by the side of a junction box, an act that wouldn't prevent a determined enemy from stealing their hard drives but would at least shut them all down. Komodo dragged her along almost before she could finish, darting through the open door and into the conference room. Behind them the sounds of pursuit intensified.

Romero spun in the doorway, pulling Smyth down with him. "Keep going," he muttered. "We'll buy a few extra minutes."

Hayden sped on, glancing back as she passed them. The leader of the attackers ran into view. Romero opened fire instantly, but the man twisted acrobatically and dived headlong out of sight. Romero's subsequent bullets took down the second man.

Return fire rattled from within the ops room, straight through the open door of the conference room, and slammed into the far wall. The large oblong front of the table was churned to splinters. Smyth extended his arm and fired blindly around the corner, then looked shocked when his rifle was shot out of his hand.

Romero swore at him, "Dickhead."

"Always works in the movies." Smyth made no effort to scramble after the lost weapon. No doubt it had been damaged by the offending bullet and besides, it was far too exposed. Instead, he reached around his back and came out with a handgun. "Ready?"

Romero checked on the progress of his new team mates. The conference room was empty. Hopefully by now they would be approaching the escape route door.

“Ready.”

Romero jammed his trigger finger down hard, splashing bullets in a wide arc. Smyth broke cover and ran across the room. A second later, Smyth laid down covering fire as Romero sprinted toward him. It was a classic shielding move, executed by professionals. Smyth turned into the corridor that led toward the shower rooms and the concealed escape door. There would be no time for any finesse here, no time to hide their exit route; it was simple, run for your life.

Smyth ran. Bullets pounded the walls, the table and even the windows behind them. The sound of hard pursuit spurred them on. Smyth saw the dogleg at the end of the corridor just as Hayden peeked around the corner.

“Hurry!”

Smyth didn’t need to be told twice. Freedom was twelve steps away. A quick glance to the left assured him that Romero kept pace. They were almost at the corner when Smyth felt something warm splash across his face. At the same time, Romero jerked and tripped headlong, sliding across the polished floor and leaving a red trail behind him.

Smyth stared, distraught. The back of Romero’s head had been blown out. Just like that, one of his best friends and colleagues had been killed. Shock turned to anger and Smyth turned quickly, unleashing bullet after bullet, spraying the attacking force with a deadly hail of lead.

Men collapsed groaning. Others fell to their knees or doubled over. Some remained standing, returning fire with a vengeance, their faces hard and battle-crazed behind their black masks.

Smyth would have died then and there if it weren't for Hayden and Kinimaka. The two agents had lain in wait; not for one minute had they considered leaving comrades behind. As Smyth fired, screamed and roared, Hayden and Kinimaka emerged behind him, guns spitting hotly, and pulled him to safety. At first Smyth fought them, but as his clip ran dry and true grief set in, he allowed them to lead him away.

"I'm okay," he said after a second, his soldier's training kicking in. All feelings would be compartmentalized until later. "I'm good."

Hayden hardened her resolve. She had seen Romero stagger by; seen the way he fell and the spray of blood; and, though she had only known the man for a few days, her heart had lurched. Romero was a good soldier, a good man. He had helped Drake stampede across Europe and destroy a human trafficking ring. He had had a hell of a future.

But the same thing could be said for them all. This was kill or be killed, and they were in no position to make a stand right now. She stared at the exit door. It hadn't escaped her notice that a cacophony of sirens *wasn't* blasting along the street outside. Something big was happening in DC tonight. Something terrible.

Her heart clutched at a vision of Gates, of Drake and Dahl on the other side of town, and of Mai and Alicia—so far away. Her mission, her goal in life now, was to send them a warning as soon as she could. She sprinted for the doorway. Karin and Komodo were on the other side, holding the big door open. She pushed Smyth ahead of her. Kinimaka ran at the other side, firing blindly.

A bullet clanged off the metal door. Another sent splinters of metal into Komodo's hair. Smyth squeezed through, then Hayden.

She turned swiftly on hearing a shout.

"You will never escape us." The words were driven at her by the attackers' albino leader, loaded with hate and a terrifying certainty. He was grinning, with Mano clear in his sights, and pulled the trigger.

Kinimaka staggered, falling hard, but his lurch was an evasive maneuver. Still, the bullet would have ended him if Komodo hadn't let the door swing shut at the last moment. The albino's bullet deflected off the closing door and buried itself in the nearest wall.

"Shit."

Hayden seconded the Hawaiian's heartfelt sigh and helped him up. "Keep going," she said. They could not afford to slow down now. Not until they were safe.

"Weapons check," Komodo said as he pushed through the group to the front. He waved for them to follow and called, "One rifle, one mag."

Karin spoke next. "Pistol. Three shots left, I think."

"Check it," Smyth urged. "I have Romero's rifle and half a mag."

Hayden and Kinimaka spoke up too, feeling sick at the thought of their meager supplies. The tunnel stretched ahead of them, slightly inclined, lit every six feet by electric lights built into the walls above their heads. The floor was smooth concrete, as were the sides and roof. It was rough and hastily built, but it served its purpose well.

The mood was subdued. No one spoke as they trotted down the slope. A boom echoed through the tunnel as their enemies smashed something against the door. After a few more seconds an even louder boom signified an explosion, and then the sound of debris clattering off the walls. Hayden made her feet go faster.

The tunnel bottomed out before rising slightly. Unlike the rest of them, Karin had been this way before and explained that the escape route exited into a tiny room. The room was security barred and keypad locked from the outside, but only required a strong push to exit. Komodo ran hard, and the tunnel soon came up against a door. Without stopping, he leaned into it and sent it crashing back against its hinges.

Hayden brought up the rear. The layout of the tunnel resulted in their assailants being just out of sight, but the sound of their pursuit was loud and getting closer. By now she knew the timbre of the albino's voice, hating the sound of the hard confidence it exuded. Unlike Boudreau, this mercenary was all about efficiency and cunning—the worst kind to come up against.

She pushed into the small cupboard-like room and pulled the door closed behind her, knowing it would only slow the attackers down for a few extra seconds. The others had already exited into the mall, and the sound of their voices echoed around the enormous space.

It didn't sound right somehow . . .

Hayden glanced around, stopping in surprise. "The mall is *empty?"*

"Closed down three or four years ago," Karin acknowledged. "Everything apart from the food court."

Hayden took in the light-green shuttered shop fronts, the dimmed lighting, the higher floor windows staring down on this modern crypt as if in judgment, the polished tiled floors and highly reflective surfaces.

"It's in the middle of Washington," she said, as if that statement might help switch the lights of commerce back on.

"Ain't nowhere safe from the bullshit bean counters," Smyth said, looking at Karin. "Where's the exit?"

Karin pointed to the right. The team set off at pace, Hayden surrounded by a sense of the surreal as the empty mall echoed to their hollow footsteps. From somewhere above them the sound of cash machines opening and kids' conversation and laughter drifted like the sounds of old, distressed ghosts. She felt a huge relief knowing the food court was on the next level.

A muted explosion chased the space behind their fleeing heels. Smyth turned in place, still running, and loosed several bullets in the direction they had come. Kinimaka ducked as return fire whickered overhead.

The leader barked a resonating order, signaling the start of a prolonged bombardment. Bullets flashed through the air and impacted against the shiny walls, cracking the hard surfaces. Hayden and her entire team dived headlong, hitting the floor and sliding with solid momentum. Komodo and Smyth rolled as they slid, coming around with guns already blazing.

The battle raged as Karin, Hayden and Kinimaka scrambled behind a round maroon-colored pillar. Chips of plastic showered through the air around them as their enemies concentrated their fire power. Smyth and Komodo rolled the other way, having to lie lengthways behind the short wall of a semi-circular water fountain. Komodo slithered until he could poke his head around the edge, and fired a few rounds.

Then he turned to Hayden. His eyes said it all. They were dangerously low on ammo.

Keep moving, Smyth was mouthing at her. She knew the military man's mantra by heart. To stop was to die. She sat with her back to the pillar and surveyed the area. Karin pointed out the exit, dangerously exposed at the end of a long, wide corridor.

"How many of those assholes are left?" she asked Kinimaka.

"Best guess? Eight, maybe a few more or less."

Karin grasped Hayden's hand. "What *is* this? What's going on?"

Hayden weighed the impact of revealing her fears and decided against it. "Not sure. Yet." Both Karin and Kinimaka had loved ones out there and to start worrying about them now wouldn't help anyone.

"We need to break for that exit," she said. "Before we run out of ammo. What we need is a diversion."

"What about that?" Kinimaka pointed overhead. Hayden took it in and looked speculatively at him. "Can you take 'em all down?"

The Hawaiian raised an eyebrow. "How long have you known me?"

"Alright." Hayden signaled Smyth and Komodo. As she peered out she saw the attacking unit creeping forward in perfect formation whilst still firing. It was going to take a miracle to get all of them out of this one alive.

She prayed. "Go."

Kinimaka rolled onto his back and fired toward the ceiling. All his remaining shots went into breaking the supporting cables that tethered half a dozen swirling plastic displays to the roof. As the displays plummeted down, the SPEAR team rose and ran.

Hayden saw the albino dive sideways as the enormous hard plastic casings shattered against the mall floor, crushing several of his men and making a noise like several RPGs exploding. Three men made it straight through by sliding, but lost their weapons and came up holding knives.

Smyth and Kinimaka were in their faces. Smyth shot the first point-blank, then upended his empty rifle to club the next across the bridge of the nose. Despite the audible crack, the merc didn't even flinch, just snorted and lashed back at Smyth. The ex-Delta soldier took a swipe across the cheek; blood flew and he hammered the butt of his rifle into the guy's teeth. The merc lunged a second time. Smyth let the knife pass less than an inch from his body, trapped the arm and broke it. At the same time, he disabled the man with a heavy blow to the temple.

Komodo dispatched his own adversary just as the albino hit them. This man didn't fight conventionally. He slid in, taking Komodo's legs, but not just tripping him—the blow almost broke Komodo's shins. He yelped in agony. Smyth covered for him, stomping toward the albino's head. When his foot landed it crushed nothing but empty space; the albino was already up, lithely twisting around behind him and encircling his neck with a thick arm.

Hayden saw the albino's power and the sudden panic in Smyth's normally sardonic face as he felt his adversary's strength. She couldn't fire for fear of hitting her team mate so she bounded over the gap between them. The roof displays had devastated the ranks of their attackers, but several were groaning and already rising to their knees.

Hayden punched the albino in the soft place behind the ear, then put a choke hold around his own neck. She expected him to fall back, but was amazed when he bunched the muscles in his neck and fought her grip. She had never known anything like it. Even as she applied all her strength she couldn't actually tell if she was making any impression.

Smyth twisted hard. The albino didn't shift an inch. His lips moved as he whispered something into Smyth's ear.

"If this were prison, soldier, you would be my boy."

The three fighters struggled hard, locked into position, as precious seconds flew by. When Komodo approached the tableau, the albino only grinned. "C'mon, boy, I'll take you too."

But then Kinimaka broke it all apart by hitting the albino with a waist-high tackle. Hayden was flung aside. Smyth hit the floor hard. The albino cracked his head against a pillar and looked stunned. Kinimaka pushed away.

"We gotta go!"

In an instant they had turned and were sprinting for the exit. The albino shook his head to clear his daze. His men picked their way through the display wreckage, bruised and bleeding, and searching for lost weapons. Hayden pushed the rest before her. She was now the only one with any ammo, and needed to cover the escape. For precious seconds they ran unhindered, seeing the double exit doors loom closer with every step. Blackness pressed hard against the glass and people strolled along the broad expanse of Pennsylvania Avenue outside. More than escape, it offered divine freedom. She couldn't believe they had all escaped this latest skirmish intact.

Hayden risked a glance back. The albino was drawing a bead on her, one eye closed. She saw his wrist flex, then felt the punch of the bullet as it struck.

She staggered, gasping. Ahead, Kinimaka turned, eyes suddenly wider than she had ever seen and burning with fear. Hayden put a hand to her waist, but felt nothing. Her legs were still working.

"Jesus," she breathed at him. "Must have ripped right through my jacket."

Kinimaka breathed deep and reached for the swinging exit doors. Cold air flowed into the mall.

Hayden slowed. The gun cracked again and this time she felt the bullet as it punched through her abdomen, felt the gout of blood explode from her body, felt her nails rip as she grasped desperately for Kinimaka and missed, falling hard to the cold mall floor.

CHAPTER EIGHT

Kinimaka ducked as another bullet passed close to his head. With one heave he managed to lift Hayden's inert body and drape it over one of his massive shoulders. He knew full well what was happening here. He had heard the albino's comment 'The Blood King sends his regards', and knew time was of the essence. He should get word to his family right away, but Hayden was his closest family now and she needed him.

They rushed out of the mall into the cool night. The bright lights of Pennsylvania Avenue bathed them in stark unreality. Life wasn't about eye-catching colors, provocative billboards and gleaming cars. It was struggle and desperation and momentary bursts of pure pleasure. It was dirty, unforgiving and ever-changing.

Komodo dashed out into the middle of the road, stopped a car and hauled out the driver. Without ceremony, the rest of the team piled in, Kinimaka holding Hayden across his lap. She was still breathing, and he kept every emotion reined in as the world passed him by.

"Nearest hospital?" Komodo cried.

"Needs to be secure," Smyth rasped, unaccountably calm.

"There's a military hospital on Georgia," Karin said, her eidetic memory useful as ever. "Should be well guarded."

Kinimaka passed his cell over to her. "Call them, and call Langley too. If they have any men to spare, we're gonna need them."

Smyth turned to him. "You think this thing ain't over?"

Kinimaka cradled the unmoving head of his girlfriend. "I think it's far from over." He was about to continue when Karin cursed out loud.

"What is it?"

Instead of answering, shocked into silence and with tears suddenly bright in her eyes, Karin turned up the radio. The broadcast filled the car.

". . . and to recap, reports suggest that the Secretary of Defense, Jonathan Gates, has been killed in Washington DC tonight. Though the authorities remain quiet, eye witness accounts speak of a professional gunman. It's still too early to speculate on—"

Smyth stared at the radio as if he could will it into submission. "Is this right? It could only have just happened."

Karin handed Kinimaka back his cell and shifted to dig her own phone out of her jeans pocket. "This is the Blood King," she said. "It's the Blood Vendetta. When we learned of the riot earlier, I wondered about it. But there were no reports of any prisoners escaping. So either he has full communications working on the inside and has been orchestrating this thing for months, or he's free."

Kinimaka's eyes were huge. "Or both."

Silence reigned in the car as Kinimaka and Karin both pressed speed dial numbers on their cell phones and listened to the dreadful, ominous drone of unanswered ringtones.

CHAPTER NINE

Matt Drake glared at Torsten Dahl across the beer-stained table.

"Face it, mate, you're *English.* Everyone thinks you're English. You sound English. You act English. Maybe not a *Yorkshireman."* Drake shrugged. "But nobody's perfect."

Dahl threw back the last of his pint. "So you think I'm almost perfect?"

"Didn't say that," Drake pointed out as he sipped at a Pepsi Max. He glanced around. The quiet pub they'd entered half an hour ago had become decidedly busy in the last five minutes. Couples crowded the bar. Some were shouting. Others sat staring into space. Drake picked up on the air of shock and disbelief.

"What the hell's going on over there?"

But Dahl was like a dog with a bone. "Do you think Mai's perfect?"

Drake flicked his attention back to the Swede. "What?"

"That's why we're here, isn't it? Mai upped and left and wouldn't take you with her."

"Is *that* why you invited me here? To talk? Shit, I coulda been watching prime time."

"You know exactly why I invited you," Dahl said quietly. "You're pissed off with her. But, mate, I have to say . . . she knows what she's doing. If she wants to do something alone, neither you, me, or the entire Swedish Special Forces can stand in her way."

Drake chortled. "The Swedish Special Forces couldn't catch an escaped monkey, let alone handle Mai."

Dahl took the barb with a fixed smile. "Don't be pissed off at her. It's obviously something she has to do."

"Heard that before," Drake said. "Doesn't mean it's right."

Dahl shrugged. "Well, matey, it doesn't mean it's wrong either."

Drake stared into his glass for a moment, ignoring the rising noise around them. "Honestly? It's the danger she's willingly walking into. These wankers who think they own her . . . they're worse than the fucking Yakuza. Far worse."

"We should be with her." Dahl sat back. "I agree. Look, if she does this her way, she's free. If she doesn't, it will never end."

"You missed the option where she's dead."

Dahl looked away, not wanting to push the issue of Drake and his woman. For the first time, the tumult around them registered on his radar. He sniffed the air. "I smell trouble."

Drake nodded and slipped off his chair. Together the two men drifted closer to the bar, joining the ever-increasing crowd.

What they saw shocked them to the core. Drake felt his mouth dry up instantly, and found he couldn't move a muscle. Dahl's gasp of disbelief was audible.

The picture on the TV screen was an aerial view of central Washington DC. The Washington Monument and Lincoln Memorial shone, and then the view centered in. Flashing lights, black vans, and cop cars jammed the display. An inset showed a portrait of their boss, Jonathan Gates, and the red ticker across the bottom spelled out the words: Secretary of Defense killed in Washington DC.

Drake backed away, fighting off a black cloud which threatened to overwhelm his vision. He turned to Dahl, but found that the words just would not come. Their eyes locked and expressed all that needed to be said.

Dahl pointed at the way out. By the time they reached the saloon-type exit doors, the Swede had found his voice. "Do you have your ID?"

Drake nodded.

"We can drive straight there."

Again Drake nodded as a dark maelstrom of scenarios whirled through his head. They knew Gates had been seeing Sarah Moxley at the Hotel Dillion tonight, but what the hell had happened? Outside, the streets were strangely quiet, eerily so. The population of Washington, it seemed, were clustered around their TVs. Dahl led the way to their parked car and set off at pace.

"He was a good man," Dahl said into a thick silence broken only by the car's purring engine. "The kind of man you could admire. The type of politician you could follow. A rare leader."

"Who would *do* this?" Drake blurted without expecting any kind of answer. The list was endless—from an opportune civilian whacko to a disgruntled general to the more likely terrorist scenario.

"We'll find out," Dahl said, slowing the car as he approached a road block. "And then we'll stuff their fanaticism so far down their bloody throats it'll hopefully choke 'em."

They ended up running half the way to the restaurant. Both men checked their phones, but although Drake had received a missed call from Hayden, neither of them could raise the rest of the team. It was most likely because the SPEAR HQ was going crazy and being run ragged, but Drake didn't like it and neither did Dahl. They would have kept trying, but the checkpoints grew more regular the closer they came to the restaurant, each one more stringent than the next. When they finally reached the scene, Drake stood back, appalled.

The whole façade of the famous, respected restaurant had been blown out. Shattered glass littered the sidewalk all the way to the curb. Tables were upturned and broken. The two men didn't enter the restaurant, but lingered on the fringes, eyes drawn toward the two inert bodies lying in the center of the room.

Drake took one more moment to grieve, then packed it away. He swallowed hard and began to look around. "That's odd," he said.

Dahl nodded. "I saw them on the way in. Secret Service. Two of them."

"I thought they only protected the President."

"They do. But Coburn was speaking across the road." Dahl rolled his eyes to the right, surveying the ground in between. "I don't like the look of this, Drake."

Drake cast his eyes over the bodies. The woman sitting in a chair near the bar, held there along with other witnesses, looked familiar.

"Sarah?" he called. "Is that you?"

She looked up, and a wave of gratitude swept across her face. She hobbled painfully as she tried to walk over.

A cop walked up to her. "Wait right there, miss."

"Could we just have a moment?" Drake picked his way through the debris and tapped the cop on the shoulder.

"Who the hell are you?"

The Yorkshireman flashed his badge. "Part of Gates' team."

A look of respect entered the cop's eyes. "Alright. Sure. Take your time. But she ain't gonna be cleared to leave for a while."

Drake enfolded Sarah Moxley in his arms. The sobs that wracked her body brought his own grief bubbling back to the surface. "I'm sorry, Sarah. I'm so sorry."

"He . . . he was a good man. He didn't deserve this. There are so many others—"

Drake put a finger to her lips. "Don't finish that thought," he said. "You might regret it later. Do you know the assassin's identity?"

"They've told us nothing."

"Once we get going on this," he said, "The bastards who planned it will have nowhere to hide. Trust me." He didn't care that he'd told himself he'd never make that promise again. Not after this.

But Moxley suddenly pulled away. Tears streaked her face and her lipstick was smudged, but her eyes bored into him with a mix of intellect and fear. "You mean you don't know?"

"Know what?"

"The *Blood King* did this. At least, he organized it. The killer said as much before someone saved my life by shooting him."

Drake felt the bottom of his world fall out for the second time in thirty minutes. He pulled further away from Moxley and held her at arm's length. *"Are you sure?"*

Her expression conveyed the words she couldn't speak. Drake fished out his phone and looked at Dahl.

"Call your family," he said. "Kovalenko ordered this."

Dahl went white, turning away as he made the call. Drake pressed a speed dial number and waited for the call to connect. The seconds passed by like hours, each one cleaving a year from his life.

"Hello?" Mai's voice, at last, thirteen hours ahead.

Drake told her everything.

"Oh, my God. Poor Jonathan. But I have to call Chika and Dai. I have to go. Matt, thank you, but I have to go."

Drake understood. His next call was to Ben Blake. In his experience, the young man never parted for more than half a minute with his phone and always answered. He waited expectantly, but this time it just rang and rang. Drake checked his watch. It was early morning over in the UK. Maybe . . .

"Hello?"

"Ben? Are you okay?"

"I'm sorry, sir. This isn't Mr. Blake. This is Chief Inspector Mills of the West Yorkshire Police. Who am I talking to?"

The world swayed, but Drake clung to hope. "This is Matt Drake. I'm Ben's friend. I currently work for the US government. Is Ben okay?"

There were a few seconds of silence. "Right, sir. You're in Mr. Blake's contacts and I can see old text messages and calls made between you. I'm sorry to have to tell you this, Mr. Drake, but Ben Blake was murdered a short while ago. He was killed alongside his parents and two other men, who we believe were active members of the British Army. Do you have any knowledge of this?"

Drake didn't even feel his legs give way as he crashed to the floor.

CHAPTER TEN

Drake became aware that he was crawling through the wreckage, looking for his cell phone. In another second, Dahl was there with him.

Drake swiveled his head, believing he couldn't feel any worse, but suddenly became heart stricken as he looked into the Swede's face. "Your . . . your kids?"

Dahl swallowed hard. A cop came up to them and ordered them to get up. A man dressed in an army uniform backed him up. One look at the two men's faces and both officials backed away.

Dahl breathed low. "They're fine. So's the wife. Special Forces are with them as we speak, taking them out of the country."

"Thank God. Ben's . . . dead. So are Sam and Jo. Fuck me."

Dahl sat down hard, deflated. "The Blood Vendetta. Kovalenko must have reactivated it. Do you think he escaped this morning?"

"Shit. I do now."

Dahl glance around the devastated restaurant, taking in the haunted eyes of a dozen law enforcement officers looking back at him. "This is like the scene of a national disaster. Nobody knows what's happening."

Drake looked up. "If Kovalenko is free, it's only gonna get worse."

Dahl flipped his phone open again. "Where the hell are Hayden and the others?" Desperately, he hit the speed dial.

"Try everyone," Drake said. "Try—" Suddenly he shot up. *"Fuck!"*

"What is it?"

"Alicia!"

Drake dialed and held the phone close, certain that he couldn't handle another tragedy. When the familiar crazy-ass tones filled the phone with life he felt utter relief.

"The Drakester! What the fuck do you want, man?"

Again, he went through the story. "You need to get the hell out, Alicia. Leave and run, right now. All of you."

"That bastard Kovalenko ordered all that? I wish I was with you right now, Drake. I really do."

"Don't worry. Just get to safety. And stay off the radar and out of contact, Alicia. We don't know how far Kovalenko's claws reach this time, but you can bet your arse it's pretty damn deep."

"I always bet my arse, Drake. And I'll do it again now. We're out of here, and once we're safe I'll come to you."

"No. Don't—"

"Fuck you."

The line went dead. Drake closed his eyes. He couldn't think about that right now. Alicia would do as she pleased no matter what he said. For once, he allowed Dahl to help him to his feet and take charge without comment.

"There's an RV point near the hotel." The Swede pointed to the building where President Coburn had been in the throes of an after-dinner speech. "We need to go there now. I just heard something about the President."

Drake stared. "No."

"It's not good."

CHAPTER ELEVEN

The Blood King, with Gabriel and several other men at his side, walked calmly into the lobby of the Hotel Dillion and fanned out. Many were looking disheveled and, feigning distress, threw themselves into easy chairs and began talking loudly about the death of the Secretary of Defense. Kovalenko and Gabriel approached reception, joining the largest of the queues which had formed for late rooms in the wake of the President's departure. The demand for rooms would only grow as word about Gates' demise got out, and when the world learned of what was about to happen.

The Hotel Dillion, closely guarded and practically locked-down, continually swept and searched during the President's brief tenure, had instantly reverted back to a well-run, well-organized business upon the departure of the last Secret Service agent. It was all part of the hotel's policy with the White House.

As he waited, the heavily bundled-up Blood King fielded a number of calls. The first was to inform about the demise of Ben Blake and two other men who had defended him. Kovalenko's mouth stretched into a wide, satisfied grin but his words didn't reflect the pleasure he felt.

"And the parents?"

"The same, sir."

A pleasant metallic taste filled his mouth as he bit his inner lip in happiness.

"And so to the next. This cursed Ninth Division, where Drake 'earned his stripes', as they say. Let their blood wash the streets clean." Kovalenko knew, though Wells had died, many more of Drake's respected superiors and team mates were controlled by the well-established British secret ops' fully deniable asset they called the Ninth Division.

"Yes, sir. In particular we're going after Crouch and Cohen."

"Good."

The next call was more local.

"DC team here, sir. Jaye is at least badly injured, possibly dead. The Hawaiian, Smyth, Karin Blake and Komodo are with her. We have a fix on their new position."

"Do not fail me this time." Kovalenko jabbed the end button, seething. There should have been no mistakes. His men had recruited the best mercenaries out there for this wild, audacious coup. Hard, fresh, unconscionable men at the top of their game. The Blood King would brook no slip-ups.

Whilst waiting for more teams to check in—notably the Kitano and Myles units—he took a few minutes to evaluate and memorize the area around him. Right now the hotel was buzzing: a bustling enterprise where businessmen and tourists, and even the staff, passed through without taking the time to appreciate the history that nestled all around them. Built in 1850, only fifty years after the completion of the White House, the Scotch and Champagne Bar had been a sparkling meeting place even back in the days of Abraham Lincoln. Kovalenko eyed the entrance to the bar just off the reception area. If he had time and the right plan he would have liked nothing better than to simply plant Coburn's head in there, but more complex strategies had been drawn up to ensure exit routes and the future prospects of his men. With that particular thought in mind he turned briefly to Gabriel, the tall African, by his side.

"Our man on the inside. What's his name again?"

Gabriel grinned widely in that unnerving way of his. "Marnich. Agent Marnich."

"They should be here soon."

"An' we be ready fo' dem."

Kovalenko again blessed his good fortune in running into Mordant and Gabriel. Two lieutenants who could facilitate such dazzling havoc as this were invaluable.

With no more calls coming in, Kovalenko pocketed the phone. He didn't know and wasn't worried that some kind of authority might be monitoring the calls. They would be late.

And then, as if in answer to his thoughts and wishes, the front door of the hotel slammed open.

The Blood King smiled, a gifted predator in his element.

Coburn.

CHAPTER TWELVE

President Coburn waited restlessly as his four Secret Service agents came to a decision. In real-time, it didn't actually take long but Coburn was already feeling an old instinct kicking in—that of self-preservation.

At last, Marnich nodded at Franks. "Gridlock's impassable both ways. Back to the hotel?"

Franks hesitated, glancing through the rear window at the other two Escalades and the snarled traffic behind them. "No way back by road. We're going to have to hump it."

Marnich made a show of struggling between dilemmas. "Hotel's the most secure place around. We just left it."

"More secure than the White House?"

"Too many people and variables between us and it. Not as many behind us. An adversary would expect us to go forward. Who knows what might lie ahead? The hotel is secure, it was checked an hour ago, and the area is now crawling with every authority from the cops to the FBI and the army. My call is the Dillion."

"Agreed." Franks spoke into his wrist mic. "We're sitting ducks out here. Prepare to fall out to the Dillion. Eagle One will be with us."

Coburn leaned forward. "Won't we be more vulnerable out there?" he asked. "The Escalade's armored."

Franks met his eyes. Marnich spoke up. "Trouble is, we don't know *if* anyone's out there, sir, and we don't know what they've got. There are plenty of weapons these days that can pierce our armor."

"In Washington?"

"Maybe not," Marnich conceded, but left the sentence hanging.

Franks took the bait. "The Dillion is one block back, and crawling with authorities investigating the Secretary's death. It's three minutes away." He glanced at the President. "You ready for a brisk run, sir?"

Coburn nodded, conceding to their decision. A President rarely questioned the Secret Service, ex-military or not. They paused for six more seconds as Franks again spoke into his comms system.

"Alpha Bird One. Alpha Bird One. We need first-class extraction outside the Dillion. ETA—four minutes."

The answer made Franks smile. "All good." Coburn assumed he had called in one of the military choppers housed close by, making it their exit strategy or, he stared cannily at Franks, a diversion. He really should learn all these multiple code words by heart.

Marnich cracked the door open first, beckoning the President over. Instantly, the crazed din of an unthinkable amount of traffic chaos blasted into the car. Horns blared and metal still crunched. Men and women yelled in anger, and from overhead came the heavy thunk of rotor blades. The news services hadn't wasted any time in getting airborne.

"Shit," Franks said, eyeing the air. "They're even quicker than we are."

It was meant as a joke, to lighten the tension, but Coburn couldn't help but shrug it away, staying frosty. There were too many bright glaring lights around, especially on the higher floors of surrounding buildings, and more than enough hotel rooms, empty offices and apartment blocks to house an army of assassins.

Take it easy, he thought. *The Secret Service have this.*

Coburn stepped into the road. Instantly, agents from the other two cars surrounded him. Franks shouldered in and pushed his head down. Coburn had no choice but to suffer the indignity of staring at his feet whilst his protective detail made their way a few hundred yards back to the Dillion. His only link to the real world was the noise—a woman trying to calm her crying baby protesting as she was moved aside by the agents, a voluble older man demanding that the agents stop and immediately sort the stoplight situation out, a man arguing forcefully with someone about whose fault it was that his brand new Jaguar had suffered damage—one of the agents having to step in and diffuse the situation before it came to blows. Coburn became acutely aware that his protective detail was undermanned—he had sent two of his best to oversee the Gates investigation, but as the seconds and minutes passed and nothing happened, he began to breathe more easily. Maybe the stoplight disruption had been a glitch; a snag thrown up because, quite frankly, it was barely ever used.

Franks put pressure on his shoulders, slowing him down. "Dillion is ahead," he whispered, then louder. "You four go in first."

Coburn looked up. A wash of golden light flooded across the sidewalk where the Dillion proudly stood. The ring of agents steered him toward the gold-paneled, wide-open front doors, passing underneath the blue-and-white-striped ornate canopy. Tourists and civilians stood about in comical poses, gawping. Cameras flashed and cell phones took video, annoying the agents no end. Every flash made a trigger finger twitch and gave the periphery agents a vital moment of focus turned away from the President.

"Alpha Bird One ETA two minutes," Marnich said.

"Inside." Franks pushed them toward the well-lit lobby. As soon as they pushed through the doors his men began to yell.

"Clear the lobby! Clear the lobby now!"

The President would be fully secured and guarded inside here. Coburn slowed and began to think about the cell phone in his pocket, wondering if a call to his wife was in order. He was reaching for the device when Franks' soft growl stopped him cold, freezing the marrow in his bones.

"It's a fuckin' trap."

CHAPTER THIRTEEN

Mai Kitano paced the floor of her hotel room, frustrated that she would have to wait four more hours before her meeting with the master assassin, Gyuki.

Her old clan, the organization which had bought her from her destitute parents, wanted her back, and Gyuki, their most formidable hitman among hundreds, had all but demanded she meet with him in Tokyo at 1300 hours today.

Men like Gyuki, she mused, *were not real men.* Born in bloodshed, ripped from their families at a young age by warfare, strife or murder, they were trained to hunt and kill from the time they could walk. They knew no luxuries, no worldly trappings or any other life. This was all they had ever known, and thus they could maintain a focus no other fighting man in the world was capable of.

Ninjas? They might be. The old concept of the word had been lost through time. Mai herself was one of them, but even she conjured up images created by the Hollywood studios whenever she heard the word. But such fantasies did not bother these men, having no real concept of the outside world. They knew only what they were told and moved through the night, cloaked in shadows, except under extreme circumstances.

Such as Mai. For Gyuki to demand a meeting in broad daylight in a public place was unheard of. The master assassin would be as distracted as he was ever going to get.

Mai's thoughts slipped back to Matt Drake. She hesitated even to think the word boyfriend. It was a somewhat alien concept to her, too permanent for their line of work. If she allowed herself to be drawn into an easier life, to relax for even a minute, she knew she would die. Just look at what had happened to Drake back in DC when she had momentarily let down her guard.

Now as she paced, the phone rang, and she shook her head to see it was Drake calling. He hadn't wanted her to come alone to Tokyo, and in his desperation had forgotten the etiquette that had built between them, trying everything short of handcuffs to make her stay. Now she considered ignoring the call to teach him a lesson, but the gracious and respectful part of her won through.

"Hello?"

She listened as Drake talked fast. Hot anger and apprehension stole over her as he spoke. "Oh, my God. Poor Jonathan. But I have to warn Chika and Dai. I have to go. Matt, thank you, but I have to go."

Mai jabbed at the phone, twice hitting the wrong button before calming her inner self and taking a deep breath. After that she depressed Chika's speed-dial button and, with a huge effort, forced herself to wait patiently for an answer.

"Please. Please, Chika, my sister." She had already saved Chika from the Blood King once back in Miami.

The tone chimed monotonously, every double ring adding a weight of worry to her heart. Mai made an instant decision and, tucking the phone between her neck and shoulder, grabbed her keys and exited the hotel room. Her rental was parked right outside. By the time she wrenched the door open and jumped inside the empty ringing of the phone was enough to destroy her composure.

"Come on!" Mai slammed the steering wheel with both hands and started the vehicle. She tore out of the car park, narrowly missing an oncoming Pepsi wagon, almost drowned by the tones of its blaring air horns. Her hotel was in the heart of Tokyo, not far from Chika's apartment.

"Chika," she said aloud. "Oh no."

Within minutes she had crossed two junctions and caused a fender-bender. She cut off a boy racer in a black Evo and slung the little rental across two lanes onto the street that led to Chika's.

Only then was the call answered. "Yes?"

Mai almost swooned with relief, but didn't let it show in her voice. "Get out. Now. I've just had it confirmed that Kovalenko escaped. It's almost certain he's sent men after you."

"I did tell you about the men who have been watching me," Chika said matter-of-factly. "I'm surprised your other people haven't noticed."

"They probably have. Now get out."

Mai had just enough time to contact Dai Hibiki before she shot to a stop outside Chika's. Dai answered with his customary curt effectiveness.

"What's up?"

"The Blood King is free. He targets family and friends, Dai. If I were you, I would get safe."

"Shit. Understood. And Chika?"

"Here now." Mai rolled the rental up over the curb and jumped out, leaving the door open. Chika ran to meet her, pouncing from the shadows of the arched entryway to her apartment block. Mai quickly scanned the area and wasn't shocked to see three shadowy figures staring down at her through Chika's apartment window.

So close . . .

Chika reached her. Mai nodded and, as she turned, saw a fourth man standing by her car, leaning over the top and lining her up in the sights of a big Desert Eagle. The man was European, well groomed, and wore a sports jacket over a casual open-necked shirt. His lips curled as he spoke.

"The Blood King sends his regards."

CHAPTER FOURTEEN

Could a person dodge more than one bullet? More significantly, could a person raised and trained as a Ninja dodge more than one bullet?

Mai Kitano employed lightning reactions, moving before her would-be killer even had a pound of pressure on the trigger. She could afford that small luxury. She knew exactly where he was aiming. She flung Chika to the ground and used the momentum of her throw to roll into a handstand and spin away. The gun boomed and the bullet flew between her flying heels. She landed in cat stance and sprung even as he realigned his aim, using the trunk of a wide tree for her next point of cover, but knowing she could not stay there for fear of the man turning his aim toward Chika. She paused for a heartbeat, allowing her inner calm and breathing to take over and speed up her reactions.

Mai knew she needed to be seen as the main threat. A second bullet slammed into the tree. Mai realized she was out of time. Chika was alone and totally exposed out here. Mai quickly stepped into view, ready to try her luck, prepared to take a bullet and still fight on to reach the shooter, already fine-tuning the zigzag run that would best preserve her life, when a white cop car shot past her vision and screeched as it swung broadside at the man with the gun.

The killer whirled, eyes wide, but it was too late. One minute the smug victor, the next the victim of a crushing incident, he lay across the hood of the car, held in place only because the vehicles were so close together. The gun slipped from between his fingers and clattered noisily to the road.

Mai stared as Dai Hibiki jumped out and beckoned both her and Chika over. “Hurry. You don’t have much time.” His gaze was turned up toward Chika’s window.

Mai stopped right in front of him. “How the hell did you get here so quick?”

Hibiki smiled at Chika. “When you called I was already on my way here.”

CHAPTER FIFTEEN

Matt Drake assessed the hell, the horror and the stunned confusion that held sway over the center of Washington DC and clamped a hand on Dahl's shoulder.

"Wait."

"What?"

"We have to get this right. Open your friggin' eyes. Not one man out here knows what he's bloody doing."

Dahl stopped, taking in the various scenes playing out around them. Dead ahead, people staggered out of the brightly lit front entrance of the Hotel Dillion amidst the sounds of gunfire. From the left, the two Secret Service agents were sprinting hard *toward* the hotel, shouting at a bunch of cops to follow them. The cops looked bewildered, their attention divided between the snarled-up traffic, the hordes of angry pedestrians, the scene of Gates' murder and the frantic Secret Service agents. In the midst of all this mayhem, it had to have crossed every cop's mind that even the agents might not be who they appeared to be. And to the right, the wide street stretched into a nightmare vision of floodlit chaos, the road snarled and jammed up, hordes of men and women thronging every available space, all the way to the White House.

"Jesus Christ," Dahl breathed, standing still for a minute. "This is just crazy. It's like . . . the end of the world."

Men, women and officials rushed all around them. Strident, purposeless cries cut the air, nothing more than blunt knives. Sirens squalled like errant gusts of wind. And the aimless and the shocked stood all around, dumbfounded, staring at nothing.

Drake ignored it, and tried to contact Hayden again. When he got no answer he decided to try Karin. The phone rang twice before it was picked up.

"Matt? Thank God, are you okay?"

Drake let out a long breath. There was no way to steal himself for this next conversation. And as badly as he wanted to know what was happening at their end, he knew he had to tell her everything he knew first.

"Karin—"

"The whole fucking world's gone crazy, Matt. Romero's dead. Hayden's dying. We're in hiding. And I can't get hold of Ben, or Mum and Dad. Why can't I get hold of them?"

Drake felt the center of his very being wobble. *Romero? And . . . and Hayden?* He wanted to speak, but found his tongue just wouldn't work. All of a sudden the craziness around him didn't matter anymore.

"Fuck me," he said at last, and suddenly found himself sitting down right there in the midst of the mayhem on the city street.

Lost.

"Matt? I'm sorry. I didn't mean to be so blunt. I'm so glad you're okay. How are the others?"

Drake ignored the half-hysterical flurry of questions. "It's bad news, Karin," he said with heavy emotion. "Ben and your Mum and Dad . . . they're gone. They were killed." The last word came out so thick with grief Drake started to cough.

Karin screamed at him. She cried and denied him until her voice drifted away and another came on the phone.

"Drake. This is Smyth. Komodo, Karin and Kinimaka are incommunicado right now. You need to get over here, bud. We could do with you and that crazy Swede about now."

Drake nodded to himself. "What happened?"

"Fuckers hit the HQ hard, man. Didn't give us a chance. Must've been watching it for weeks. We're lucky any of us got outta there alive."

"And Hayden? Romero?"

Smyth drew a breath. "They got hit," he said irritably. "It happens."

Drake relayed the news to Dahl as the Swede squatted next to him. "Where are you, Smyth?"

"Gray's Military Hospital. I haven't the slightest idea where it is. It's pretty well guarded and they're working on Hayden right now. Got a bad feeling though, Drake, like . . . safe ain't safe anymore. Something don't feel right, you know?"

Drake did. If the Blood King's men could find the SPEAR team's HQ, he felt they sure as hell could track them to a hospital, military or not.

"We're on our way." He was about to end the conversation when the phone bleeped to warn him of another incoming call. Drake checked the caller ID and was shocked to see the bat phone symbol flashing, the one he had assigned to Jonathan Gates' most secure emergency line. It had never rung before.

His mouth dropped open yet again. "Smyth. Wait. Just wait."

Quickly, he flipped over to the new line, answering, "Yes? This is Matt Drake."

An official-sounding voice spoke in hard impassive tones. "We're calling all active agents from every agency together right now to attend a crisis meeting at the Hotel Lewison Park, Conference Room 1B."

Drake noted Dahl answering the same call. "What's this about?"

"Go there now. The VP will address you."

"Now? I—"

The connection broke. Drake stared at the phone. *VP?* he thought. *As in Vice President?* His phone had a tracker, so they would know he was close by the Lewison. For a second, he just stared at Dahl.

"Can Kovalenko really do all this?"

"I don't know." Dahl pointed out the Lewison, not a hundred yards away. "But that's one call we can't ignore."

Drake explained the situation to Smyth and told him they would be in touch as soon as they were able. "What happened to the President?" Smyth asked.

"I don't know," Drake said. "But I think we're about to find out."

CHAPTER SIXTEEN

Mano Kinimaka sat down heavily in the plastic seat, aware but not caring that its legs were splayed dangerously close to collapse. Before him, Hayden struggled to turn her head on the pillow, her pasty white face scrunched up in pain. The hospital had done a good job of patching her up, but the bullet had taken a heavy toll on her strength.

Kinimaka wiped his eyes.

Slowly, Hayden's lips moved. Kinimaka caught a whisper. "What is it, Mano?"

The big Hawaiian stared at the far wall. "My mom," he said in a voice that sounded like he had a mouthful of knives. "Kovalenko got to her."

Even in her critical state, Hayden struggled to sit up. Her gasp of pain alerted Kinimaka and dragged him back from the brink of shock. "Stop." He moved over to sit on the bed and leaned over, feeling the entire apparatus shift and hugged her hard. "Stop, Hayden."

"Is she . . . ?" The feathery whisper was like a dream voice in his ear.

"Okay?" He spoke into the bed cover, his voice muffled. "No. They murdered her. That bastard murdered my mom."

Hayden kissed him softly. Kinimaka felt tears flood his eyes and shook his head. "It ain't worth it. All this shit we put ourselves through? It just ain't worth it anymore."

"I know. And with Jonathan gone, what will we do?"

Kinimaka turned his head so he could look into his girlfriend's eyes. The sparks that had twinkled there, glittering by-products of an energetic vivacious heart, were now dulled almost to obscurity. The pallor of her skin spoke of her nearness to death. But she wouldn't give in. Still, she fought.

Kinimaka steeled himself, using her strength to rally his own resilience and courage. "You are my mentor," he said. "And my idol. You always will be, Hayden Jaye."

Her attempt at a smile broke his heart again. When the phone rang he slammed it to his ear without once breaking their eye contact.

"Yes?"

"Mano. This is Agent Collins, your CIA liaison for LA. It's about your sister, Kono. You just rang to check on her?"

Kinimaka could barely bring himself to speak. "Yes."

"She's fine and under close guard. Without going into too much detail, Mano, we got there just in time."

"Thank . . . you," he managed, "Agent Collins."

"Don't thank me," she said. "It was your call that prompted the op. Thank yourself." The agent hung up; tough, strict and to the point.

Hayden brushed his hair with a shaking hand. "She's okay?"

"Yeah. She's fine."

"Thank God."

Kinimaka looked up, then around the room; for the first time noticing the lack of security, the open undraped windows, the well-lit office blocks that surrounded the hospital, the tree-lined entry road.

"God ain't here for us today," he said, standing up. "We're going to have to look after ourselves."

CHAPTER SEVENTEEN

The Blood King poured himself a precise shot of vodka, expecting very little from the relatively famous French brand and receiving exactly that. He tipped the shot back in one go, the way his Russian fathers and forefathers had always done. He yelled out a toast, as was his ritual.

"To freedom," he said, speaking to Gabriel and the other mercenaries about the room. "Let us hope it tastes better than this fuckin' vodka, dah?"

The men saluted. The Blood King chased the shot with a salty pickle, obtained from the in-room mini bar. "Gods," he said, spitting the bits out. "I have tasted better prison food." He stared at the quiet occupant in the room. "How about you? What exactly is your poison, Mr. President?"

Coburn eyed Kovalenko with disdain. "You won't get away with this."

"I won't? But I already have, Mr. Pres. I already have."

"What the hell do you want?"

"Ah, sixty-four million dollar question. But that number is so out of date in modern times, yes? Let's see, how much did it cost you to become President? Six hundred and sixty four million, perhaps?"

"You're crazy, Kovalenko."

"So they tell me," the Blood King said wryly. "Too many years at sea playing the salty dog. Same as Blackbeard, yes?"

"So you still think you're a pirate? You won't be able to disappear this time, Kovalenko."

The Blood King poured a second shot, contemplating the President's words and weighing them against the recent pleasurable scene he'd witnessed in the hotel's lobby when his men had decimated Coburn's Secret Service detail. This was something new for him, weighing someone else's opinion against his own. After so many years of fulfillment without consequence it was actually a breath of fresh air. But he had discovered the ability in prison whilst recruiting Mordant and Gabriel to the cause, and had found, to his surprise, that other people had clever ideas too.

But the Americans were weak at their heart and unimaginative. They had allowed a covert enemy force to plant an operative deep inside their capital city's Department of Transport—to the point where he been able to pull off a one-time infiltration of their secretive hi-tech VIP traffic control system.

All lights green, was the maxim, meaning 'clear the way for the particular dignitary', but not this time. On this occasion, the saying had become an absolute—all lights, all roads.

And there was still something *far* better to come.

Kovalenko threw back the shot, toasting under his breath, this time to his lieutenants and the men they had selected. The Secret Service agents had ordered the lobby to be evacuated, but had been understandably uneasy, and when armed men had stepped forward from several different parts of the room two of them had choked, others had died instantly, three had thrown themselves at the President, and the rest had simply started blasting away.

No mind, Kovalenko thought. It didn't matter. They had all died. Coburn was unharmed, and even that hadn't been a prerequisite of the op. The Blood King had shot several wounded men in the head, satisfying his blood lust for that part of the day. At last, life felt right again, almost worth living.

"What *do* you want?" Coburn said again, interrupting his reverie.

"What do you get man who has everything?" Kovalenko said in his thick Russian accent. "A president?" He chuckled. "Heads of men who have betrayed him? Imprisoned him? Well, that will do to start."

"You're still pursuing this damn vendetta? So that's why you killed Jonathan. We should have ended you when we had the chance."

Kovalenko looked a little surprised. "I see you are a fighter, not a whiner, yes? Well, it is good. I would hate to have to cut out your tongue so soon."

Gabriel caught his attention. "Dis ting is ready, mon. You want it over dere?"

The Blood King grinned and moved over to sit by the President. From his waistband, he produced two huge guns and set them down on the table. The suite was situated on a high floor, prepped weeks ago before being cleared out for the inevitable Secret Service sweep. It was perfect for their needs, and just one of many rooms their enemies might figure they were occupying.

Gabriel positioned a large-screen laptop on the table before him. The Motion Eye—its webcam—was already activated.

"Will this stream live?"

"When y' push de button." Gabriel indicated the enter key. "You will broadcast to YouTube, and after that Hulu, UStream, Blinkx and a hundred others. De right channels have been informed dat a broadcast be imminent."

"They will not try to shut it down?"

Gabriel shrugged. "Unlikely. Dey need dis information. Dey might try to censor it. Gag us. But the American news channels, dey are bold, mon. Dey will sink dere claws in. Dey will get dere story." Gabriel smiled widely, making the President's eyes widen. Kovalenko didn't blame him. The African was one scary, unhinged, but absolutely brilliant fellow and had shown his proficiency time and time again whilst plotting Coburn's downfall from prison, through intermediaries to powerful men on the outside.

Men who were just starting to rise in ways of their own.

Kovalenko tossed back one more toast. "To Blood Vendetta."

Then he hit the enter key and positioned the webcam's eye so that only the President and he could be seen. As a broad smile broke out over the Blood King's face, he calmly and noisily loaded his guns as the nation watched.

He stared into the camera the whole time and spoke only four words. "Come and get me."

CHAPTER EIGHTEEN

"Fuck."

Alicia Myles slammed her phone down on the bedside table and shook Lomas. When the bearded biker didn't twitch a muscle, Alicia sat up and delivered a hard blow to his ribs.

"Urrghhh," Lomas groaned, coming out of a foggy sleep. "Let me sleep. What—"

"Get the fuck up," Alicia was already shrugging on her clothes. "Or I'll squeeze your balls until your eyes pop."

Lomas rolled over. "Again? I didn't even enjoy it the first time."

"Come on. Drake called. The bloody Blood King escaped. There'll be a vendetta out on me, you and the entire crew."

"The *bloody* Blood King? Is that Kovelanko's crazy brother or something?"

Alicia sat down to buckle her boots. "Just hurry."

"Christ, Myles," Lomas leaned on an elbow, watching her. "There's *always* a vendetta out on us. We're bikers, for shit's sake, every one of us a one-percenter. What's so different about this vendetta?"

A one-percenter was a biker belonging to that small ratio of bikers who didn't abide by the law. Alicia turned to Lomas and, as she had anticipated, the deep anxiety stretched across her face was almost enough to get him going. She added more, "He's killed some of my friends, their families, the Secretary of Defense, and has kidnapped the President in the last hour."

"The President?" Lomas looked blank for a second, then shot up. "What, *the* President? Of the US? But . . . but what makes you think he'll have time for us?"

Alicia bit back her frustration, taking a second to clear her head. To protect the bikers, she would need Lomas. These guys were tough and wouldn't be moved easily; certainly not through mere threat. "I was part of the team that put him away. Even before that, he swore a blood vendetta on our lives and the lives of our families and friends. This is the man who taught the CIA new lessons in how to disappear. The man who led a terrorist attack on Hawaii. Remember? And now," she reached out, "Now he's after us."

"But he's just a man."

Alicia nodded. "He is. But he's better connected than Parliament and Congress put together. Look, I already seriously doubt everyone will survive the next few hours." She paused. "The longer we wait the more of us will die."

At last, Lomas seemed to get the picture. He pulled away from her, stared a moment longer, then seemed to remember exactly who was saying these things to him—the strongest, hardest, most capable warrior he had ever met. "What should we do?"

"Get the fuck gone. Off the grid."

Alicia grabbed her gear and padded over to the window. They were three floors up in yet another luxurious European hotel paid for by a grateful US government. Outside, the night was black; the glaring hotel lights showed no activity save for the flitting of a little white electric security car.

"These people wouldn't show themselves," she said. "They'll be total pros. Mercs. Disgruntled commandos. Top-class fighters. I hope we're not too late, I already fought my way out of a hotel against Kovalenko once." It seemed a long time ago now since her boyfriend had been murdered.

She suddenly felt isolated, being so far away from the team. Since she had quit the SAS and the British Ninth Division, Alicia had been more than happy to go it alone, but then

SPEAR came along with its many diverse personalities. Among them, Alicia had felt needed, even protected. When there was no immediate threat, leaving them for a while hadn't seemed much of an issue. Now, even with her new biker family, she felt strangely alone.

Shit, what the hell is wrong with me? Is it something to do with Drake?

From the moment she had met him in that undignified way in Africa he had become a part of her heart.

Where did she belong? Never with a father who got fall-down drunk and beat her mother. Not even with the Army. With Drake? She thought about that one for a second, remembering that first meeting in Johannesburg during the firefight to end them all. She, Drake and two SAS teams had taken on an army of African commandos and lived to tell the tale. But no—she didn't believe there was a future for the two of them.

Besides, now he had Mai.

Behind her, Lomas was calling the guys on his phone. It was quicker than trying to wake them up by knocking on every door. After five minutes of haranguing and sermonizing, Lomas had ordered them all to be gathered along the corridor in five minutes.

Alicia turned to him. "Good. We all need to enter the lobby together."

"We have no weapons," Lomas reminded her. "Short of your pistol and mine, Whipper's whips and a truckload of knives. Maybe a couple of old Uzis somewhere." He shrugged seriously. "Not much to fight with."

Alicia smiled wistfully. "Then we'll adopt one of Drakey's tricks. We'll pry them from the fingers of our dead enemies."

****

The biker gang, looking messy, tired and bedraggled, yawned their way carelessly toward the lifts. Everyone had their belongings and bike keys at the ready, hands inches from concealed weapons. Laid-Back Lex viewed it all through slitted eyes while Ribeye scouted every meandering turn of the corridor.

"Three teams," Alicia said. "One in each lift and one down the stairs. Ready?"

"Wait," Dirty Sarah said. "Who made you Bitch Queen? This ain't no democracy, dear."

Lomas waved her off. "Stop. Any of you shitheads get accepted into the SAS?"

Most of the bikers shook their heads. A couple looked as if they were thinking hard, trying to remember their old lives.

"She did. Let her take the lead till we're out of here."

Alicia didn't tell them again, just headed for the stairs. The stairwell was empty, the whole area as quiet as a mausoleum. She peered quickly over the rails, but saw no sign of movement.

"Come on."

Lomas stayed close behind, followed by the veggie Ribeye, the young and pretty Trace, Whipper and several others. Whipper had no way of furtively carrying her whip, so she let it unfurl beside her, holding it close to her body.

Alicia led the way down three flights and put her face to the glass aperture in the door that led out to the lobby. "Nothing," she said. "Stay close."

With fingers wrapped around the butt of the gun in her jacket pocket, the Englishwoman stepped boldly out into the lobby. Silence greeted her; a silence wrapped in worry and stress. They heard the lifts ding and moved quickly to cover the automatic doors.

Nothing happened. The lobby was empty. Alicia crossed the carpeted floor, tense, expecting at any moment to hear the opening salvos of a fusillade of shots. The blackness of 0300 hours smothered every window, and the sparse pools of light outside shone on big puddles of nothing.

But beyond them . . . beyond them were landscaped gardens full of trees, bushes and undergrowth. And the major roads past that. She scanned the skies. No sign of movement.

Lomas took the time to check out. "That much for Pay-Per-View? Really?"

The woman behind the desk looked a little embarrassed. Lomas smiled. "Ah, I read your mind, honey, faster than you can say Jurassic Pork. *That* kind of Pay-Per-View? Well, we're bikers. Unofficially, of course. We take it where we can get it."

Alicia turned. "Time to go."

She cracked the front door and walked out into the chilly night. The hotel's parking area was right out front, which helped enormously. The gang picked their way among the silent cars, spreading out and taking different routes to where their crowd of two-wheeled machines sat waiting.

Alicia never stopped assessing. If anyone was out there they were good. She sensed nothing out of place, nothing that sent her radar twitching. And that radar had been fixed into her by the best mentors in the world. What could they be waiting for?

Nothing, she thought. They weren't here yet.

Or spectacle, she thought again. Kovalenko was all about the spectacle. Well, fuck him. The more time they were given, the better their chance of survival. She watched as the gang slipped astride their bikes, weapons now exposed, and looked over to Lomas. The next step would be a noisy one.

Alicia climbed aboard Lomas' Ducati Monster and squeezed his ribs. "Do it."

"Which way?"

Alicia thought about it. A good adversary would already have the variables covered. "Head for the airport."

Lomas inclined his head. The whole noisy ensemble started their engines en masse. The sweet music of throaty Sportster V-twins, Hondas, Suzukis, low-slung choppers and big Bark-o-loungers mingled into an earsplitting cacophony; a deafening roar and snarl of purpose. Lomas peeled out first, and the gang streamed after, satisfied to a man and woman now that they were back in their element. The night was dark, the lights low, and the long road was already beckoning.

The hotel stood at their backs, all but those occupants too drunk or drugged woken up and dragged out of bed by the noise, but by now everyone except Alicia barely remembered its name. Lomas guided his Ducati along a roaming path and through the hotel's gates, out onto a wide service road. Two miles ahead stood a set of stoplights and a junction that led to Autobahn 8, a significant three-hundred-mile stretch of road that led from Salzburg to Luxembourg. Lomas powered down the two mile road, Alicia studying the blackness that blasted past. Every inch of tarmac that flashed by made her breathe a little easier. Within minutes, the entire gang had entered the Autobahn and were starting to open their throttles.

Lomas tipped his head back. "Looks like they couldn't find us fast enough. We never actually registered under real names, you know."

"Maybe you should have. Authorities wouldn't know them."

Lomas coughed. "Interpol might."

Alicia saw meager amounts of traffic behind them. A helicopter hovered in the lighter skies toward Stuttgart. It all looked perfectly normal.

"Just don't spare the horses."

****

Alicia allowed the winding road to take her attention away as the turbulent stream of bikes tore through the night. It wouldn't do to stay perfectly primed every step of the way; she needed to find time to unwind. The rest of the crew was constantly surveying the area, though of course in the dark every light looks the same.

Alicia tried to quell a flustered feeling, something totally alien to her. Drake's call hadn't been long, but it had intimated that the SPEAR team was falling apart. Even now, people she had come to like, even care about, could be dying. And she was over here in freakin' Germany hanging with a pack of knuckleheads. She should be over there, in the fray, fighting their greatest battle yet. She needed that release.

Well, maybe I can get there before it's all done.

Glittering lights emerged out of the utter dark ahead. Alicia saw a long bridge stretching over a deep chasm, floodlit every few feet. Three lanes to both carriageways and a barrier down the middle. It stood like a glaring oasis in a land of shadow. As the growling procession poured across the bridge, a sudden shout rang out, passing through the gang's hissing Bluetooth helmet microphones.

Lomas slowed and looked back. "What did he say?"

Alicia had already seen it. "Big black vehicle just blocked the bridge behind us."

"Probably a BMW," Lomas speculated. "Some of those Bavarian Motor Works car drivers can be real wankers."

"Make that two."

Alicia didn't have to employ her sixth and seventh senses for trouble to know this was about to get way beyond ugly. The floodlit bridge was a spectacle Kovalenko and his men wouldn't pass up. As the bikers powered on, it soon became obvious that the way ahead was also blocked.

"Shit." Lomas pulled up. "There ain't no way off this bridge, Taz."

Alicia scanned in both directions, trying to discern their enemy's intent. The biker gang gathered and formed a rough circle like the cavalry at Custer's Last Stand. Laid-Back Lex was as calm as ever.

"What are we doin' here, Lomas? Waitin' around to be rat-packed by these fuckers? Tell us to do something!"

Lomas ignored him, along with everyone else. If Lex wasn't bitchin', politicians weren't on the take and local councils were in it for the people. Alicia watched and waited and then both sets of vehicles parted no more than a car's width and four powerful Nissan coupés shot through the gaps.

"Here they come."

Front and behind, the fast cars blasted clear of the road block and spread out across the three lanes, attacking the circle of bikers head on. Men leaned out of every window, rifles in hand, taking aim.

"This ain't gonna be pretty," Ribeye said.

Alicia made eye contact with Lomas. "Not everyone will survive. Just do the best you can."

Lomas revved up the Monster. "Take 'em apart, boys."

CHAPTER NINETEEN

Mai met the master assassin, Gyuki, in the green depths of Shinjuku Park, close to the Hilton in central Tokyo. At any other time, the scenery would have called to her. Multi-hued tall and short trees, sculpted bushes, temples, bridges and acres of lush greenery offered a tranquil place for her mind to dwell, but not on this day.

The place of their meeting was a low, arched bridge spanning a narrow body of water. Trees overhung both sides, and natural vegetation had built up all around. It was a good place for a clandestine meet.

Mai saw the figure standing in the center of the bridge as she approached. It had been a long time since she had seen Gyuki; a long time since she had even *heard* of him. When he looked up, pinning her with his gaze, she saw the fire in his eyes was as furious and fanatical as ever.

"Your prayers were not answered," were his first words to her in so many years she had forgotten. "I did not die."

"Master Gyuki." She inclined her head. "The years have not changed you, though perhaps the world has?"

"Is that your way of inferring that *you* have changed?" Gyuki spat the words, the deep furrows across his face creasing. "In what way? To consort with our enemy?"

Mai watched him very carefully, mindful of every fluid change in his body. His hands and arms were hidden deep inside a flowing black cloak which reached to his knees, and his face was partly shaded by a wide-brimmed hat. "I consort only with those I wish to," Mai said evenly. "Just like any girl who is not owned. Tell me, Master Gyuki, do you have the same luxury?"

The assassin's eyes widened. Mai slipped into a defensive stance. She knew her friend, Dai Hibiki, was observing the exchange through the lens of a high-powered rifle, but Gyuki was quick.

Was he quicker than a bullet?

Of course, she thought. A man didn't become the greatest Ninja assassin of all time through tardiness in battle.

It isn't being faster than the bullet. She remembered his teachings. *It is offering the person behind the barrel many distractions.*

"The Clan made you," Gyuki said. "Yet you show your disrespect."

Mai shook her head. She had been determined not to get into a slanging match with Gyuki, it would do her no good, but his visionless words spoke purely of blind faith. Here was a man who had never loved anything, owned anything, or experienced the happiness of childhood, even his own. Here was a machine, made by older machines that should have died out long ago.

Extinction would be good for them.

"The Clan *bought* me. Imprisoned me. Molded me into a killer with no soul, no heart. They killed with impunity and, I daresay, probably still do. Some of those old jobs I heard about, and the one I observed," she shook her head, "still haunt me."

"It is our life," Gyuki said simply. "It is what we were born to do."

"Not me," Mai said. "I was dragged from the arms of my penniless parents. I, who had known only adoration and love, was suddenly told it was fight or die. Survive or perish in adversity. You had no right to impose that law. You still don't."

"You will return to the Clan for the rest of your life," Gyuki told her harshly. "And you will do our bidding, whatever that may be. We own you and always have. There will be no other life for you, Mai Kitano."

"And how do you intend to enforce your words?"

Mai faced off the master assassin, confident in her own ability, but knowing he was probably better. The odds still stood at two-to-one, though. She was sure he hadn't spotted Hibiki.

Gyuki didn't move. His fiery glare bored into her own eyes as if he was trying to set her on fire. Maybe he could do that. Mai wondered if she'd played too many video games in her past. Then Gyuki did move, but it was only a step toward the edge of the bridge. He clasped the rails, deliberately not looking at her.

"Your parents are with us now."

Mai gasped. Nothing could have shocked her more. Chika had disowned her parents when she found out about Mai, and Mai herself had not known them since she was a child. Neither sister knew of their whereabouts and had privately thought they might have passed away. The broken hearted tended to die young.

Mai grasped the rail, trying to steady herself. "You mean you have them imprisoned? In your village?"

"They reside in the Clan village," Gyuki acknowledged. "We have a job for you." He produced a manila folder from deep inside the folds of his cloak. "Everything is in there. Do this job, Mai Kitano, or you will never see your parents alive again. And even after them we would sacrifice Chika, and Hibiki, and then you. For the Clan"

Gyuki turned to walk away. "The quicker you get it done, the quicker you will see your parents."

"You must let them go!" Mai called after him. "If I do this you must let them go."

Gyuki did not answer.

CHAPTER TWENTY

Lomas gunned the Ducati forward so hard Alicia was thrown backwards and almost dismounted. Blood lust coursed through the man's veins, mixed with more than a little fear. Alicia steadied herself and yanked out her pistol. She leaned around her boyfriend's bulk, sighting down the barrel. A blue Nissan sped toward her with a man hanging out the passenger side, rifle in hand. The driver toted a small handgun through his own window. More Nissans stretched across the three-lane Autobahn. Half of Lomas's biker gang peeled out beside him, filling the road; the other half shot off in the other direction.

"Crash an' burn, boys," Lomas breathed into his helmet mic. "It was always gonna come down to this."

Both enemies raced toward each other at reckless speed, the cluttered row of bikes grumbling toward the screaming pearl-blue line-up of cars. Lomas shouted over the uproar, "So here's another first for you!"

"Oh, I've been in a charge before," Alicia said, remembering Czechoslovakia. "But never whilst riding a Monster!"

Lomas ducked his head even lower. "Crazy beautiful," he mumbled. "Now I know what Slash meant."

Alicia fired, destroying her enemy's windscreen. Shots drilled back, zipping overhead. A single bullet clanged off the engine block, ricocheting harmlessly away. Alicia switched her aim to the tires and fired twice, mindful that she only had one spare clip. Both her shots bounced off the tarmac.

To their left a bike went down, scraping along at high speed with a noise like a felled leviathan. Its rider, JPS, spun beside it, shredding his leathers as he went. He was one of the unarmed bikers, but determined to help distract their attackers. In seconds, the bikes and cars ate up the ground separating them and came together. One bike struck the side of a car, bouncing off and sending its rider screaming over the parapet of the bridge. Lomas cursed heavily. The car veered across the path of another, sending both vehicles into a slide. Two more bikes went down, one with its rider shot, the other through sheer bad luck.

Lomas hung low over his engine as his bike shot through the gap between two cars. Bullets flew horizontally. Alicia ducked to the left, firing blindly to the right. They were past in less than two seconds. When she breathed again and turned around, all four cars were already lining back up, preparing for another charge. Beyond them, the rest of the bikers hustled through their own bullet-strewn gauntlet, taking fire.

The blue Nissans screamed in unison. The vehicles spurted forward, laying down acres of rubber. Clouds of bluish smoke obscured the scene behind them. Lomas blipped the throttle of the Ducati, looking across the line at his men and women.

"Hit it."

The column surged ahead. Whipper's bike ran next to theirs, letting her notorious weapon unfurl behind as she took off. Alicia popped a Nissan's driver-side tire with her first shot this time, then the tire of the one running beside it. One of the cars started to swerve crazily toward them.

"Shit," Lomas all but yelped, speculating on the best way to go. The Nissan swung sharply about. Alicia took out a rear tire and then suddenly the whole vehicle flipped, its occupants rattling crazily around the interior as the three-ton runaway killing machine bounced straight for them.

Alicia saw Whipper to her right unleash her whip expertly toward the arm of the driver who sought to shoot her. The hard twined rope slashed through the air at the speed of sound, lashing the gun from his hand and severing two fingers. The man's scream was lost as that car also turned sharply.

Now Alicia had two death traps tumbling toward her.

And no way to save herself. It was all in the hands of Lomas, a situation she rarely faced and absolutely detested. The biker leader laid it down, leaning the bike over hard and sliding, scraping the big machine along the ground. Sparks flew from the bike, the fairing, and from the metal heel-tips of his boots. The first Nissan slammed down with an almighty crash no more than six inches before them, then rose just enough for the Ducati to slide right under. The spinning car bonnet glanced off Lomas's helmet, knocking his head back hard. Alicia saw the Nissan's occupants with their faces pressed hard up against the windscreen and bodies hanging loosely. Already dead.

She fought to help Lomas, angling her weight so the bike ground its way beyond the path of the second Nissan, but their combined weight wasn't quite enough. The blue car struck the ground hard just as the Ducati grated by, smashing down on its front wheel and flipping both Lomas and Alicia into the air.

Alicia flailed as she flew and landed heavily, tucking on impact. The air rushed from her lungs. The biker's suit saved her flesh from being churned to Swiss cheese; the helmet protected her skull. She rolled with the momentum, decreasing the impact, and came up on one knee.

Both vehicles smashed into one another with a thump like a house falling down. Debris scattered across the carriageway. She spotted at least two unmoving bodies and several rifles. But that didn't matter for now. Quickly, she turned to Lomas and shook his shoulder.

"That was close. C'mon, this ain't no time for a nap, dickhead."

Lomas rolled over, but only through the momentum caused by Alicia's shaking. His form lay inert, still. Alicia pulled his helmet off and stared at his face.

"No."

She slapped his cheeks before thinking to check for a pulse. As her heart rose into her mouth, Alicia Myles did the one thing she had shunned since childhood.

She prayed for another person.

"Please, God. Please, God. Please . . ."

Lomas's eyes flickered open. The pulse beneath her finger was weak, but tangible. "Christ," he muttered. "That hurt."

Alicia scanned his body. There were no obvious injuries: no blood, no crooked joints. If Lomas was in pain, the damage was on the inside.

"Wait here. I'll get help."

She took in the situation. The bad news was that many of the bikers were down, at least half of them clearly wounded or unmoving. The good news was that only one of the Nissans remained. She skimmed across the scene at both ends of the bridge, not liking what she saw. All four BMWs were still in place.

To her side, Lomas's Ducati still rumbled. A germ of an idea entered her head.

"I think we—"

The hand that grabbed her wrist was desperate. Alicia started and flicked her gaze back to Lomas. What she saw turned her insides to ice. Bright-red blood bubbled up through his open mouth. The biker tried to talk, but the gush of blood made him cough and choke.

"Lomas." Her voice was emotionless.

"If this . . . if this is the last . . . fight of the Slayers," he managed. "Make sure . . . we win."

Alicia held his hand and moved her head close until their noses were touching. She knew her lover was about to die and no one could save him. She took in the last moments of his life, his breath, and savored them. His last gasp came, but it was the sudden silence that was most overwhelming. The abrupt absence of sound.

She sat back, looking up, searching the black skies for an answer, a plan. Anything. If there was one time in her life she thought her prayers had been answered this had been it. But nothing existed up there. It was all shit.

Forged in adversity, born to battle, Alicia rose to stand over the body of the biker leader. Fast as a fox she hefted up the Ducati and gave a huge bellow, a great rallying call.

"To me!" she cried. *"You want to win? Come to me!"*

The weary and the half-dead, the bleeding and the broken, those on their last legs and last bullets, all stood up. Ribeye and Whipper, Laid-Back Lex and Knuckler, Dirty Sarah and Trace, rose like heroes among the ashes. Alicia revved the Ducati and leaned over as it spurted forward, scooping up two of the rifles. The surviving bikers dashed to their machines, jumping astride the seats and gunning them toward her. Alicia spun the Monster on its back wheel, leaving a cloud of dust all around her.

"Go to hell, you bastards."

As the rest of the bikers drew level with her, Alicia opened the Ducati's throttle, sending it zipping forward at an alarming pace. As she rode, she laid both rifles across each other, balanced on the front of the bike, their barrels facing forward and stocks nestled into the pit of her arms. The gap between her and the BMWs decreased fast, and soon she could make out moon-like faces staring through the half-smoked windows. Another two seconds and Alicia took her hands off the handlebars, steering with the weight of her body and pressure on the rifles, and let loose a double salvo from hell.

Bullets spewed from the barrels, firing in two directions, decimating the sides of the big SUVs. With an effort, she concentrated her fire toward the gap in the middle, destroying the front and back ends of the respective vehicles. Metal chunks cleaved away. Doors flew open as men scrambled to safety. The rear car collapsed, its wheels destroyed. To her left and right the surviving biker crew fired and slashed and threw whatever weapons they could at the fleeing men, taking out as many as possible for the friends they had left behind. Alicia's focus was the narrow gap and the stream of bullets. She could allow nothing else to enter her thoughts right now. It was all about death and escape, blood and vengeance.

The Ducati shot through the breach, twitching as its tires hit debris on the way through. Alicia let go of the rifles, but didn't stop. She turned in her seat, seeing her comrades shimmy and swerve in her wake as they negotiated the small opening. With the road open before her again, she opened the throttle and keyed her Bluetooth helmet mic.

"Is this thing still working?"

"I hear you." Trace's voice. The others joined in one by one.

"We should take a moment for our friends." Alicia waited in silence, seething as the dark skies began to lighten.

"I'm heading for the nearest airport," she then said; anger, passion and loss thickening her voice. "The crazy bastard who sanctioned this is walking free in DC. Who's with me?"

CHAPTER TWENTY ONE

Before Matt Drake entered the Hotel Lewison Park, he took one more call. The initial plan was to ignore everything, get to the meeting, and find out what the hell was happening, but when he saw the caller ID he simply stopped and stared in disbelief.

"Bloody hell. I don't believe this."

Dahl looked over his shoulder like an annoying parrot. "You don't believe what? Who is it this time?"

"Stop squawking." Drake turned away and pushed the green button. The call connected instantly and, despite the distance, the voice that spoke sounded crisp and clear.

"Is this Matt Drake?"

"Yes sir, Mr. Crouch. How are you?"

A moment of silence followed. Michael Crouch was the highly respected leader of the British special ops unit known as the Ninth Division, a secret section that specialized in dangerous missions, usually involving traitors and extractions, and with the perpetual support of the SAS, though they could literally call on anyone inside the British Isles and more than a few outside the borders. Drake had not spoken to Crouch in eight years.

"Good, Drake, good. We're all gutted to hear about Sam and Jo. They were . . . stalwarts." Crouch wasn't a big speaker. What he had to say was usually summed up in just a few words. But the meaning behind them was always straight from the heart.

"Thank you, sir." Drake wanted to say more, but with thoughts of Sam and Jo came thoughts of Ben and his parents, and Hayden, Mai and Alicia, and everyone else who might be under threat from the Blood King. "They were."

Crouch sighed. "Been a while, Matt. Been a while. I've heard all about your latest exploits. Just remember, lad, you're British."

Drake knew Crouch wouldn't expand on that statement and, in any case, he didn't have to. There was a certain reserve associated with and expected from a British soldier. The SPEAR team didn't usually display it.

"Yes, sir. Sorry, sir." All the time he was thinking *what the hell are the Ninth Division calling me now for?*

Drake waited. Crouch was the deserved top dog of the supreme and most secret unit of the British Special Forces. He was the man everyone wanted on their side, many steps above what Wells had been. He hadn't just called for a chat.

"What exactly are you into, lad?"

Drake stared at his reflection in a nearby window. He hadn't expected that. "I'm not sure what you mean, sir."

"We know about the Secretary of Defense, the President and Kovalenko. But what's the bastard's plan? What's the feel over there, Drake?"

The Brits were after an inside man then, probably shitting themselves over in Whitehall in case the Blood King had any special plans for them. Crouch must be under immense pressure but, good man or not, Drake wouldn't betray the people he worked for.

"We're heading into a meeting right now, sir," he said. "After that, I'll tell you what I can, but only that."

Crouch sighed again. "Thought you might say that. Here, you talk to him."

Drake blinked at himself in the window. *What next?* Then the dulcet tones he remembered from many previous ops soothed their way across the airwaves.

"Hey, Matt. Shelly here. How about lending us a hand on this one?"

Drake almost shivered. Shelly Cohen possessed the type of voice you might hear on a late night radio show—sweet as honey, melodic and very comforting. She was the beating heart of the Ninth Division, warm but at the same time as hard as nails, your friend but always pushing you toward that next great goal. Along with Crouch the two were a formidable team.

"Hi, Shelly. Always good to hear your voice. I told Crouch I'll do what I can."

"I see. Well, the PM has our balls in a vice with this one. Anything you can do will help."

Jesus, he thought. *How can she make the phrase 'balls in a vice' sound so sexy?*

"I will," he said. "For you. Um, for you all, I mean."

"Of course. Well, speak soon. And stay frisky."

It was her motto, the phrase she used with the boys in the field when they were in harm's way. It was a double entendre of course, but one that helped endear her to every soldier. The other thing that defined her was her penchant to venture into the field quite regularly herself, often unsupported and on dangerous missions. Shelly Cohen was a bit of an unattainable legend back at the Ninth Division. Drake couldn't believe he hadn't thought of her in eight years.

"Friskier than ever," he said, then realized she'd already hung up. Dahl was at his side, staring at him.

"Who are you talking to? One of those sex-talk call centers?"

"Yeah." Drake pocketed the phone. "It was Swedish. Your wife answered."

"Well, the VP is waiting," Dahl said impassively. "The wife will have to hang on."

They trotted toward the heavily guarded hotel, IDs at the ready.

"Jesus, Drake," Dahl said. "I thought we'd encountered almost everything. But this." He shook his head. "All this that's happening tonight. It just takes the fuckin' gold medal for batshit crazy."

"Don't worry," Drake replied, stress thickening his Yorkshire accent. "We're gonna find Kovalenko right quick and stick a grenade down his gob."

CHAPTER TWENTY TWO

Drake entered Conference Room 1B not knowing what to expect. The first thing he noticed was the heavy security; at least twenty Secret Service agents stood around the raised dais at the end of the room when only half-a-dozen normally surrounded the President. They wore black suits and blue ties, and bore little gold pins on their lapels. To a man, a white earpiece dangled from their lobes and disappeared under their collars. Even more stood about the room, automatic weapons in full view. Drake knew the Army was gathering outside—several of its highest ranking officers were already here.

The room itself bustled with agents from every division, many stood around in groups discussing the crisis. Drake just hoped they weren't already deciding which poor bastard would take the fall for all this.

Several large TVs and monitors had been hastily erected above the stage, each one showing the face of an important-looking individual, depicted by their uniforms, medals and bearing.

Dahl pointed to the dais. "You know any of those men?"

"No more than you. Vice President Dolan in the flesh. Chairman of the Joint Chiefs, Sanford, on telly. I bet those guys are the other Joint Chiefs. Not sure about the rest."

Dahl nodded to a sandy-haired man to the far right. "I know him. Commandant of the Marine Corps, Tom Liddell. Good man."

Drake glanced across the room and headed over to the water table. Several jugs were scattered about and he helped himself to a glass. As he drank, the Vice President rose and called for quiet. The casual unceremonious way in which he did it confirmed as much as anything the level of threat they were up against.

"My friends, I don't have long here. The Secret Service are about to whisk me off." He waited until every last murmur subsided. "They would rather I be long gone already. But I wanted to say—this will not stand. This is free American soil, my friends, and *no one* will dictate to us our way of life. This is free American soil, hard-fought for by every serviceman and woman every day of their lives. This is free American soil, and we *will* fight for it tooth and nail, blood and bone, until every last breath has been forced from our bodies. We will fight and we will never stop, for our way of life, for our dignity, our honor, and for our children."

The Vice President nodded and turned away, quickly surrounded by the Secret Service. The room erupted into applause. Drake put down his glass to join in, and Dahl clapped loudly at his side. After a minute, another man spoke, the Deputy Secretary of Defense, William Massey.

Massey, on camera, held up a remote control and flicked it at his own screen. A blank TV at the front of the room glimmered into life. "This is what happened a few minutes ago."

Drake watched as, unbelievably, Dmitry Kovalenko, seated beside President Coburn, calmly laid down a four-word challenge to every serviceman, cop or gung-ho citizen in the United States.

"Come and get me."

Massey leaned into the camera, but another voice spoke up first. The voice of the Chairman of the Joint Chiefs, John Sanford.

"It must never be said that the United States watched indolently when we were tested. We will not stand in disarray and watch a public execution. By God, we will accept that bastard's challenge and go get our president."

Now Massey held up a hand. "But first we need *your* input." He acknowledged every man and woman in the room. "You were all brought here today—and yes, some are still en route—because of your past service to this country and the special skills you can bring to the table. This—" he clicked an unseen button. "Is the blueprint of the Hotel Dillion. It is overlaid with every known facelift and upgrade. Put your heads together, gentlemen. We're going in to get President Coburn within the hour."

CHAPTER TWENTY THREE

Mai Kitano turned her back on the small picturesque bridge where she had met Gyuki only when she was sure the master assassin had left the area. She made her way warily out of the park and around to the prearranged meeting point with Dai Hibiki. The terse little Japanese agent was waiting for her and spoke as soon as she approached the open window of his car.

"What did he say?"

Mai waited until she had climbed into the front seat and sat down. She remained suspicious. The parking area was very public, jam-packed with dog-walkers, shoppers and people on their lunch breaks, but such manic activity could just as easily hide a tail as reveal one.

"They have my parents. They won't let me go, Dai."

Her friend gripped the bridge of his nose. "Your parents? Good God. Even Chika doesn't know where they are."

"Chika disowned them when she found out what they had done to me. That decision only piled one more heartbreak upon them. It doesn't matter why or how, it only matters now that the Clan have them."

"Where?"

"Their village." Mai shrugged. "I have no idea where it is."

"But you do have a plan?"

"Yes and no." Mai sighed. "It's not only my parents they are threatening. It's Chika, and you. And me. If I follow my plan to the end, a lot of people will get hurt, and not all of them deservedly."

"This may help." Hibiki switched the car's radio on. A news channel, NHK World Radio Japan, was reporting that the President of the United States had been abducted and played a recording of Dmitry Kovalenko's challenge. Mai stared through the car's windscreen and into the middle distance, unseeing.

"I should be there. It is bad enough that I do not know the fate of all my friends. Now, they also have to deal with this."

Hibiki squeezed her shoulder. "There is no shame in fighting here too. You are still fighting for your family and friends."

Mai nodded. "You're right. My fear is unfounded." She put a hand out and patted his knee. "Be careful, my friend. Keep Chika safe and look after yourself."

Hibiki scowled. "What does that mean? Surely you can't—"

"I'm doing this alone." Mai said quietly and forcefully. "For one, you need deniability. And more, I need you with Chika. If this goes down the way I see it . . . you may never see me again, Dai."

Hibiki swallowed hard but said nothing.

Mai reached for the door catch, still clutching the file Gyuki had given her and already planning her next move. She paused as Hibiki began to speak.

"I remember you," he said softly. "From the first few months around the office to that damn Coscon where you took out the whole of the local Yakuza. I was there, I know, and I helped, but you came through, Mai. You took the risks, you stole the show. Deservedly, you became a legend."

"Thank you."

"That damn costume," he chuckled. "When you walked into the station dressed in that cosplay outfit there wasn't a stick of work done for a whole six minutes. And even when you were kicking the Yakuza from here to hell and back, not one of them knew whether to worship, fight or photograph you. An honorable respectful real-life super hero."

Mai cracked open the door.

"Whatever you have to do," Hibiki said to her back. "Make it moral and honorable, and make it count."

Mai travelled by taxi to Tokyo Bay, ignoring the file Gyuki had provided, instead gazing through the grimy window at the busy sidewalks and streets she knew so well. Barely an inch of road was visible beneath the myriad buses, cars, bicycles and minivans which flew in all directions. Trees lined the streets, masses of scooters parked beneath their overhanging branches. Long, colorful banners hung down the side of every shop front and from the buildings above, advertising everything from sex to sushi. The noise was filtered by the closed window, but Mai's ears still reverberated from the din outside. The taxi driver had the radio tuned into NHK so Mai asked him to turn it up.

"No further details at this point, though it is known that Vice President Dolan is currently in crisis talks with the Joint Chiefs and members of the Cabinet. To recap, the YouTube broadcast by the man known as the Blood King, Dmitry Kovalenko, subsequently removed, is thought to be genuine. We—"

Mai tuned out, her thoughts with Drake and the rest of the team. By the time the taxi had threaded its way over to Tokyo Bay, her calm center was anything but. Of all the times for something so critical to happen . . .

Mai comforted herself with the knowledge that she had been able to save Chika, and that Hibiki too was safe. She paid the taxi driver and stepped out into a stiff Tokyo breeze blowing in across the bay. A tiny coffee shop stood forlornly on a nearby corner, scruffy tables and chairs, and indeed the entire trashy façade, in need of enhancement, but offering just the kind of anonymity Mai needed. She paid for a bottle of water and sat down, opening the file. An initial glance had already told her where her target was likely to be for the next three hours. Now it was time to read and digest the rest.

Akio Hayami was a local businessman, chiefly an accountant, who laundered money for the Clan. They wanted rid of him because of 'anomalies'. It was that simple, except Mai knew it would be anything but. The Clan would not furnish her with the full picture, only with what they thought was in their own interests. The Clan would never change for the better.

Mai read the information, scrutinizing every last detail of the man, Hayami. On paper, he looked guilty, just as much a criminal as most of the inmates of Fuchu, but Mai held her judgment. The problem was, what other choice did she have? The job, according to the file, was to isolate Hayami and make him 'disappear'. That was it. No questioning, no investigation. They were, quite simply, ordering her to commit murder.

Mai sat back, casting her gaze across the bay. Blue water rolled and undulated out there, the wave tops caught by the sun and made to glitter. White yachts dotted its surface, tacking into the wind. Closer at hand, dozens of various-sized vessels lay at rest, tied up to the nearest dock. Hayami would be on one of these, alone, working for the Clan. Mai cast her own eye down the figures. Hayami was well paid for his work. If he was cooking the books, he was a greedy, stupid man who probably deserved all he got. But then, he was helping one of the most ruthlessly efficient and murderous groups in the world. Mai wondered if Hayami even knew what they did to survive. He was not one of their vicious bunch, and was far removed from their terrifyingly bloodthirsty inner circle. *Did he deserve to die?*

Mai put her morals aside. *What choice do I have?* The only way into their village was with Gyuki, and the only way to fool

Gyuki was not to fool him at all. She had to go through with this.

Mai finished the last of her water and rose, eyeing the slips where yachts were docked. Signage told her that Hayami's boat was moored behind the coffee shop to the right, and her careful surveillance of that area whilst drinking the water told her that only one CCTV stanchion overlooked it. Mai wandered warily over, eyeing the camera and trailing wire as she approached. The coaxial cable dangled loose and flapped intermittently against the metal stanchion. Mai leaned against it, pretending to look through her mobile, and quickly cut through the wires with a small foldaway knife.

One thing about the advent of mobile phones, she reflected, *They make loitering around appear so much more authentic.*

She continued along the dock, unsure how quickly the guards would respond, if indeed there were any live guards and the whole thing wasn't run by automaton. Hayami's yacht swayed and swelled a little way down, gleaming white under the lowering late-afternoon sun. The deck was empty, but she thought she could spy lights on inside. She cast about, seeing no signs of anyone but figures in the distance. Gyuki, she was sure, would be somewhere around, but she held out little hope of being able to spot him.

Mai walked down the slip alongside the yacht, secured the file, and pulled herself aboard. Without sound she padded toward the back of the boat, careful to stay low and cast no shadows across the wide windows. At one point she ended up crawling, but eventually came around a blind corner and saw the rear sliding doors standing slightly open. To her right, a winding staircase led to the upper deck. Mai crawled forward, waiting behind a conveniently located potted plant, and tried to peer through the smoked glass. Beyond the doors was a small aft deck, dominated by an eight-sided table, more flowers and a small leather sofa. If Mai's yacht knowledge was any good, the doors beyond the aft deck would lead to the saloon and wet bar. Hayami probably liked to drown his sorrows in there while working for bad men.

Quickly, she slipped through the smoked-glass doors and skirted the polished table. Through the second set of doors, she discerned the bright glow of a computer screen and the shadow of a man sitting in front of it. The man's head was bowed, held between both hands, and the crystal tumbler at his side was empty but for a few cubes of ice.

Mai cracked the last set of doors, poised in case they made any sound, mindful that the Clan may even have devised this scenario as an elaborate trap. The fastest way out was by following a chair through one of the side windows and out into the bay, but no one stepped forward.

Mai advanced all the way until she could almost touch Hayami on the shoulder. She paused, riddled with doubt, but there was no going back now. She prepared to punch one of the nerve clusters at the base of Hayami's neck, took a breath, and then paused.

The file had not mentioned children.

Nestled beside Hayami's computer, inside a tiny silver frame, sat a photo of the man and two teenagers. The resemblance was undeniable. Hayami swung around at that point, perhaps sensing her presence or catching a reflection. The man's eyes were huge.

"Who . . . who are you?"

"You have children?" Mai remained poised.

"Y . . . yes. Emiko, my girl, and Jien, my boy."

"How old are they?" Mai was playing for time, thinking hard.

"Emiko—she is sixteen. Jien is eighteen. Why?"

Hayami raised his hands and stood up slowly. There was nowhere for him to go, and he didn't even try to conceal his work.

Mai fought to hide her trepidation. "You know why I'm here?"

"The . . . the Tsugarai?"

Mai felt a rush of distaste at the very mention of the name. For her, it remained unspeakable. "You have angered them."

"I've done nothing wrong!" Hayami looked flustered. "For them, I mean. I clean their money. I don't even know what they *do.*"

"Then you should ask more questions," Mai hissed. "If only to test your conscience. If only to ensure you don't end up in Hell."

Hayami's mouth worked but no sound came forth. Mai set her jaw. "What did you do to anger them?"

"Nothing! I swear, I would never do anything to upset the Tsugarai."

"I thought you didn't know what they did. You are lying to me."

"I don't. But, the men they send—" Hayami shuddered. "I would not want to upset them."

Mai studied the man. For the most part she thought he was telling the truth, but Hayami wasn't being completely honest. If he'd met several clan members he must have guessed they weren't exactly video game programmers. If he was capable of one lie to her face he was capable of more.

She shook her head. "I don't believe you."

She struck and he fell, dead before he hit the floor. All she was left with was utter silence, the gentle sway of the yacht, and the face and eyes of his children, staring almost accusingly from within the confines of their small frame.

Her thoughts turned to Gyuki and the clan village where her parents were being held.

CHAPTER TWENTY FOUR

Drake sat back as Vice President Dolan appeared on videophone, linked to a large monitor. They had been cooling their heels and recuperating for a while whilst the Americans got their communications running smoothly alongside their current chain of command. Drake and Dahl had confirmed that all living members and families of the SPEAR team were safe, for now, but that Kovalenko's Blood Vendetta was still up and running on all of them. Hayden was slightly more comfortable in hospital.

Alicia had contacted Drake some time ago, almost speechless and seething with anger. She had told him she was about to jump on a plane bound for DC, and Drake had known it would be pointless to argue with her. Instead, he had offered all he could at the time. "See you soon."

Still reeling from the deaths of Ben and his parents, from Sam and Jo, still stunned by the murder of Mano's mother and Gates and Romero, and now most of the biker gang, he was finding it hard to string together a full sentence let alone more words of consolation. What he needed—what they all needed—was to string Kovalenko from the highest building.

Vice President Dolan interrupted his despondent ruminations. "Gentlemen, give me scenarios and probable outcomes."

The strategists spoke up. The men of action followed. The Secretary of the Army, Navy and Air Force all had their say, along with their seconds. The Director of the FBI was present in Conference Room 1B. The Joint Chiefs and cabinet members were available on monitors. As Drake listened and constantly scanned his surroundings, he soon realized that this innocuous little room inside this hotel was actually one of the many secret crisis centers the United States government had set up throughout the country after the events of 9/11; a secure environment where all local or visiting VIPs could be taken to liaise with other VIPs anywhere in the country in times of emergency.

The overriding consensus was that something had to be done and done soon, through an offensive against the Hotel Dillion. The same blueprints that had previously been handed out were revealed again, signaling the start of a tactical discussion.

"Kovalenko may have the capability to upload anything to the public, at any time," one of the cabinet members pointed out. "We can't let the President go out that way. The eyes of the world," he said. "Are watching."

"Can't we kill the area's immediate broadcast capabilities?" Someone asked from the assembled agents.

"We *can,*" was the answer. "But it's risky. We'd have a potential blowback against ourselves and we can't be sure he hasn't already gotten something out."

The Commandant of the Marine Corps agreed, "And folks, don't forget the eyes of our enemies are also watching. We simply cannot look inadequate here today."

"A man who escapes a secret prison, kills the Secretary of Defense and then abducts the President, in my opinion, has a long-term plan," the Vice President said. "Which we must bear in mind."

"The city is as secure as it's ever going to be," the FBI Director said. "More forces are being drafted in."

Drake held up his hand and, when noticed, was acknowledged by the VP. "Yes?"

"Matt Drake, of SPEAR, sir," he said, for the benefit of those who didn't know. "Dmitry Kovalenko is *obsessed* with what he calls his Blood Vendetta," he pointed out. "It's something we can use to catch the man, if we can just get a step ahead."

"Good. Work on that. Your team is still active?"

Drake had no time to wonder if Dolan's meaning was twofold. "Yes, sir."

Dolan switched to another question. Drake sat back down and leaned toward Dahl. "What did that mean?"

Dahl stared ahead. "I don't think he liked you."

"With Gates gone," Drake ignored the glib comment, "We have no leader. To paraphrase Jonathan, 'the sharks will already be circling'."

Dahl nodded. "I know. Have you noticed that General Stone – Jonathan's harshest critic – is conspicuously absent? So we'll make sure we stay useful and join the strike team," he said. "Truthfully, it's where we should be. In the front line."

Drake sipped from his bottle. "I hate to say it, but you're right. I'd much rather be helping Hayden and the others right now—"

"They're safe. In the military hospital, right?"

"Aye. That they are, we hope. And Kovalenko's right here, across the street."

Dahl cast his eye across the rows. "See if you can figure out who's in charge." His tone, whilst laced with a little prep-school sarcasm, was genuinely uncertain.

Drake stood up. "In the corner. See that door? Some guys are already mobilizing in there."

Dahl smiled. "Time for your just desserts, Kovalenko."

CHAPTER TWENTY FIVE

Mano Kinimaka remained by Hayden's side as Smyth stalked out of the room to inspect the security arrangements and request a stock of 'heavy' hardware from someone in charge. This was a *military* hospital after all, the touchy ex-Delta solider argued, mostly to himself. Komodo sat with Karin in the corner of the room, hunched over his girlfriend as she sobbed her heart out. Their genius computer geek would be of no help to them for a while, and Kinimaka couldn't blame her. It was all he could do to hold it together for Hayden after learning about the death of his mother. If their whole situation wasn't so dire, he would be curled into a dismal ball next to Karin or on a plane bound for Honolulu.

Hayden spoke in a soft whisper, and Kinimaka had to lean over to hear the words. "Are you okay?"

He smiled, up close, and kissed her lips. Feeling the dryness, he held a glass of water for her to drag up a few sips. He smoothed the hair away from her forehead. "Here you are, shot to hell. And you ask me if *I'm* okay. God, I love you."

Hayden smiled weakly. "I was only shot once. I'm a Jaye. It'll take more than that to put me down."

Kinimaka silently sent a big thank you out into the ether, then felt guilty because his mom had not been so lucky. Life wasn't hinged on fate or design. Nobody out there had a complete plan. It was a giant dirty smorgasbord of chance and probability, shot through with prejudice, fanaticism and greed. Life was happenstance, nothing more, and you made of it what you could. Those who got really lucky were among the chosen few who could say they had won.

Kinimaka glanced up fast when the door opened, heart suddenly racing, and felt a rush of relief when Smyth walked in. The scowl on the soldier's face had not diminished.

"C'mon, you guys. I could've been the fuckin' enemy and taken you all out. Right there and then. Bad news is—the security in this hole sucks. Good news—they're issuing us a few weapons. Probably relics from the Jurassic age, but all they have to do is kill bad guys, right?"

When no one answered, Smyth made his way over to the bare window. "I can't believe Romero's gone," he said to his reflection. "Thought that maniac would have little Romeros of his own one day that I could train up to kick his ass."

Kinimaka was about to slide off the bed and wander over when an unmistakable sound delivered harsh shock treatment to every set of frayed nerves in the room.

"Gunshot," Smyth said and ran to the door.

It was muffled, probably emanating from the first floor two stories below, but was quickly followed by several more. Smyth listened as the two guards stationed outside the door received a report through their earpieces.

Kinimaka came to his shoulder. "What's going on?"

Smyth waved towards the guards. "We're waiting."

The closest guard turned. "Shots fired in the parking area and now in the lobby. A large force of men—"

Kinimaka turned away, his eyes and thoughts switching immediately to Hayden. "We have to assume," he said. "That they're gonna get up here. We have to go. Now."

"We can't move her." Komodo turned.

"We have to." Kinimaka walked over to the bed. "We'll all die if we stay here." He leaned over and spoke quietly. "You ready to check outta this place, Hay?"

"I am if you are, Man."

As gently as if he was lifting a newborn, Kinimaka picked Hayden up and cradled her in his big arms, making sure her head was nestled into his shoulder. Komodo urged Karin to her feet at Kinimaka's insistence, supporting her with his arms. "Where do you plan to go?"

Smyth answered that one without missing a beat, "The only way is up."

Outside the room, the guards were listening to their comms. Smyth tapped one of them on the shoulder. "You should come with us. Radio your colleagues and tell them to get the hell out. Those guys will kill you all."

"But this is a hospital," the guard answered. "There are patients here."

Smyth shook his head. "They ain't bothered about your patients, bud. They want *us.* And the only danger to you or your patients is if you try and stop 'em."

Point made, Smyth made a beeline for the nearest set of stairs. Kinimaka followed close, Hayden's weight not causing him any bother as he padded along. Smyth cracked the doors and listened. No sounds of flying feet echoed up the stairwell.

"Three floors up," he said. "Then to the roof."

"Are we trapping ourselves up there?" Kinimaka asked.

"We're Delta, bud," Smyth rasped, indicating Komodo and himself. "We don't get trapped."

From back down the corridor came the sudden burst of automatic weapons.

"Didn't take long," Smyth murmured.

"Hospital is unprepared," Kinimaka said. "They have no support. And I'm guessing this is a first. Attackers are prepared and unmatched. Only one outcome."

Smyth stared. "CIA teach you that?"

"What?"

"That kind of 'lie down and die' bullshit. There's always a chance, man. You just gotta grind it out for yourself."

Smyth started up the stairs. Kinimaka followed at pace, Komodo urging Karin along behind. Explosions rattled out at their backs, sliced apart by the screams of the guards. Smyth bounded up two sets of stairs and came to the next floor. Without pause, he ignored the stairs and barged through the doors and into the corridor beyond.

"Where the hell's he going?" Komodo asked. "I thought we were headed for the roof?"

Kinimaka leaned against a wall. "Just give him a minute. I have an idea what he's up to."

Three nail-biting minutes later, Smyth came back. In his arms he held three rifles and two handguns. Quickly, he distributed the load. "Knew they kept the armor on the third floor," he breathed. "And shit, these friggin' SPEAR IDs are like laminated gold bullion. One scan and you're in. Think I'll start using mine at Walmart."

Karin held her head up long enough to accept her handgun, then Smyth held the last piece out to Hayden. "Wasn't sure if you could use it, but hey," he shrugged, "Can't hurt to try."

Kinimaka took the gun and fixed her hand around it. A smile lit her eyes, and Kinimaka winked. "Always happier with a gun in her hands."

Smyth took off again, now pounding up the steps. He didn't stop until he reached the top floor, then held the door open for the rest. "Roof access is at the end of the corridor," he said. "We'll have to break down the door."

"Not a problem." Komodo led the way now, still with Karin at his side. As the team moved into the corridor, they heard the sound of feet battering the stairs below. The attack team was minutes behind.

A shot fired up the stairwell, impacting with the wall. Smyth let the door close behind and searched for a way to block it.

"Forget it," Komodo called. "Won't last more'n a few seconds anyway. We need to get to the roof."

The broad soldier looked nothing like the mild-mannered, clean-speaking, easy-going chef that Kinimaka had grown used to back at the HQ these last few days. Instead, the new image had been sloughed like an old skin, leaving the raw, hard-hitting ex-Delta soldier to take the reins. Komodo hit the stair-access door hard with his shoulder and watched it splinter, then kicked it off its hinges.

"Up."

He urged Karin inside, then the others. Smyth passed him last as the stairwell door flew open. "We don't have much time."

"Shit." Komodo ducked back in. The team climbed one more stair switchback, then pushed open a final door that led out into the night. Kinimaka pushed it wide with his shoulder, already studying the roof area. The first thing he saw were the bare tops of scaffolding poles sticking up above the rear of the building.

Komodo slammed the door shut behind them. "We have two minutes at most."

"No cover," Smyth took it all in. "Damn. What's that?" He sprinted past Kinimaka and reached the edge of the roof first. "Scaffolding goes all the way to the ground," he said, peering over. "But I don't see a ladder. Can you jump with that load, big man?"

Kinimaka pursed his lips. "Can't guarantee the landing. It's risky. The whole scaffold could collapse under my weight."

"Staying here is riskier."

"About a minute," Komodo warned as he took aim on the access door. "Make a decision."

"Crap." Kinimaka wrapped his arms tighter around Hayden's body and walked to the edge. "I'll protect you as best I can." He glanced into her eyes.

The smile told him she already knew and drove another spike through his heart.

"Ready?"

"Wait!" Karin's piercing cry froze them all. She was standing at the roof's edge, toward the side, overlooking the adjacent building. "This would work better."

Kinimaka was glad to hear her voice again. He'd been scared one of their most essential team members would collapse into shattered little pieces and never let herself be put back together again. But she was made of sterner stuff, this Englishwoman, and had dwelled deep in grief before.

The harshest lesson to learn was also the simplest one—sink or swim.

Karin told them her plan. Within seconds, Smyth had rushed off and jumped down onto the scaffold to grab hold of one of the scaffolding planks. With Komodo's help he managed to heave and haul it onto the roof. Together, they laid it across the gap between both buildings, forming a makeshift, unsteady bridge.

Then bodies hit the inside of the access door, each blow accompanied by shouts.

"Crap." Smyth raced across the bridge, arms out, swaying as he ran and adjusting to the warped wobble of the long, rough plank. As soon as he was over he took cover, lining up the access door with his rifle and calling the next person across.

Kinimaka stepped up. The black night above him was no more than a reflection of the yawning abyss below, and a sharp crosswind gusted past his bulk. He fixed his concentration on the two-foot-wide plank of wood that rested unevenly before him, but countless overriding factors tore at his concentration. Questions made a pincushion of his mind.

A stiff gust buffeted his body, sending him off balance. His heart juddered. The access door crashed open and Komodo opened fire. Kinimaka almost turned and unslung his weapon, but then the quietest of sounds broke through his turmoil, a sweet whisper on the wind.

"Mano, it's okay. Whatever happens, I love you."

Kinimaka looked down at her. "I will always protect you."

"I know." Hayden's eyes closed, sending daggers through his heart. The Hawaiian stepped up and walked resolutely across the shifting plank. When its unsymmetrical base rolled to the left he saw it coming; and, concentrating hard, when it shifted suddenly to the right he shifted with it. When the wind slammed him halfway across, as he knew it would, he leaned in and kept moving. Before long, he stepped off the other end and laid Hayden carefully down onto the hard ground.

"We made it."

No answer.

A bullet whizzed past his head. Kinimaka barely noticed, but quickly took Smyth's testy advice and ducked.

"Hay?"

Her lips moved. "I'm okay. Just . . . resting."

Kinimaka breathed a heavy sigh and took the opportunity to ease out the muscles of his arms. He might not get another chance for a while.

"They need your help," Smyth hissed through the corner of his mouth. Kinimaka turned. Komodo was kneeling, firing steadily at the steel door, its surface already peppered with holes. Two attackers lay half-in half-out the door, weapons discarded, unmoving. Blood had splashed the rusty frames. Karin had taken cover behind the big man's back, two feet behind, and was aiming her revolver around the side of his head.

Kinimaka sucked in a breath. *Shit,* he thought. *They're confident.*

"Gotcha covered!" he yelled, and Komodo waved a hand, ordering Karin away. The young woman shouted back at him, clearly agitated, and Komodo immediately began to edge away with her. Kinimaka spotted a man's head sneaking around the far doorframe and fired a couple of rounds to keep him at bay. They were lucky the access was small and impossible to protect, but he had no doubt that pretty soon the freak of an albino would come up with some kind of gnarly plan.

Karin balanced on the scaffold plank and fairly skipped across. Komodo jumped on straight after, and then the night exploded. The little access door bloomed outward, chased by shrapnel and fire. Its surrounds shattered under the detonation, spinning and skimming off into the night. Komodo paused before he negotiated the plank, unsure what would come next.

But Smyth knew. "Run!" he cried.

Too late. The enemy swarmed up through the widened gap, firing as they came. Smyth and Kinimaka ducked beneath the brick parapet as bullets thudded all around them. Karin remained kneeling, shooting hard, hitting one man's arm and sending his gun soaring, kneecapping another and sending him down hard. Komodo charged across the plank, at the last minute leaping for the edge of the other building as the deformed wood rolled. His hands caught the edge, scrabbling for purchase. Bullets struck brick all around and between his flailing legs.

"Fuck me!"

Smyth and Kinimaka popped up and laid down covering fire. Komodo heaved his bulk up over the edge, landing hard.

Once safe, the team wasted no time in retreat, first upending the scaffolding plank and letting it fall to the ground far below.

Kinimaka, staying low, scanned the roof. "I hate to say it, but this roof ain't any better than the one we just almost died on."

"Sure it is." Smyth crawled past him at speed. "The bad guys aren't on it."

Kinimaka scooped up Hayden's body, feeling the shallow breaths she was taking vibrate up his arms, and scrambled after Smyth. Komodo and Karin thwarted their assailants by discharging a measured, slow and steady stream of bullets.

Kinimaka reached the far end of the roof. More scaffold poles poked up over the edge and, beyond them, a bright yellow crane. When Smyth glanced over the parapet he gave out a loud cheer.

"There's a ladder. Double wide, so even you should fit, big man."

Kinimaka stared at him. It was clear that, if they survived tonight, the ex-Delta soldier and he were going to have to talk. Hawaiian hula girls and surfer chicks had previously gotten away with calling him 'big man'. Dudes did not.

This time Smyth motioned Karin and Komodo to go first. Without pause they jumped down onto the scaffolding, feeling the whole structure rock, and headed for the ladder. Kinimaka went next, securing Hayden tightly and with great care, then leaping and landing on two feet. The planks groaned under his weight, the metal poles whining under the pressure, but the construction held.

"No fuckin' about," Smyth yelled. "They're coming across now!"

He picked off the first few as they laid a fresh plank, but the hail of covering fire he withstood soon sent him scrambling over the edge of the building. Nevertheless he tarried, still firing, mindful that their attackers carried grenades and could quite easily and happily blow the scaffolding apart before the team reached the bottom.

The sound of Komodo's clattering came to an end, then Karin's. Kinimaka was understandably slower. Smyth fired a last volley as the enemy leapt onto the roof, then turned and sprinted for the ladder. It was wide, with platforms at every level, and switch-backed, so provided a decent amount of protection. Smyth saw Kinimaka's bulk hammering at the stairs far below, then a shout came from above.

"Say hi to your little friend!"

Smyth glanced up through the gaps. Faster than him, quicker than even the Special Forces man could calculate, the vicious albino had raced to the parapet and now perched there like some nightmarish gargoyle.

In one hand he held a pineapple-shaped grenade.

Smyth put his head down and ran hard. In less than a second, he heard the clatter as the metal object hit wooden planks and knew he had no chance of outrunning the explosion. No chance at all. But he had managed to cover his team's escape.

In that last second he ran faster than ever before.

The grenade exploded with an ear-splitting clap of thunder, sending out a supercharged blast of fire and energy. Part of the brick wall of the building crumbled inward. The scaffolding all around was blown away, poles and planks shooting like arrows into the darkness, causing the whole structure to collapse.

Smyth felt the entire configuration shifting beneath his feet, swaying away from the wall and crumbling into oblivion. He flew, fleet of foot, with a fire at his heels.

One more second . . . one more step . . .

The scaffold collapsed in on itself with a clang and a roar. The albino's cackle sounded above it all. Smyth took one more step, then launched his body away from the disintegrating structure and out into empty space.

Sheer blackness and a drop of almost thirty meters lay directly below him.

He hit the bright-yellow crane hard. His forehead smashed into an upright, making him see stars, but his hands found purchase on a cross support, arresting his fall. Smyth stared up, meeting the shocked eyes of the albino.

"Mother—"

The rest was lost as the albino opened fire. Smyth placed his feet to either side of the stanchion he was clutching and let himself freefall, using his thickly-clothed arms and legs to control the descent.

He landed hard, crumpling and groaning, thankful that at least he had landed on grass and not the concrete.

Komodo held out a hand, looking impressed. "Nicely done. Thought you were a goner."

Smyth managed a rare grin. "Yeah. I bet even Mai Kitano couldn't have pulled that off."

Komodo led him away at a jog. "Mai? Are you kidding? She'd have caught the grenade in her teeth and spat it right back into the bastard's face."

Smyth acceded gracefully. "Good point."

"I mean, crap," Komodo went on. "Torsten Dahl would probably have just chewed it up and spit it out. This ain't Delta anymore, Smyth. These fuckers are the meanest, most expensively trained fighting machines on earth. They ain't normal warriors."

"I get it, I get it," Smyth grumped. "Where the hell are we going?"

"We're getting the fuck outta here."

CHAPTER TWENTY SIX

Kinimaka ducked his head and shoulders as low across Hayden's body as he dared. Any lower and he would lose his balance and go sprawling. Smyth and Komodo were ahead, tearing across the parking area toward an old but still sleek black Camaro.

"No!" Karin hissed from behind. "We won't all fit in the bloody thing." She shook her head. *"Men."*

Smyth veered to the door of an old Suburban. They were certain the albino would have left men stationed down here and were expecting resistance at any minute. Sure enough, as Smyth smashed a side window and gave their position away, several heads popped up no less than a hundred yards distant.

"Got 'em!"

The radio went flying as the man broke cover, compelled by urgent orders. Smyth jumped into the Suburban and fiddled with the ignition wires. As he fought to twist the engine into life, rounds smacked into the Suburban's bodywork. Kinimaka jerked open the rear door, lifting Hayden. At that precise moment, a heavy volley struck the car, smashing windows and shattering plastic, tearing through upholstery and cloth. Kinimaka could neither duck nor turn away. He managed to drop his arms, laying Hayden down, and then Karin and Komodo returned fire, shredding the enemy.

Smyth twisted the wires once more. The engine roared to life. Karin jumped in, then Komodo, lying flat out on the back seat. Kinimaka climbed into the footwell, letting Hayden have the seat, and found his body wedged there. It was all he could do to bring an arm up to wipe the sweat from his face.

Smyth peeled out of the lot, cheering and giving the enemy the finger through the rear view. Karin and Komodo heaved sighs of relief, then the young woman's face collapsed into grief as, again, thoughts of Ben and her parents flooded back. Kinimaka looked at the back of his hand and wondered where the blood had come from.

He tapped his head. Nothing hurt. That could mean only one thing . . .

Smyth threw the Suburban around a corner. "Where to?"

"CIA safe house," Komodo said. "One of our old ones. One of SPEAR's old ones, I mean."

Carefully, Kinimaka rolled Hayden on to her side.

"No. Oh no."

Blood stained the seat. Fresh blood.

"Got an address?" Smyth was concentrating on the road ahead.

"Yeah, hang on."

Kinimaka pulled Hayden's shirt up. The bullet wound was still bandaged, untouched. So where . . .

Hayden's eyes fluttered open. Kinimaka nodded at the bandage. "Does it hurt?"

"Nah. It doesn't hurt at all. It went straight through Boudreau's old knife wound." Her eyes smiled.

Kinimaka sighed with relief. "Then what—"

Hayden coughed harshly. "It's the new one just under my heart that's killing me."

CHAPTER TWENTY SEVEN

Mai Kitano walked away from Tokyo Bay, drifted for a short while, then ducked into a quiet alley. She dug out her phone and noted that Hibiki had called. *What now?* Her heart wanted to return the call, to make sure both he and Chika were safe, but her head told her that they should both be kept out of this, well away, and that contacting them would do no good. She couldn't help them at the moment.

There was nothing from Drake, and she failed to quell a pang of worry. It would only take her a second to log on to a network and scan the news channels, but even that small luxury was forbidden. In her heart the road was clear. The way forward went in only one direction.

She was theirs. She belonged to the Clan. Her parents were being kept under lock and key. These factors could not be avoided and needed to be addressed directly before she would allow herself to dream of a future.

Mai hit the return call icon next to Gyuki's phone number.

"Yes?" the flat voice instantly answered.

"It is done. I have completed your work."

"Of course you have. We already know. Where have you been for the last twenty four minutes?"

Mai shuddered at the expectant tone. This man truly believed he owned her. "Getting lost. Making sure I was not seen nor followed."

"You have let your standards slip so far, Mai Kitano? These issues are not a concern if the job is prepared for and executed in the approved manner."

"Time was not on my side."

There was a long pause, then Gyuki said, "We gave you no time constraint."

"Hayami was there. Alone. Sometimes a job is best done on the first pass to ensure your face does not become familiar to the area. And you have my parents."

"Ah. You do not trust us."

Mai resisted an urge to reply in the manner of Alicia Myles to that one. Swearing, mocking and taunting would not help her case. Instead, she remained silent.

"Well, we are true to our word. As men of the Clan have always been. As tradition has taught us. Meet me here," he reeled off an address, "In half an hour."

Mai met Gyuki for the second time that day in his first-floor hotel room. Behind closed and locked doors and draped windows, Gyuki was a different man. Stripped to the waist, he bowed without taking his eyes off her.

"Come inside. We will leave soon."

Mai skirted him warily, eyeing every movement of his rippling body. "How about right now?"

"You are scared of me." Gyuki nodded. "I understand. But don't be. You are still useful to us."

"Scared of you?" Mai repeated. "Why would I be? I could take you, Gyuki."

The master assassin gauged her movement. "Have you grown so much?"

"You're a fossil, Gyuki. A product of Japan's past. You should have long since disappeared with the Samurai, the Shoguns and the fucking dynasties. And with the Ninja clans. They should also be long gone."

Gyuki faced her, deliberately making his muscles dance independently of themselves. "Fight me for your body," he whispered malevolently. "As we used to do."

Mai stood very still. This was one of the memories she had kept buried all these years. And despite her words, she wasn't sure she could take Gyuki. She would not be bated into trying before she located her parents.

"Maybe later," she said with cold detachment. "When do we leave?"

Gyuki shrugged. "The clan village is two hours away. If we leave now we can be there before lights out."

They exited the hotel, found Gyuki's car, a mundane white Honda and joined the slow-moving traffic. Once away from the bright lights and bustling attractions of central Tokyo, the roads grew quieter and Gyuki made better time. His driving was unremarkable and he did nothing to make himself stand out, just one of many homecoming minions. Mai studied his visage in the repeated wash of oncoming headlights and found it to be unkind, merciless and devoid of emotion. The world could only become a better place when this man breathed his last.

High rises gave way to office buildings, then to rows of houses and, eventually, to patches of undeveloped grassland. After two hours Mai looked thoroughly lost, and Gyuki didn't even mention blindfolding her. It was one of his failings, this arrogance, this all-encompassing clan belief that he, and they, were superior beings. It may eventually prove his undoing.

At last, Gyuki pulled the car off the road at a turn marked by two overhanging wizened old trees and an abandoned church, and drove about three more miles. The tree-lined road was pitted, overgrown with roadside shrubbery, and extremely unappealing. Designed to keep the curious away, no doubt. Gyuki circumvented several nasty potholes, bounded across a few more, and then pulled into a blind road to the left. He powered up the double-rutted dirt track, then slowed as the trees grew sparse and a flat space opened out.

Mai saw a dirt-topped parking area where several other cars as nondescript as Gyuki's sat waiting for the next assassin. Or maybe just for the next grocery run. Who knew what womb-to-tomb assassins got up to these days?

Gyuki parked and got out, signaling that Mai should follow. The Japanese woman was happy to do so, taking in every twist and turn of the emerging village as she went. The Clan had extended since she had left. What had been a long shed billeting a dozen mixed men and women, girls and boys, was now two. A fighting arena sat between the two; square and marked by hanging red banners adorned with the golden symbol signifying the name of the Clan.

Tsugarai. It was only a family name, but it should have meant *devil.*

Mai familiarized herself with the place. Beyond the two sheds were dotted half a dozen small dwellings, no doubt the homes of the clan chiefs, and one small temple. Further over near the tree line stood one final building, a long low structure with barred windows and doors. This was also new. The village had never needed a jail before.

Gyuki pointed Mai to the temple. She tried to shake off the sense of unreality which had clung to her since she had stepped out of the car. Not only was she stepping back in time to a place she feared and hated, but where *was* everyone? The village was deserted, as quiet as Hayami's boat now that the man was dead.

"Quiet day, Gyuki?"

The man ignored her, his attention captured by the temple before them. It was by far the fanciest building in the village, tastefully adorned with golden flags and with two lion-head statues that stood to either side of the entrance.

"Shoes off at the door. Bow when you enter," Gyuki reminded her. It was like taking a terrible trip down the haunted highways of her past. By most standards the clan temple was simple, little more than a large and gently curving roof traditional in Japanese architecture with thin, movable, non-load-bearing walls. The oversized eaves gave the interior a classic dimness, contributing heavily to the temple's foreboding presence. The interior consisted of only one room, commonly called a moya, though the movable walls could partition small areas off.

Mai was aware that most temples were sacred places and business would never be conducted there, but the Clan held mostly to their own rules and broke them when it pleased. As she crossed the threshold, she paused for a minute to let her eyes adjust. Figures slowly materialized out of the gloom beyond.

The clan master, Bishamon, looked as old today as he had over twenty years ago, not a day younger than three hundred. Mai wondered if his stick-thin right hand could still whip out with a quick cuff as fast as it used to.

"Hisashiburi, Hanshi. " Mai saw no reason to antagonize the elder too soon, allowing him the high honorific which roughly translated as 'Grand Master'.

"Your family misses you, Mai."

She bowed her head, aware that Bishamon's statement had nothing to do with the feelings of her parents. "I have returned," she murmured at the earthen floor. "To do your bidding."

The clan master unfolded his body from where he sat, cross-legged, upon a raised dais. He wore only a loin cloth and a white robe open down the middle. As he crept toward her, Mai was reminded of a spider slinking across its web on thin, spindly legs.

"You returned to save your worthless sister and her koshinuke boyfriend. You have far to go before we will allow your true rebirth."

"Of course."

"But for now it is good." Bishamon waved dismissively at her. "Gyuki tells us Hayami is dead. Go see your parents now, Mai, and see what you fight for."

Mai spun immediately, anxious to get away from the evil old man and his private lair. The place stank of deep buried things; bad earth, sweat and old blood. Not a whisker stirred in there, not a whisper went unheard. The deep shadows concealed more than dark corners, she was sure.

Outside, the pitch black night was not as sinister. Clouds scudded across a quarter moon. She paused to get her bearings and Gyuki's voice whispered close to her ear. "Looking for something?"

"No," Mai said quickly. "Waiting for you."

"We have eighteen warriors," Gyuki told her with a smirk. "Two master assassins and the Grand Master. If you held any notions about freeing your parents—and yourself—Mai, I hope you are no longer courting them."

"Two master assassins?" Mai was surprised. "I thought you were the only one."

Gyuki hissed. "Then you are an idiot. The Tsugarai never stagnate."

Mai fell in behind him, wondering who else might have made the grade to master assassin. She could barely remember any of her old classmates. Truth was, she had tried to forget about all of them and held serious doubts that any had actually survived. Questions regarding the prison-like building struck her again.

Gyuki led her around one of the big sheds. Nestling close to its treeward side, small, squat and built in perpetual shadow, was a single story structure which could be labeled as little more than a hut. Gyuki waved her toward the door.

"Go. I will wait here. You have thirty minutes."

Mai stared at the door. Legs which never failed her in battle suddenly started to shake. *My parents?* The couple who had sold her in order to put food on the table. Sold her, albeit unknowingly, into a violent form of slavery that she was still trying to escape. For a minute her feet refused to move, and she almost turned around, but the sight of Gyuki's amused face galvanized her body and will.

Before she knew it, she was knocking on the door, heart pounding. The first thing she heard was shuffling, then a man's voice—*my father's voice*—and the sound of the door being dragged open.

Words failed her. Emotion slackened her face. The old couple staring out at her wore expressions of utter amazement. The woman acted first.

She fell to her knees. *"Mai?"*

Her father fell onto her, sobbing, and it was all she could do to hold him up. Behind her, the callous voice of Gyuki cut through the night.

"Twenty minutes."

Mai carried her father inside.

Five more minutes passed before anyone could speak.

"When they said they could find you, we didn't believe them," her mother somehow strung a sentence together. "But they . . . they have taken good care of us."

Mai supported her father as he tried to lower himself into a chair. "Wait. They've *taken good care* . . . you mean you're here voluntarily?"

Her mother, Chie, spoke quickly, her accent so thick Mai could barely follow. "They found us many months ago. Your father . . . he was not doing so well. They took us in. They knew your sister, Chika, she . . . she—"

Disowned you, Mai thought, but said nothing. She could see the agony they had been through. It was etched on every single line and curve of their faces, it limited their every movement. It had all but destroyed them.

The Clan had given them hope. Again. For the second time. And the Clan would dash that hope on a whim and gladly hand her parents the poisoned swords upon which to throw themselves.

Mai bit back her thoughts and feelings. "It is good to see you again," she said simply, and reveled in the pure happiness that flowed across her parents' features. For now, it was enough.

Mai walked out into the night, making sure her parents knew she would return soon. In what capacity, she didn't know, but she intended to be back within days rather than weeks.

Gyuki stood unmoved, quietly laughing at her. "A wonderful reunion."

Mai walked right up to him until their breath mingled. "What's next?"

"Next? You will show your true worth to the Tsugarai Clan. Today was but a test. Tomorrow—" Gyuki actually began to laugh.

Mai gaped at him. Never before had she heard the master assassin laugh, and never again did she want to. It was a truly demented sound, like a mental patient finally freed after being forced to watch *Coronation Street* or *Days of our Lives* for twenty five years straight.

"Tomorrow," Gyuki got a hold of himself. "You revisit the Coscon."

Mai staggered. "I what?"

"You remember it well, I am sure. The Tokyo Coscon where your name became legend. The great Mai Kitano will return once more. Tomorrow we need a job completing." Gyuki chuckled. "It so happens that our target will be there. How very fitting."

Mai struggled to articulate.

"And more. Your target is a prominent member of the Yakuza. A leader. You must make a spectacle of him, teach them a lesson. They have dishonored the Tsugarai."

Mai turned away from his manic laughter. The last Coscon had all but killed her, left her a wreck, and made her name. She had almost destroyed a branch of the local Yakuza, turning herself into a lasting target, and now they wanted her to do it all again.

Within the halls of law enforcement, her name was legend because of the Coscon. Her rise through the ranks had been meteoric. A sudden idea formed in her mind as she stared into the face of Gyuki's insanity.

Maybe, just maybe, she could pull this one off too.

CHAPTER TWENTY EIGHT

Drake heaved a sigh of relief as word finally came down the chain of command.

"Mission is a go. Repeat, mission is a go."

The VP had taken his time, but had eventually signed off on a plan devised by every one of the Joint Chiefs and their advisors. No single man wanted to be lumbered with formulating the strategy that could potentially save or sacrifice the President of the United States, but something had to be done. It had finally come down to the military men and their lifelong experience.

Dahl clapped him on the shoulder. "C'mon, matey. Time to chuck Kovalenko back through the gates of Hell."

The men rose. They were a large group, involving many agents from the FBI Counter Terrorism Division, Hostage Rescue, and Special Weapons and Tactics. The hotel consisted of twelve floors, over three hundred rooms and around forty suites. Cutting edge technology had been used to penetrate the hotel's walls, technology that Drake had encountered once before. The secret base over in the Florida Keys had used their advanced camera to determine the President's location. Once redirected it had examined every room, floor by floor, finding civilians hiding in fear behind locked doors, tourists closeted together and watching CNN's live feed, a turn-down maid engaged in a little discreet robbery, a manager surfing the Net for the best odds to gamble as to whether President Coburn lived or died, then the rogue Secret Service agent Marnich, and finally Kovalenko and his band of mercenaries. The Presidential Suite was on the top floor, but Kovalenko had set up his twisted sideshow one floor below. It was noted that

Kovalenko stayed well away from the windows and used no unnecessary lighting, so they assumed he knew nothing about the American's see-through-walls technology. But the harsh truth remained—they would only get one crack at this.

Marnich's family had been contacted. It had been verified that they weren't under duress and that the US agent was officially a traitor. Everyone in the room knew the Government had been compromised, the stoplight scenario upheld that hypothesis, but no one knew to what level. The Department of Defense was sweeping DC itself to ensure no other surprises remained in the form of radiological or biological signatures. The NSA reported no particular increase in anti-US chatter around the globe. The airspace above DC had been partially restricted and military flyovers were underway. The country's threat level had been raised. In addition to the top-secret camera feed, an infra-red SaTScan had been ordered of the hotel in case the advanced camera passed outside its range of influence.

Drake craned his neck to view the live feed being bounced by satellite from the hidden facility in Key Largo. Kovalenko sat alone at a little round table, a shot glass and mini vodka bottles arranged before him as if they were on parade. Half a dozen of his men roamed the suite, each man dressed in a similar suit to the President, passing from the bedroom to the main room and through to a second bedroom. Two captives could also be seen, trussed up in the back bedroom, also wearing dark suits. The bar area was manned by a wiry African, who appeared to be Kovalenko's second-in-command.

President Coburn rested with his feet up on a leather couch, looking remarkably calm and relaxed. His eyes were fixed upon a wall-mounted TV, watching minute-by-minute reports of the night's events.

Now, Drake slipped around the sheer outer walls and then the courtyard of the Hotel Dillion, concealing his movements from and ignoring the raucous choppers hovering above. The news cameras had been allowed to stay, at a safe distance, to help fuel any overconfidence Kovalenko might be starting to feel. They knew the Blood King was pretty well isolated up there, but they also knew he would have some kind of a plan. Shot through with craziness or not, the situation wasn't going to get any better.

Drake followed Dahl and half a dozen members of SWAT through a side door into a restaurant and dimly lit bar area that let out close to a rear stairwell. Each one of the hotel's three stairwells were being negotiated at the same time by mixed forces, kept in constant contact by a central comms command. The central comms would orchestrate the clandestine assault whilst constantly analyzing every single scrap of information pinging around out there.

Drake paused as the team leader's fist punched the air. He didn't like the thought of being nothing more than a play piece, shuffled about a strategic board, dependent on the whim of others who might give the order to abort or strike at any given moment—he thought those days had shrunk to a distant speck in his rearview—but the mission objective surpassed all his sensitivities. That and the chance to avenge Gates and finally put Kovalenko into the ground in return for everything that had been committed in his name.

"All perimeters clear. Proceed with caution." The command came down the line. The team leader stepped out, hugging the wall all the way to the stairwell door. His men followed. Communications were constant, passing between command and all three teams. FBI experts of all shapes and sizes were being utilized on the outside, from Hostage Rescue specialists, who analyzed Kovalenko and his men and President

Coburn's every move, to respected pros from America's most elite tactical divisions. This truly was a fluid mission in all senses of the word, and under extreme scrutiny. Drake hit the stairwell as the sixth man in line and stayed against the wall, looking up as far as he could, but only able to see as high as the third floor. One flight of stairs up and they were halfway between the first and second floors. The team leader signaled another pause. Drake listened to a flurry of information. All three teams had infiltrated to the same level and, so far, met no resistance. This was expected. Every floor of the hotel had been scrutinized; the dilemma was that the rest of the mission had to be executed expeditiously.

Whilst Kovalenko's men had enjoyed months of preparation toward this exact moment.

Drake followed as the team scaled another set of stairs and then two more, bringing them up to the third floor. Dahl turned and tapped him on the helmet, pointing to the window nearby. Drake glanced out to see flashing blue lights parked haphazardly for entire blocks and washing the streets and stone walls all the way to the White House.

Crazy mayhem.

It hit Drake then that there were times in the UK's and America's histories, nights like this when everyone was glued to the television or the radio or the Internet, and these were the moments that went down in history, never to be forgotten. These were the moments when you always remembered where you were and what you were doing. Moments that changed the world, and your life, forever.

Drake turned away from the window and steeled his resolve. Not only were the police, the FBI and the Army out there, so were his closest friends, all part of the only family he had left. This nightmare would only end for everyone by cutting the head off the snake.

With no contrary orders, the team progressed further up the staircase. The SWAT team advanced on whisper-soft feet, the whole black-clad group looking like a team of Ninjas. Drake had heard the term *ninja* used by the FBI, referring to a ready-to-go SWAT team member, but it only reminded him of the real thing. Although kept to a minimum, the sound of their passing still echoed. The fifth and then sixth floor came, then another squawk of static signaled a halt.

"Sit rep. Check."

All three team leaders radioed the all-clear. Command furnished them with a blast of information—nothing had changed 'upstairs', but they sounded confident that no news was good news.

Drake watched as the team leader raised his hand, then paused as a new sound reached their ears. It was a sound every single man on the stairs knew by heart and by experience.

An explosion ripped through the hotel.

CHAPTER TWENTY NINE

Drake dropped to the floor.

"Hold position! Hold position!"

"Ya don't fuckin' say!" The unnerved team leader shouted into his mic.

Drake heard the deep rumble die away. The explosion had come from the other side of the hotel, barely shaking the structure and doing little real damage. A frantic exchange was taking place over the comms.

"Team Echo, come back. Team Echo, come back."

Two teams, including Drake's, had returned the summons already, but the third had not responded. Their comms channel was still open though, its airwaves thick with the muffled sounds of pain and distress. Drake listened while staring up the staircase as the survivors finally managed to speak.

"Trap. Goddamn pressure pad or something triggered a shaped charge down the staircase from the landing above. We have wounded—"

Suddenly the comms system and its operators changed their dispositions from anxious to hysterical.

"Kovalenko! It's Kovalenko. He's calling the emergency number right now."

"Jesus Christ! Get a fix on it!"

Drake settled back on his haunches, feeling helpless. He began to creep back down the staircase, each man following in the others' footsteps as the team leader retreated from his highest point—three steps from the landing. Maybe Team Echo had been the first to make it to that level.

"We're piggybacked onto the call! Listening in. . ."

Drake couldn't hear what the Blood King said, but the sudden deathly silence on the line attested to its magnitude. Every man stopped moving, fingers to their ears, weapons lowered, listening. Every fist was clenched, every ounce of breath held. The tension soon became as thick as jungle heat.

"No . . ." an operator breathed.

"Alpha team here," Drake's team leader spoke gruffly. "What the hell is going on up there?"

"Kovalenko has Coburn . . . I mean, I mean the President. They're pulling him . . . across the room. No—"

Drake gritted his teeth. The Blood King stood not five floors above him, yet stayed firmly beyond his reach. Hot blood and a thirst for vengeance surged through his body, making him want to run up every stair and burst in through the bastard's door, all guns blazing, but one simple booby-trap had stopped any chance of that happening. Men were dead, and now Kovalenko was revealing the next part of his master plan. It was all staged, Drake knew. Every part of Kovalenko's plan would have been thought through to the finest and bloodiest detail.

"Oh no . . . the President is now positioned before the window. The commandos are around him. Kovalenko just put the phone down, said something like 'you want to test me? Here's what I do.' And . . . and . . . *my God!"*

"What is it?" most of the team cried. "What's happening?"

"That madman just threw President Coburn out of an eleventh story window."

CHAPTER THIRTY

The Blood King evaluated the mood of his men. The focus was still high, the expectancy soaring. They had made it this far, but the toughest part of the plan was about to unfold. He looked to Gabriel behind the bar, pleased to see the African's ever-present malicious optimism. If luck and success could be garnered through sheer will and belief, then the African would see them through a hundredfold.

Kovalenko made another call, this time to an FBI number. When the operative answered he asked to be put through to the leader of the on-site Hostage Rescue Team. Within minutes the call was live.

"You had to test me, you American assholes, didn't you?" he said. "I warned you, did I not? Will you now try to test me again?"

"Our teams have been ordered to stand down," came the expected reply. "What is it you want?"

Kovalenko paused for a second. *Why aren't they asking about Coburn?* "Did you recover the body?"

"We know it wasn't the President. In fact, it was an English book critic, in town for the East Coast Book Fair. Congratulations, you murdered an innocent civilian."

"Ah," Kovalenko waved it away. "You see, in my war there are no innocents. You people," he spat. "You live in a world where everything is taken for granted. You shop at your food markets and whine at an empty shelf. You complain about stale bread. You have," he paused to think, "Reality TV? You assholes need to learn that you know *nothing* about reality. Nothing."

"Hey, I hate that shit as much as the next guy. What is it you want, Kovalenko?"

"You failed to stop me so now I will leave. You must have a kind of infra-red or tracker wired to President's heart? You have something, that I do know, otherwise you would have asked about his welfare. Now, a chopper is approaching Washington airspace. My chopper, dah? Let it pass through. Let it land on hotel roof or President dies. You hear me? I read President Coburn earned his wings in battle. We will see if they help him fly out of the fucking window, dah?"

"We can't just let a chopper through. The chain of command goes all the way to—"

"Let it through," Kovalenko hissed. "Or Coburn dies right now. On this open channel."

"If you kill the President you lose all bargaining power."

Kovalenko signaled Gabriel. The African moved faster than a puma, slinking around the wet bar and hauling Coburn up by the neck. The President yelled in surprise and pain, unnerved by the sudden violence.

"Do you want death of President on *your* head?" Kovalenko whispered into the phone.

"Just . . . just wait. Hang on." The fearful voice cut off.

Kovalenko smiled. "Happy to."

CHAPTER THIRTY ONE

Drake hotfooted it back to the Hotel Lewison Park and Conference Room 1B just as Kovalenko's latest demands were being discussed. The buck stopped with the VP, but all the Joint Chiefs and their aides, several Chiefs of Staff, the FBI, and others were involved in a hot debate.

"Let him go," said the White House Chief of Staff. "We can track it and the President with ease. Where can they go?"

"With all due respect," the Chairman of the Joint Chiefs muttered. "This is a military operation. You can't—"

"John." The Vice President waved him down. "I asked everyone for their input here."

"You can't let the bastard go," the Secretary of the Army said. "It'll send a message to every potential nutball out there—'c'mon boys, it's open season on the US'."

"Where would it end?" someone else put in. Drake saw the VP had now been joined in his secure location by various military leaders, not all of whom were on the monitor.

"Let it take off and shoot it down," the Secretary of the Army proposed, his face as hard as Kevlar.

Several faces blanched. The VP's voice rose an octave. "With the President on board? You can't be serious."

"They've tricked us more than once today," the Secretary said. "Who's to say what else Kovalenko has up his sleeve?"

"Does anyone have another suggestion?" the VP asked. "Preferably something that doesn't involve killing the President?"

"Track it. Follow it." Tom Liddell, the Commandant of the Marine Corps, said firmly. "And accept that Kovalenko isn't finished yet. Not by a long way. But he will slip up. I believe we should try to contact Agent Marnich and offer him a deal. It is possible he's realized the error of his ways and is looking for a way out. And . . . the man does have family. I also—" Liddell paused as the VP gasped.

"Tom. Are you suggesting—"

Liddell half smiled. "Sir, this is not television. I wouldn't condone terrorizing a man's family, no matter what he's done. I simply meant that he may want to protect his family name."

Drake leaned over towards Dahl. "Give Kovalenko some rope and he *will* hang himself."

"It's not in their playbook to risk the President's life," Dahl returned. "They'll struggle with it. But eventually, they'll agree to track the chopper. There is no other choice."

Drake looked around. "So like it or not, we're redundant. Maybe it's time to start looking after our own."

Dahl pursed his lips in thought. "That actually makes sense. Which is strange, coming from you."

Drake ignored the gentle ribbing as his cellphone vibrated. Quickly, he moved to the back of the room and fished it out. "Yes?"

"It's me. Where the hell are you? I'm outside the Lewison. Even the SPEAR ID won't get me inside."

"Alicia? You're in DC? Has it been that long?"

"I only came from Germany, dickhead. Now get your arse out here and find me."

Drake listened as she narrowed her location down. He didn't try to cheer her up or console her, just took it all in and then signaled Dahl over. "Alicia's arrived."

"Shit. Now there'll be trouble."

The two men exited Conference Room 1B and left the hotel through a side door. Other members of the assault team were milling about outside, some staring at the skies or texting loved ones, but most were watching the eleventh floor of the Hotel Dillion, wondering what was going to happen next.

Drake breathed deeply, taking a moment to relax. He hadn't even begun to assimilate most of the night's events yet. And now here came a blue-eyed blond-haired warzone, stalking right up to him with half-a-dozen dilapidated bikers in tow.

"I'm sorry, Alicia," he said straight away. "About Lomas."

"Thanks. Sorry about Ben and . . ."

Drake knew there were too many casualties to list right now. He nodded at the bikers. "Did many survive?"

"Not even enough for a good fuckin' orgy."

Drake shook his head. "Well, not by your standards anyway."

Dahl pushed past to pull Alicia into a hug. The blond woman allowed it for a few seconds, then pulled away. "Hayden? Mano?"

"We don't know." Drake waved at the scene around them. "It's been hell around here."

"Shit. I leave you alone for one friggin' week and you lose half of America."

"Not quite." Drake looked to his phone. "Now let's—"

But at that moment a chopper blasted low overhead. Drake looked up, glimpsing what looked like a Sikorsky S-92: an executive chopper which could hold several men in luxury. He watched as the bird hovered over the Dillion; a perched beast.

"They gave him the bird," Dahl said, not surprised.

Drake tuned back into reality, dipping his head and tapping the ear mic. The transmissions were still coming through strong and dispersed throughout the attendant teams.

"Chopper has arrived. Repeat, chopper has arrived. Wait ten. Wait ten."

"Ground units, make ready. Teams Alpha, Bravo, Echo—ground units make ready."

Drake pinched the bridge of his nose. "That's us. We're part of Team Bravo," he said. "Bollocks. Looks like they want us to track the chopper's progress from the ground."

Dahl shrugged. "Makes sense, mate. It's another failsafe. They have plenty of other ways to track it through the air."

"I'm coming with you." Alicia looked prepared to knock out the closest SWAT team member in order to get his kit. The man saw her eyeing him up and warily backed away. Drake radioed for another set of gear.

"You can't bring the Motherfuckers."

"That's *not* their name. Don't let 'em hear you calling them that, Drakey."

The chopper slowly settled onto the roof of the Dillion, its huge rotors in constant motion. Drake assumed Kovalenko, his men, and the President were heading topside, but the command center would know for sure. They could follow Coburn through the tracker implanted in his body.

Minutes passed. Alicia quickly suited up and then went to speak briefly to the remainder of the gang. The ground units began assembling around the plaza surrounding the Lewison Park, checking weapons and gear. Dawn had broken over DC and the skies were lightening by the minute. Clouds sped overhead, chased by chill errant breezes. A severe moon watched over it all, as desolate as the heart of the country. Drake imagined how many Americans were waking up right now and going straight to their TVs, ignoring preparations for the school run and the morning commute; and how many others had persisted through the night; and how many more around the world.

The ex-SAS man braced himself against a sudden shiver, not sure if it was the creeping cold wind or the state of his mind. On top of all this he was still snowed under with unresolved questions. How was Mai faring in Tokyo? How the hell could she hope to defeat a clan of Ninja assassins? Were their friends and team mates in DC still alive? How was

Hayden? The last they'd heard, she'd been close to death.

And on the back burner, still a raging craving inferno of need, were the unanswered questions surrounding Coyote. Did clues remain in Zoya's house? Every minute they spent not investigating was another minute when evidence might disappear. And did it all really matter? Through the last six months they had faced one crisis after another. He had started to wonder if the emergencies would ever end.

But Jonathan Gates' death changed everything. The Secretary had been the driving force behind the construction of the SPEAR team and the primary glue that held it all together.

What next?

"Hustle up," the comms barked in his ear. "Chopper's lifting off."

Drake sprang into action. Dahl and Alicia ran by his side as he re-joined Team Bravo and hurried toward a cluster of parked vehicles. Humvees all, they had been provided by the Army and were military spec, all with Up-Armor capabilities. Drake caught a glimpse of the tracking system as he climbed in. It seemed even the President of the United States could be reduced to a flashing red dot these days.

"Wait a minute," Alicia said as she settled. "They can't have sealed off every road in DC. What happens when the chopper flies over a traffic jam or something?"

"That's why there are three teams," a man seated beside her said. "And more birds in the air than kites at the Blossom Kite Festival. Plus re-tasked satellites, infra-red, and some toys that ain't even been made public yet. We won't lose the President again."

Drake kept his silence. One thing was certain, if Kovalenko could snatch Coburn from under the noses of the elite Secret Service, then he could get him out of DC. "You know," he said. "If Kovalenko hadn't hit our HQ and our team we'd know the bastard's plan by now. Karin would have used his own men to get close."

"We're all hopping around on our back foot," Dahl agreed. "But the FBI will be on top of that, mate, I'm sure."

"Let's hope." Drake peered out the window and saw the Sikorsky lifting off. Straight away it veered onto a northwesterly course and the comms system yowled into life.

"Ground units. This is command. Take Constitution to Virginia and await further instructions. All roads as far north as F Street and east to 21st are clear."

In addition, more teams were ordered back into the hotel, this time to perform a meticulous sweep. Every scenario had been imagined.

The Humvee lurched forward, propelled by a heavy nervy right foot. The seated men clutched their weapons harder, muttering. The black vehicles, five in total, blasted up the wide road between stately buildings and rows of bare trees, aiming for the fork that would take them to Virginia. A convoy of vehicles followed, many loaded with men in army uniforms. All around them stood empty streets, empty sidewalks, and closed buildings; to their left stood the floodlit, scaffold-surrounded Washington Monument, stunning by night or by day; on every roof sat an 'eye in the sky', a sniper with a spotter beside him, ears attuned to the comms. The route of the chopper was being tracked at every level and by every means. Drake started to wonder what Kovalenko would pull next to cover his escape.

The possibilities scared him. One thing was sure—it would go down in history.

CHAPTER THIRTY TWO

The Sikorsky flew unhindered through the dawn skies, carrying with it the nightmares, hopes and immediate future of the United States.

Drake watched it fly straight as they sped up Virginia Avenue. The road was like most in DC: wide and practical and straight. The way forward was perfectly clear as they passed statues and offices, heading into the university area. As far as F Street the way stood clear, but beyond that the driver was already calling for the DC cops to stop more traffic. The operation was entirely fluid; the chopper could change course at any time but, unless the VP and his advisors wanted to sacrifice President Coburn, this was as tight as it was going to get.

Alicia craned her neck. “Dammit. We’d have been better off taking the bikes.”

“Bikes already had riders,” Dahl told her. “Trained ones.”

The five-vehicle convoy shot up Virginia past Anniversary Park and the F Street turn-off without slowing down. Not surprisingly, the streets were quiet this morning. Drake stared. “Is it starting to come down?”

Instantly, every man and woman slid over to the right-side windows. The Sikorsky was losing altitude and fast. Drake watched the tracker and the blinking red dot, overlaid by a 3D map of Washington DC. The dot was descending into a wide greenish circle.

“What is that place?”

The driver clicked his fingers and threw the vehicle up New Hampshire Avenue. “That’s Washington Circle Park. Good cover. Four exits. And then a shitload of roads leading away. A ton of getaway scenarios. Can't believe that madman's coming down in DC."

Dahl leaned forward. "How many roads is a shitload exactly?"

"Dunno. Eight maybe."

"That does qualify as a shitload. Get your foot down, driver."

Dahl sat back, stroking his chin. Drake shook his head. "From now on you should start all your sentences with 'I'm sorry, I'm Swedish, but . . .'"

"Only if you start yours, 'I'm a dumb Yorkshire knob'."

The Sikorsky continued to descend. All eyes were fixed to the hovering chopper and its vague, indistinct payload. Team Bravo had hands on every door, weapons ready, and total focus. Their driver squealed to a stop at the top of 23rd Street outside an orange-signed Burger Tap and Shake, on the crosswalk between black iron glass-topped signal poles. The seven-story brick edifice of the George Washington University Hospital stood to their left, identified by its big black signage and fronted by holly trees and planters. The Washington Circle was empty of traffic, a surreal sight even at the quietest of times, but the park inside the sizeable roundabout was anything but.

Drake leapt out of the vehicle, chasing the first two teams who were already pounding across the road and through the nearest wide entrance. Broad grass strips and big sycamores and oaks stood all around, barren but still hampering their efforts and obstructing their vision. A four-foot-tall, chain-link fence ringed the interior of the park. Drake saw the usual water fountains, black trash cans, and black iron benches as he rushed along, all apparently designed to complement the tall broad-based street-lights that had colonized most of central DC.

Gunfire erupted ahead, bullets flying in all directions. Drake doubted it was the attacking force and flung himself behind the nearest waste basket. When he chanced a momentary glance, a scene of bizarre and deadly chaos met his eyes.

The chopper rested on its skids, its rotors spinning at full speed, the resulting wash buffeting hard at anything nearby. The horsed bronze statue of George Washington stood just behind, sword bared, the horse's green nostrils barely out of rotor range. Six men knelt in a circle around the chopper, guns raised, firing indiscriminately. Four more men stood by the open chopper door.

Everyone wore identical black suits, gloves and balaclavas. It was impossible to tell who was who. The shooters might be prime targets, but Drake knew it would be a brave man who fired on them for fear of a luckless ricochet or even a through and through that might strike Coburn.

Before the attackers had time to settle or take stock, a shout went up from one of the men surrounding Kovalenko, maybe even the Blood King himself. Instantly, the whole contingent started to run.

"What the—" Alicia blurted.

But Drake was watching carefully. The four men nearest the chopper were joined by one shooter and broke to the south, the closest point to his position. Two other men broke to the northwest, and the remaining three to the southwest. All ran for park exits, firing hard as they went. Two unlucky soldiers took bullets, folding where they stood. In each fleeing group one man did not fire. Even now, they couldn't tell each man apart. Would the techs at command be able to pinpoint the President's signal?

"Hold fire!" the call screamed through the comms. *"Hold yer damn fire!"*

Fleet of foot, the Blood King and his men disseminated through the park. Reports came in through the comms from all surrounding areas, between the snipers and spotters on the roofs and the teams on the ground, the FBI trackers and the countless army patrols. It was more a case of too much information than too little.

Drake watched the craziness unfold, making a fast decision. "That group." He indicated the cluster of five men, but looked to the Team Bravo leader before moving. The man nodded quickly, not consulting his comms. It was fast becoming clear that someone's decision-making capabilities were somewhat lacking.

"Trust the goddamn suits," he muttered as he pushed past Drake. The team crossed a paved area and ran onto a concreted exit path. Bullets slammed into a man's vest, sending him to his knees with a grunt. Drake understood it was an unusual situation. No one could fire on Kovalenko's men, but at the same time Kovalenko couldn't directly threaten the President. What the hell else did the man have up his sleeve?

Choppers thundered overhead. Army vehicles screeched to a halt at hastily erected police barriers all around the Circle. Like gasoline on fire, this was a situation fast raging out of control. Drake pursued the fleeing group, Dahl and Alicia at his side. When he turned to them he noticed, for the first time since she'd returned, the fresh scars on Alicia's face.

"Looks like you put up a major battle."

Alicia's eyes were windows looking onto a black death. "These," she said, rubbing a hand across her cheeks. "I'm proud of."

Drake jumped off a curb, now crossing the road. The fires of dread burned bright in his heart. They couldn't care for all of their people right now. *He* couldn't care for them. Not even Mai. Sometimes silence was seen as inaction, but today it was an imperative.

The five-man terrorist group ran carefully but quickly

alongside buildings. If the President was one of them, then he was under a constant threat of some kind. Drake rounded a corner, ducking back as gray stone exploded where bullets struck. Another team member went down, wounded.

"Orders?" the team leader repeated into his comms. "What are my orders?"

Kovalenko's men slowed alongside the big hospital building and threw a grenade at a shop front, blowing out the doors and proving they had more than just guns in their arsenal. The team charged inside. Drake pulled up close by, noticing the green Starbucks sign.

"This part of their plan?"

"Good friggin' idea," Alicia said. "An extra-hot latte might just save my bollocks from freezing off out here."

One of the other team members studied her strangely, as if wondering whether to call her on that one. Wisely, he held his peace and looked away. Drake listened as the team leader consulted a digital blueprint on his handheld scanner.

"Shop exits onto a parallel street," he said. "Yeah, they planned this one."

The soldiers dashed inside, knocking over chairs and metal tables. Almost without thought, Dahl grabbed a handful of caramel waffles as he passed a big brown wicker basket, throwing one each to his colleagues. The mirror-clean pastry case was empty. Once through the café they exited onto a narrow street just in time to see Kovalenko's men blowing their way into another shop.

"We have them," the team leader reported. "They're not exactly trying to hide their movements."

Drake glanced at Dahl. This wasn't right. Kovalenko's men couldn't do this all day. It felt more as if they were waiting for something to happen.

Something big.

Drake entered the next shop on the escapees' boot-heels, surprised to find it was a large bookstore. They quickly crossed the open-plan area where big publishers paid small fortunes for their books to be stacked on tables designed to attract the eye and the wallet of incoming, unwitting consumers—the nearer the door the more expensive the table—and started to thread through the high stacked shelves beyond. With a high-pitched whistle, bullets began to thud and fly into the bookshelves, shredding wooden surrounds and paper pages alike. Drake hit the deck as books fell and spun all around him. One of the larger cases, shredded, collapsed into a tumbling pile, shedding heaps of mashed up books like trickling sand. The team leader muttered into his headset.

"Keep 'em in sight," came through the comms system.

"Taking heavy fire!"

"All these freakin' books," Alicia put in. "Don't they sell Kindles in Washington?"

"Apparently," Dahl said, inching forward on his elbows. "Some people still prefer paper."

"Dinosaurs in a digital age," Alicia said.

Dahl laughed. Drake peered around the edge of a sturdy looking bookcase. Paper still fluttered all around, fighting clouds of dust for airspace. The rear of the store was empty.

"Go."

Running again, Team Bravo was now down to a total of five. None of the men they had left behind were seriously injured, but all had sustained some kind of wound. The damaged bookshop exited through a constricted back door which led to an alleyway, still within the shadow of the George Washington University Hospital building. The Blood King's men were already racing along the alley's length, heading for the sliver of daylight that beckoned from its far end like the exit of a tunnel. Drake could see men running parallel along the rooftops above, tracking the runaways.

The team took off in pursuit, using dirty doorways and grimy dumpsters to duck behind when they came under fire. Bullets clanged and fizzed from every surface. At one point they were forced to take cover behind a big Dodge truck. Drake shook his head sadly as gunfire riddled its front end.

Alicia noticed the gesture. “For fucksake, Drake. Don’t worry. It’s not one of those Cobra things.”

“You mean an AC Cobra.” Drake glared. “Like the one you shot up in Hawaii.”

“Whatever.”

The alley gave onto another wide thoroughfare. By the time Team Bravo reached daylight, Kovalenko’s men were over a hundred yards ahead, but it was immediately apparent where they were heading.

“Metro,” someone said. “Shit.”

“Metro’s closed,” the team leader said. “Don’t worry.”

Drake raced on. Something was coming and rushing headlong toward them at a terrible pace, but what?

CHAPTER THIRTY THREE

Kinimaka knew instantly that Hayden was dying, bleeding to death, and that he only had one chance to save her life. Everything came down to this. All his training, every scrap of his experience. Act fast. Push everything else aside and work like he'd never worked before.

He would still have to go through the motions, but following those procedures saved lives more often than not. The new gunshot wound underneath Hayden's heart was a through and through; it appeared not to have rattled around inside her body since the entrance and exit wounds were in perfect alignment, but sometimes even that assumption had been proved to be a mistake. Kinimaka had known bullets chew people up inside, bouncing from bone to bone, and still line up when they came out.

Her airway was fine; she was breathing raggedly and even muttering. Her eyes were bright, so bright they made his heart lurch and his nerves rattle. Kinimaka felt such a rush of anxiety and love he began to doubt his ability and almost stopped what he was doing to call Smyth to take over. But no, this was Hayden. His boss and his friend for so long, now his lover.

But battlefield medicine was about as precise as the name suggested. He recognized she was strong enough to place her hands over the wound to control the bleeding, and laid her out in the back seat.

"Drive steady," he told Smyth.

Then he turned back to Hayden. "Hold your hands tightly here. I know it hurts. Press, Hay, just press."

As she groaned, Kinimaka looked around for something to make a seal. The first thing he saw in the rear footwell of their stolen car was a CVC plastic bag—not good enough, but inside it were several items. Quickly he tore open a package and grabbed the plastic, placing it over the wound. There was no tape around so Kinimaka forced Hayden to hold it in place. Using a plastic seal this way slowed the bleeding and helped prevent the development of a collapsed lung. It would ensure that, if she came out of this okay, she would have every chance to get better without some kind of disability. He wrapped her up warm, minimizing any exposure, and let her lie in the most comfortable position.

Karin stared over the back of her seat. "Don't elevate her legs, Mano. She'll bleed easier."

Kinimaka bit his tongue. He knew that, but Karin was only trying to help. "Thanks."

Smyth swerved around a slower car. "Sorry," he said through gritted teeth. "How's she doin'?"

"I can't tell. We need to get her to that safe house."

"Doin' my best."

With no pursuit and quiet roads the Suburban made good time. Once they entered the restricted area, using their SPEAR IDs, the roads truly opened up and Smyth soon powered down the street where their old safe house sat. Komodo called ahead, using an old CIA code that Kinimaka remembered, and forced a laugh.

"Looks like they sent everyone here. Place is gonna be crowded."

"Never mind," Kinimaka said. "So long as we can make her comfortable."

Hayden's eyes fluttered. Her breathing came in shallow gasps, but even that was better than it had been before. Kinimaka had done all he could for her, short of finding a surgeon and an ER. Contrary to popular TV, the bullet didn't need to be removed straight away. To do that would only increase the blood flow.

What remained of their team climbed wearily out of the black Suburban, taking a second to bask in the rays of the rising sun, then positioned themselves to help extract Hayden from the car. It was a slow process and risky, but she couldn't stay there. By the time they approached the door it was already open.

Lauren Fox greeted them, "Hey."

Smyth made eyes at her. "Hey."

"We cleared a room for her."

Kinimaka moved slowly, taking every ounce of Hayden's weight and trusting Komodo to protect the area around her wounds as best he could. They moved through a dimly lit room and paused.

"In here." Kinimaka recognized the Russian thief, Yorgi, standing waving in a doorway. As he started to move again he saw Sarah Moxley sitting in a cloud of depression on one of the sofas.

"Sarah?"

The woman barely looked up, her thoughts still dwelling on the dreadful scene that had started this night off— the murder of Jonathan Gates.

Kinimaka moved on, addressing Lauren, "You three don't seem like the likeliest of roommates."

"I was staying here already." She shrugged. "Bit of a long story, but let's just say I ain't exactly some five-star general's flavor of the month. Jonathan was going to sort it all out." She paused. "Shit."

"What did you do?" Kinimaka squeezed his bulk through the bedroom doorway and carefully maneuvered Hayden between Komodo and himself.

"Not *me,* exactly. Nightshade. My alter ego. We needed information from General Stone but then Jonathan's good conscience got in the way. By the time he pulled me out we think Stone had gotten wise."

Smyth was following hot on her heels. "You're a hooker aren't you? We got a hooker on our team. That's just fuckin *awesome.*" Then he sobered. "Poor Romero. He would have loved that."

Lauren ignored him. "It's an old story I guess now, involving General Stone. Not worth resurrecting again and again."

Kinimaka placed Hayden on the bed and stared down at her with anguished eyes. He thought her breathing had grown even more ragged, but was that just his imagination? Komodo looked over the bed at Lauren.

"An old story, huh? You mean it's last week's news, don't you? I've come to realize that's how fast this team moves. But Lauren, a five-star general? That ain't just gonna go away."

"I know, man, I know. But I've been taking pretty good care of myself all these years. I can sure do it again."

"You think just because you're streetwise you can handle this man's influence?"

Kinimaka tuned the conversation out, leaning over the bed, closer to Hayden. Damn, how they needed her expertise and leadership right now. The harsh breaths she took, lying down, told the story of how near death she was. His mind, usually so clear and concise, was in pieces right now. He knew he should be doing something, but couldn't quite focus on it. Should Hayden's welfare come first? The team's? The civilians'? Or should they be trying to help Coburn? What would Kovalenko do next?

He sat on the bed, wincing as it creaked under his weight. Hayden's eyes fluttered open.

"Mano?"

"I'm here. You're safe. I'm going to use the tech in here to find a safe hospital and call an ambulance. They can't follow us everywhere can they? How the hell do they keep on finding us?"

"The . . . the Grid," Hayden whispered. "I figured . . . it has to be . . . it's compromised—"

Her eyes closed again and she stopped talking. Kinimaka leaned in. "The what? The *Grid?*"

"It's the only . . . way—"

Hayden's words rattled like a last breath. Kinimaka pulled away, heart flipping, but saw her eyes wide open and staring. The life in them was vivid, the will to live dazzling. Quickly, he checked her dressings.

"You think the Grid's compromised?"

Hayden gave a bare nod.

"But that means . . ."

Kinimaka stared around the bedroom and through the door at the other part of the safe house. All seemed well, but an icy sliver of dread slipped down his spine. In that single quiet moment he felt every hair on his body stand on end.

"Oh no."

The safe house door exploded.

CHAPTER THIRTY FOUR

Drake pelted along the street, all thoughts of his own safety put aside, as the five-man terrorist team fell into disorder at the top of the Metro steps, right underneath the long metal and glass canopy that curved above the Foggy Bottom GWU Station. Some kind of internal battle was going on. One man tore away from the rest, ripped off his balaclava and started to shout.

"The President!" the team leader shouted. "Right there! That's him!"

Drake took off like a missile, Dahl and Alicia at his heels. The rest of Team Bravo divided around them, spanning the street, and sprinted as if they were inches away from winning gold.

Which they were.

President Coburn wrenched himself away from the grip of a man and backed off. Another man ran at him, but Coburn punched him in the nose, stopping his advance with one blow.

Drake almost cheered.

The team leader screamed into the comms. *"Send everyone! Coburn's here! Send fuckin' everyone!"*

Drake raised his rifle. He breathed deeply, letting the habitual custom relax him. He ran at full speed, without compromising his skills, and felt the presence of Team Bravo all around. Ahead, the President swiped at another hooded figure, but this one stepped away and around the blow, showing practiced ability. The figure danced around behind the President and caught him around the throat, halting all his movements, then forced him roughly down the steps. The rest turned, firing a quick burst before following.

The team leader's voice reflected his anger. *"Hurry!"*

Alicia was the first to fire back. Drake mentally kicked himself for not following suit. No one had shouted out a change of the original no-fire orders so he had just gone with it. Once a soldier . . .

But not Alicia. She had opened fire, probably hoping she took out Kovalenko and ended this whole clusterfuck. They hit the top of the steps just in time to see legs disappearing into the circular space of the station below, and started to leap down three or four at a time. The words Foggy Bottom—GWU Station shouted at him as he passed beneath a thick concrete roof. When Drake saw a rifle pointing up from the wide-open space below, he threw himself to the side, hitting the wall hard. A volley of shots passed among Team Bravo, striking no one, but slowing their pace.

Drake started down again, trying not to look at the shiny escalator sides. The team gained level ground, now standing in the surprisingly small entrance to the below-ground station. Ticket machines bordered the small space in a blue-and-silver half-circle. Yellow 'Wet Floor' cones lay scattered about. Through a wide opening Drake saw several barriers that led to the tracks and a couple of information-cum-guard stations. Large-scale maps dotted the walls amidst advertisements and electronic signs. The area was deserted apart from the five men they were pursuing, who even now were racing across the station at an angle to put as much distance as possible between them.

"Move!"

Alicia ran with her rifle tracking one of the fleeing figures. Drake watched her closely. "Be careful."

Alicia tracked her enemy but didn't fire. The men were too close together. Dahl pulled his trigger, but fired high, ruining a sign that read 'Elevator to Street'. As the fleeing men slowed near the top of an escalator, a shout went up and all five of them turned.

And stopped.

Drake put the brakes on. One enemy gun was pressed hard against Coburn's head. The rest of the rifles were trained on Team Bravo. Drake zeroed in on the man closest to the President. It was possible to kill a man so that his finger didn't twitch on the trigger, but a millimeter to either side of the kill point and you risked a catastrophe.

And this was the President.

The team leader spoke rapidly into his comms. Drake stopped not eight feet from the terrorist group. Behind and above them, they heard vehicles screeching to a halt and the sound of many thudding feet approaching the station. Sirens wailed and the sound of military choppers landing was loud even down here.

The man standing in the middle whipped his balaclava off. Dmitry Kovalenko, the Blood King, faced the man who had become his nemesis.

"Matt Drake." The guttural growl was hatred incarnate.

"Fuck you. Let the President go."

"How are your friends? And young Ben? How're his mommy and daddy?"

Drake tightened his finger on the trigger.

"Oh, and your army mates." Kovalenko spoke in mock English. "Spiffy are they?"

One more ounce was added to the pressure.

"Don't shoot!" the team leader cried. "Stand down!"

Kovalenko grinned devilishly. "Shoot me and your President dies."

Drake gritted his teeth so hard he tasted blood. The arm holding his rifle shook. He heard Dahl whisper a quiet "hold," and Alicia's indifferent grunt, saw the mocking challenge in Kovalenko's eyes, but it was the look in President Coburn's eyes which stopped him.

The Blood King's men removed their masks. The one holding Coburn was the dark-skinned African. The man's quiet smile revealed a wealth of confidence.

"Gabriel here and his brother, Mordant, are better than you will ever be, Drake. Better than you all. They would take title—" Kovalenko laughed. "Oh, and Mordant, even now, has just crashed party at CIA safe house. Your friends die as we chat, dah? How nice."

Drake's finger twitched again. He concentrated solely on Coburn's eyes, seeing the intelligence there, the calm confidence, but most of all, the tactical prowess which said this man was a heroic strategist, a player in their game, and was just awaiting his moment . . .

Tension flooded his body like never before. This was the game of games, and with a reward beyond imagination.

"Da best is yet to come." Kovalenko grinned. "Your mistake was to ever know my name, Drake. Now, my Blood Vengeance will take everything you ever loved and drive it into ground."

"Excuse me," Alicia said. "Do you have a point to make? These boots are friggin' killin' me."

"And your disgraced biker gang, Myles? Did they die well?"

"Funny thing," Alicia said emotionlessly. "I ended up killing most of the bad guys. Can you guess what I'm gonna do to you?"

Kovalenko raised his own gun. "So I shoot you now, dah? You can't shoot me. I have the President."

The gun discharged point-blank into Alicia's face. She had no chance. Her body fell backward. Drake fired at the African, but he had already slipped down onto the escalator, the bullet fizzing above his head as he pushed President Coburn before him. Kovalenko's men whirled and jumped in the African's wake, dragging Kovalenko with them.

"Whoops," the Blood King smirked with open arms. "Never was the best of shots."

Drake fell to his knees, cradling Alicia's head. He was surprised to find her shocked eyes staring into his own.

"Are . . . are you okay?"

"Yeah. I think so. Bullet passed by my helmet. I think it even glanced off."

Drake breathed deep. *Thank you, God. Thank you. Thank you.*

Dahl was by his side. "Don't do that again," he said sternly. "You gave me a goddamn heart attack."

Alicia climbed to her feet. The team eased forward past the ticket barriers and stared down the giant escalator at the escaping terrorists. Dahl clenched his fists.

"Balls to the wall." He grunted. "Live or die. Shall we go save the President?"

"Fuck, yeah." Alicia sprang forward.

"This ain't happenin' on my watch." The team leader jumped after her.

Drake slammed Dahl on the back. "You with me then, mate?"

The mad Swede simply leapt onto the middle of the escalator and threw himself headlong down the curved shiny surface, firing as he picked up pace.

"Jump on, Drake! It's crazy time!"

CHAPTER THIRTY FIVE

Kinimaka pulled his handgun out and fired even before figures burst through the breached doorway. Two men ran into his rounds and sprawled half-way across the room, lifeless; but more quickly followed. This was a full-scale breach. Smyth was closest to the door and used the smoke created by the blast to launch a surprise attack, wrestling with the next two attackers. One he punched so hard Kinimaka saw his face cave; the other he spun around and grabbed in a chokehold.

Komodo slid belly first across the floor, reaching for the weapon he had left lying on the sofa. Karin kicked it toward him, at the same time scrambling over the back to find shelter. Komodo caught the gun and shot another attacker in the knees, then the head.

Already that was five down. More surged inside the house.

Smyth used his captive as a shield whilst wrestling away his gun. Kinimaka was shocked to see Yorgi step up and stand in front of a dazed Sarah Moxley. Not even the closeness of her own death penetrated her stupor. Yorgi fired as a bunch of attackers burst into the room.

Kinimaka stood at the bedroom door. The attackers were bunched together, expecting sheer numbers to win the day. And it just might. At this rate the SPEAR team would be overwhelmed in minutes. Then the battle took a turn toward something much worse.

Kinimaka saw the albino arrive, slip like a wraith around the shattered door and square up to Smyth. To his credit he waited until Smyth threw his current assailant to the side, but then he hit like a cargo plane. Even Smyth staggered under the onslaught, barely able to defend himself; each defensive deflection seeming to cause him pain. When he found a second to attack, his strikes were blocked, turned aside, then punished.

Kinimaka emptied his clip and rammed home another. Hayden was trying to sit up in bed.

"Mano?"

"No. Lie down. You'll die if you move, Hayden."

"I'll die if I don't. It's the Agents' Grid, Mano. And no way . . . no way to shut it down unless . . . unless Karin can—"

"Got it. I know." Kinimaka saw Yorgi shoot a man and Smyth's huge bulk lifted into the air as if he were a rag doll.

"Shit," he said. "We're in trouble. That fuckin' albino could take us all out."

Smyth crashed down, crying out loud. Komodo scrambled toward the door. Bullets laced the air. Rounds struck the sofa, the floor, the walls, and the windows. The safe house was a crazy melee, swarming with hired madmen and their bloodlust; heavy with death.

Kinimaka saw Karin crawling around the back of the sofa. He beckoned her over, covering her brief run with gunfire. When she gained the bedroom she went straight to Hayden's side.

"What can I do?"

"Nothing. But we might have to move her, so get ready. There are two more ways outta here. One through a trapdoor, the other out the back. Hayden can't go down the trapdoor, that's for sure."

"Okay."

Kinimaka loosed another bullet. "And Hayden seems to think they found us by using the Grid. That sound right to you?"

"The *Grid?* You mean the Special Agent Grid? That's unhackable."

"So's the DOT's secret traffic signal system. But they broke into that."

"Bloody hell. I'm not even sure *I* could—"

"We need you to unhack the hack," Kinimaka said. "And fast."

"Well, I need a computer first. And how do they even know the Grid exists? Very few are privy to that kind of information, Mano."

"This bastard, Kovalenko. He has his fingers into everything."

"No. He has a major insider—"

"Not now." Kinimaka saw they were losing the battle. The team was on the defensive. They only had scope for one more gigantic effort. "Gotta go."

The big Hawaiian plowed into the room, lining up his targets. In a matter of seconds he plucked Lauren from the floor and threw her bodily back into the bedroom, sending her tumbling through the open door. In another second he was level with Yorgi and yelling at him to take Moxley and retreat. The Russian thief took her weight and dragged her away. Kinimaka held strong as a bullet smashed into him, striking his Kevlar vest. He charged at the crowd of men, splitting them apart like bowling pins and then, when he reached the other end of the room, he ripped the shattered, dangling door right off its broken hinges.

The attackers turned toward him. Kinimaka swung the big door like a baseball bat, smashing every man aside. The timbers shattered, falling apart as they hit. Kinimaka was left with shards of wood in his hand and an open front door behind him.

Could they . . .?

But then Smyth collided with him, bouncing clear. Kinimaka locked eyes with the albino.

"Fancy a shot at the title, big boy?"

He didn't. Kinimaka grabbed hold of Smyth and hurled the ex-Delta soldier toward the far door. At his feet, felled men were beginning to stir. He had dropped his gun when he wielded the door and now didn't have time to look for it.

"Back away," he said to the albino. "Now."

"You ever been to jail, big boy?"

Kinimaka felt pissed. Suddenly, it was okay for everyone to be sizist was it? "No. And stop calling me 'big boy', you vile white devil."

"In jail, you speak like that, it's like issuing a challenge. You need to learn more respect . . . *big boy.*"

Kinimaka never stopped moving, easing carefully past the one remaining attacker, knowing that he didn't want to provoke this man. Now was one of those times when retreat seemed more prudent than wading into battle. Not only that, he had seven bruised buddies about to wake up.

Komodo rose unsteadily, giving the Hawaiian a hard look. Kinimaka realized he might have inadvertently taken his own man out too. That sure wouldn't help his clumsy reputation. Smyth finally managed to compose himself and turned, reaching for a weapon.

Kinimaka backed away. "You good enough to take all three of us, chalky?"

The albino's eyes raised and narrowed, red-rimmed and bloodshot against his pure white skin. *Shit,* Kinimaka thought. *The crazy bastard's up for it!*

Faster than thought, Kinimaka turned and ran. Komodo moved with him. Smyth squeezed off a round. Maybe they could have stayed and defeated the albino, but Hayden's life was more important now. They flew into the bedroom. Karin already had Hayden sitting in an upright position, and had wrapped some duct tape they had found in the kitchen around both her wounds. Hayden's head hung low, but rose when

Kinimaka ran to her.

"Let's get outta here."

He started to scoop her up, but then Smyth held out a hand. "Wait," he said.

"We can't wait."

The angry man glared over at Kinimaka. "I said wait. I didn't say it for fun."

Komodo's stance changed. His whole demeanor altered from one of aggression to one of relief.

"They're gone," Smyth said. "They just got up, listened as the albino took a call, and left."

Kinimaka sighed with relief. "Now we can get her to a hospital."

"For that to happen," Karin said. "Kovalenko must have called them off. Only he could do that. And that means . . ."

"Something huge is going down," Komodo said. "Only that would make the Blood King feel the need to interrupt his vendetta."

"Fire up a computer," Kinimaka told Karin. "See if you can take down the Special Agent Grid. And Komodo, grab a satnav. I want the nearest hospital programmed in. And Smyth—"

The soldier still glared at him.

"Go outside. Take a look around and over the city. Maybe head up to the roof. I wanna know what happens the moment it hits."

CHAPTER THIRTY SIX

Drake felt like a man leaping to his own doom as he jumped onto the escalator's central divide and sailed down in Dahl's wake. The surface was slippery smooth, contributing to a swift increase in their speed. Drake heard a whoop from behind and knew that Alicia had climbed on too.

One after the other, the three SPEAR team members slid toward the Blood King, his men, and the President at high speed, firing high but still making them duck their heads and lose focus. One man tripped and fell headlong down the escalator. Dahl smashed through an oblong-shaped upright in the center of the divide, but barely noticed. His balance was perfect and never altered. He flew down the entire escalator at high speed, in just a few seconds hitting the end with his legs high and tucking to control his inevitable tumble. He landed, rolled and came up with his gun raised just as the Blood King's men jumped down the last few steps.

The African leaped at him. Drake landed in a tangle. Alicia cheered, enjoying the air time as she flew off the escalator, landing on her knees and sliding across the polished floor. Dahl stood up to the African, offering no quarter and giving no retreat. The Blood King and two of his men ran straight at Drake. The other man collapsed at the bottom of the escalator, right onto his face. It appeared his hands were tied.

President Coburn stooped down to help him.

Drake rose and waded right into Kovalenko, welcoming the attack. It felt good to pound the Blood King's flesh. He doubled the man over with a strike to the plexus, broke his nose with a rising knee, and smashed an elbow into the upcoming neck. All standard stuff, but Kovalenko staggered away, gurgling. The next two men looked to be a tougher prospect. Drake sidestepped a knife thrust and broke the wielder's wrist, then maneuvered the man so his colleague couldn't get past. The first man was far from finished, however, and propelled Drake back against the wall. Once there, his colleague stepped around. Drake ducked a stiffened fingerstab, letting it strike the wall, then grabbed hold of the man by the back of the neck and smashed his face against the hard surface. He turned once again to the man with the broken wrist.

To find President Coburn in the act of stabbing a piece of jagged plastic hard into the man's neck from behind; an act that took some solid balls.

When the man folded, blood spraying, Drake nodded. "Mr. President."

Kovalenko cried out in rage. In a moment of frustration he lunged toward Coburn, but the President stood his ground, shrugging off the Russian's attack. Kovalenko staggered, seemingly bowed by defeat.

But it was far from over. Dahl traded blow for blow with the African, both men standing toe to toe and refusing to back down. Kovalenko held a gun and fished a phone out of his pocket.

Just then, Bravo's team leader barged down the last few steps of the escalator. His face beamed a bright shade of crimson.

"Late to the fuckin' party," Alicia murmured as she came up behind Dahl.

"Don't you guys listen to your goddamn comms?"

"We've been kinda busy saving the President's ass."

"Well, do you remember Kovalenko's other two teams? They also dropped into the underground a while back, through other Metro stations. No trains means empty tunnels. And they're all converging here, *now*!"

Drake's eyes widened and he risked a glance behind him, where a wide-open, empty platform led to the train tracks. Sure enough, men were starting to climb onto the platform. *Kovalenko planned this?*

Seconds to decide. *What to do*?

"And not only that," Kovalenko said with a grin, having regained his composure and holding up his phone. "DC's about to go boom." He spoke into the phone. "Send in the drone!"

CHAPTER THIRTY SEVEN

Soldiers pounded down the escalator.

Drake knew he only had seconds to weigh the options. The Blood King was right there, backing away slowly and with a confident grin stretched across his craggy face; his remaining two backup teams mere seconds away. President Coburn stood behind Dahl and Alicia, staying quiet for now, but already signaling to the descending soldiers that something was wrong.

Gabriel stood between Drake and the Blood King, bruised and bloody but none more so than Dahl, still with that manic grin stretched across his face. If anything, the wiry African looked even more delighted.

Drake pretended to wrestle with his inner self, but pure common sense dictated the right thing to do. America needed its President back in one piece—and the SPEAR team had helped to accomplish that. The Blood King would wait for another hour, another day.

"I'll see you soon," he said as Kovalenko backed away.

"The Blood Vendetta will never end. Not whilst I live. I have already ruined you, Drake. I have ruined my great enemy. I too look forward to the last act, dah?"

A clatter of grenades bounced across the floor, followed by a loud explosion. Debris erupted from the blast point, a small chunk slamming Drake in the vest and doubling him over, the jolt of pain so intense he could barely breathe. He fell to his knees, losing focus, but battled to stay conscious. Shouts sounded from all around. Shattered brick, timber and stone continued to rain down from the ruptured walls and surroundings.

Drake crawled forward, barely able to see two feet in front

of him. His outstretched hand touched Alicia, who was kneeling and shaking her head. Beside her, Dahl sat as though in a daze. Drake slapped his face once, twice.

Dahl blinked and sighed. "That's enough."

Drake made it three times the charm, to Dahl's annoyance. Alicia looked to be planning a fourth when Dahl rose carefully and slowly to his feet.

"Bollocks."

Drake followed his gaze. The arched entrance to the train tracks was completely blocked off. The damage had been almost completely localized.

"One more failsafe for Kovalenko," Drake said.

The President still stood, shoulders covered in dust and little bits of rubble, and shouted at the first soldier who reached the bottom of the escalator. "Warn them up top. Something's about to hit. *Warn them!*" he shouted into the wavering soldier's face. *"Give them a chance!"*

"Mr. President, my orders are for the sole—"

Coburn wrenched the man's comms away. The Bravo team leader had already reported a possible strike, but the President's voice would add immense potency to the threat. The rest of the soldiers surrounded the President, completely ignoring the Blood King's mode of retreat, Drake, and his team.

Alicia eyed a man who shouldered by her. "You're welcome."

"They're just doing their job." Dahl steadied her. "Soldiers do that."

"Let's go." Coburn threw the comms device back at the luckless soldier and started toward the ascending escalator. Drake watched him walk away, then turned again to track Kovalenko's retreat.

"Bastard's gone."

Dahl came up beside him. "Op's complete," he said. "Time to go up top and find out what the hell's happening up there."

Drake reached for his phone. "And to call our friends."

If anyone had had any conventional thoughts and plans about tracking and capturing Dmitry Kovalenko through the miles and miles of underground tunnels, junctions, cross-passages, old stations and rabbit warrens which snaked beneath Washington; if anyone had pointed out that the lack of running trains aided his escape; if anyone had realized that the team led by Mordant, his other lieutenant, would eventually meet with him, then those generally uninspired thoughts had been ripped to tatters by the time President Coburn saw the rising sun.

Smyth and many others saw the menace first, the UCAV, the Unmanned Combat Air Vehicle, rise up and swing in low across the heart of the city. If it had been near the White House, Capitol Hill, or other major buildings, it might have been shot down by their defenses, but it swooped in an arc over the Dupont Circle, then settled into an unwavering flight pattern.

Kovalenko would have known where the main forces and main players would be situated by now. Had he ever actually intended to take the President any further than this Metro station? Had he intended to kill him there? Conceal him in the blast? No one would ever know. Maybe Coburn's death had been planned as the last act in the Blood Vendetta and the drone was a distraction technique.

Smyth had seen this kind of drone before, a US Hunter Killer. It operated under real-time human control, boasted a big payload capacity and hours of flight time. The subject of unmanned drones was a highly sensitive one, and this fiasco sure wasn't going to help. Even the new ones, called 'full autonomy', which could think and learn for themselves, continued to rack up collateral damage in various war zones. If

Kovalenko had somehow managed to get his hands on one he must have a mole inside the United States Air Force.

Not exactly the biggest surprise of the day. And, as Smyth knew, anything could be stolen. It just took the right minds and enough ruthless men.

Smyth watched with eyes that had seen it all before. These things used stealth technology and were able to deploy a range of munitions over a number of targets, all with surprising speed. It could defend itself against manned and other unmanned aircraft. It could deploy countermeasures to foil missiles. There was nothing he could do except watch and report.

"Is Hayden prepped?" He spoke directly to Karin.

"Ready to go. You're on speakerphone."

"I'd wait a while. This won't last long, but Washington's about to come under attack."

Smyth ended the call as gasps of disbelief bombarded his ears.

Drake sprinted hard up the escalator, taking the metal risers two at a time. When he emerged from the shadow of the underground and reached the top, he found a station in chaos; the entrance leading to the street thick with soldiers, FBI agents, SWAT, almost every acronym Drake could think of, and plenty more that probably didn't officially exist. The President was surrounded by a force of soldiers, and a small detachment of Secret Service agents were making their way to his side. Though 23rd Street was wide there was barely a space to be had between the Metro entrance and the Circa restaurant and Citibank across the road and along the road to the right that led deeper into the University area.

Drake, recognizing men of his own natural vocation, strode over to a group of Special Forces soldiers. The men who eyed him nodded after a few seconds, before returning their attention to a small screen held by their captain.

"Snipers have a bead on it," one of them breathed. "Wait. Gonna take it out."

"Fucker has to be guided by a hacked military satellite," another muttered. "Command should just take *that* out."

"It might not *be* a satellite-controlled drone," someone else answered. "Could be hacked locally, retrofitted with some kind of GPS software."

"Even," another man said. "Stolen or hijacked from one of our private security companies. Someone like Blackrock. They have drones all over the world guarding their mercenaries."

Then Drake looked up as the drone blasted overhead.

Smyth watched the drone employ its super-agile air defenses as it came under fire. Switching between precision-guided and precision-miniature weapons, it suppressed the army defenses and strafed the open spaces around the Metro Station. High-velocity rounds stitched a curving line through the massed forces down there, continuing through Washington Circle Park, taking chunks out of the monument and peppering the walls of nearby buildings.

Smyth hung his head. "God help us."

The drone swooped, then rose almost vertically and made to come around for a second pass. Fighter jets would have been scrambled almost immediately, but even those already on alert would take two to three minutes to hit the skies over Washington.

A fully armed drone could do a lot of damage in two minutes, depending on the skills of the human controller. No doubt he was just aiming for mayhem, and was cruelly accomplishing just that. The drone flew down like an attacking hawk, firing its lethal projectiles at a terrifying rate. Parked cars jumped and shook as they were torn apart. Running men fell in the street. Glass windows and the sides of buildings shattered and fragmented, pouring debris down onto the men below. Even the hospital came under fire, along with the ambulances and white FBI cars parked outside. Street lights, trees and exterior stalls collapsed, crashing down among a group of soldiers. Outside the Metro station, I Street was clogged with vehicles and personnel, most in disorder and chaos as they tried to deal with the first few minutes of Kovalenko's newest strike. The drone came in at about treetop height, a deadly black-painted predator, and mowed a wavering line from one side of the street to the other. The sound of bullets discharging and plowing into hard concrete and solid steel was overwhelming as the UCAV felled all in its path. Before it began to pull up again, an echoing boom was heard as two F-22's sliced through the skies.

The drone swerved between buildings.

Drake ran toward the madness, Dahl and Alicia at his side. When they burst out of the furthest station entrance the drone had already blasted overhead, stitching the ground along its flight path with a good chunk of its payload. Drake saw snipers on the roofs and soldiers on the streets, all with rifles aimed high, along with black-suited agents pointing their guns to the skies, all standing in the face of the onslaught and returning fire. They put up a stiff, heroic resistance but the drone passed by intact. Seconds later, the F-22's tore the clouds apart as they spotted and locked on to their target. The drone vanished along a wide street but couldn't just sit there. It soared out of the far end, hurrying to get some altitude before it began a third devastating run.

Drake could imagine the frantic communications passing between the fighter pilots and command. All they needed was the go-ahead to destroy the drone over downtown Washington and the battle would be done. All they needed was a man with a set of brass balls.

To his right, Drake heard President Coburn ask for an immediate line of communication to be opened to command. When the mobile comms was passed to him he ordered the drone to be shot down, no bluster, no airs, but also no doubt. "Just take that bastard out."

The drone lined up for another strike. One of the F-22s fired an AMRAAM, a fire-and-forget air-to-air missile with full active guidance.

"Fox Three . . . away." Drake heard the pilot's voice clearly through Coburn's open comms. The missile streaked toward the drone, hitting and blasting it apart in under a second. A cheer went up as smashed pieces of the drone fell to earth, scattering across rooftops and a good part of I Street.

Drake breathed a sigh of relief. At last, he could point his gun at the floor, a sign that the threat had lessened.

For now.

Dahl made a quick gesture. "Now," he said. "Call the others."

CHAPTER THIRTY EIGHT

Kinimaka listened to his head and not his heart, and waited for the ambulance to turn up. It arrived accompanied by a military escort. Karin, using newly established local contacts, and Kinimaka, using his juice as an ex-CIA agent, had pulled every string in their respective bows to get Hayden escorted to the nearest best-guarded hospital. The men they had spoken to had won their confidence and come through with the prompt ambulance and heavily armed escort. The SPEAR team was still under threat, a point acknowledged by all, and were permitted as much security as the authorities could spare.

Kinimaka watched with a pained expression and an aching heart as Hayden was carried away on a stretcher. He held her hand until the last moment, its limp weight almost breaking his heart. The paramedics didn't need to say that his impromptu field surgery had saved her life. He just hoped they could keep it that way. He glanced up into the morning sun as the ambulance drove away, seeking solace in its warmth, then returned to the ruined safe house.

"I'll see you again," he said under his breath: a promise, a wish.

"Tell me again," he added, louder, "Why I can't go with her."

"This is why." Karin held out her phone. "The team needs you more than Hayden does right now. So does this country. I have Drake on speakerphone. Listen to this."

"Kovalenko got away, Mano. He blew up some underground tunnels, used some kind of drone and escaped through the labyrinth beneath Washington."

Karin knitted her brows. "They'll still have him on CCTV,

Matt," she said. "There's surveillance cameras below DC too, and most other major cities."

"I know. But the arsehole's got some tech wizards working for him. They disabled some remotely, destroyed others. We have some patchy footage, but nothing that tells us where he and his psychotic band of brothers came out."

"Tech wizards for sure," Karin said. "Covert agency standard at least. Controlling that drone must have been almost as hard as stealing it. Then we had the traffic light fuck up. The Special Agent Grid incursion. What next?"

"He hit hard and fast," Dahl said. "He put everyone on the back foot. Especially us, with all the extra suffering we've had to face. Now he's on the run. This is our chance to pull together and end this the right way."

"You have everyone with you," Kinimaka said. "We all owe that bastard."

"Damn straight," Smyth rasped quietly, a look of sadness on his face. "What's the plan?"

"Head for the Foggy Bottom Metro and use your IDs. Coburn's calling together the meeting of all meetings. I have an idea . . . a good one," Drake paused. "But I need all of your support to help me pull it off and make it look good."

"On our way." Kinimaka looked around. "C'mon, guys. It's time to make Kovalenko pay. Time to shed some blood."

Smyth snarled, "And get a fuckload of vengeance."

CHAPTER THIRTY NINE

Lauren Fox sat listening as the SPEAR team made plans to go after Dmitry Kovalenko. Her head spun. Ever since she'd been attacked in her New York apartment, impressed Jonathan Gates, and then accepted a role in the team, her life had been anything but regular. Not that she led the most ordinary of lives anyway. *But hell,* she thought, *There's gotta be a limit.*

Lauren was streetwise, quick-witted and, when necessary, somewhat of a smooth talker. But she was not polite. Maybe it was being dragged around foster homes all her childhood, maybe it was the New York vice, but Lauren could not bring herself to kiss ass.

Unless she was being paid two thousand an hour, of course. For that kind of money she'd pretty much kiss anything that presented itself.

Kiss ass or kick ass? She thought back to her time on the streets. It had always been the latter.

Now, with Jonathan gone and the future of the team uncertain, Lauren's instinct was to bolt. She had the experience to look after herself. She had money saved in a Grand Central locker. The only reason she didn't was because she knew Stone was an influential five-star general and thus held a lot of clout on the Hill. He *would* track her down when he had the time. SPEAR, or whatever element remained after today, was the kind of family that would have her back, no matter what. They would stand against the general and find a way to help her. The team that Gates had formed would be her salvation.

She had originally made contact with General Stone during the Babylon affair, prepared to use her wiles, but later been told to stand down by Gates. Almost past the point of no return,

Stone had guessed something was off and had made stronger enquiries. That was until Kovalenko struck at the capital. Tomorrow, if Kovalenko vanished . . . who knew?

Now Lauren looked around. The team was about to split up. Yorgi the Russian, Sarah Moxley the Washington Post reporter and herself would be dropped off at the hospital where Hayden was being treated. The place was heavily guarded, totally secure, and if Kinimaka had allowed Hayden to be taken there then Lauren had no problem joining the wounded team leader. Plus, Kovalenko was on the run and so were his various cells. Maybe he had a plan for another day and maybe he didn't.

Anyway, she thought. *Life's at its best when it's unpredictable.*

The team gathered together. To a person they looked disheveled, shell-shocked, even downtrodden, but sparks of life and hope still lived in their eyes. They would learn to live with their losses and come fighting back.

Literally.

Kinimaka took a moment. "Look," he said to Yorgi, Moxley and her. "I know you three guys have stuff that needs sorting out. Stick with us, and we'll get into it right after we fry Kovalenko's ass. Please, just give us a few days."

Yorgi nodded vigorously. "I really have nowhere else to go. I'm good."

Sarah just nodded absently. Lauren untied then retied her dark hair. "Only Gates knew how to help me." She said. "It's . . . very sensitive."

Smyth looked up from his phone, thumbs suddenly still. Lauren wondered who he was texting in these significant moments. "Sensitive, huh? Can I help with some ointment?"

"Do I even know you?"

"I guess not. But there's always tomorrow."

Lauren looked away. "Not for some."

Smyth looked down. Before the mood sobered any further, Kinimaka pointed to the door. "Let's move out."

Lauren followed Karin and Komodo, keeping her thoughts to herself. The morning light hit her like a balm, the chill wind like a cold shower. People were moving around outside. Civilization, it seemed, had returned to the world after taking the night off.

News reports blared from open windows. Entire families sat around listening. Lauren could see them as Komodo drove them down the block. Newsstands were open, papers racked up out front with glaring headlines designed to sell thousands of copies. The brave few who wandered the streets did so with sad, subdued faces.

The nation was in mourning.

Komodo drove ten city blocks and pulled up to the hospital entrance. They were challenged almost instantly and made to show their IDs. Kinimaka called about Hayden's progress and received the same unhelpful answer.

She's in surgery right now. No change.

Lauren exited the car without saying goodbye, not sure what to say, and stood and watched as Komodo drove Karin, Kinimaka and Smyth away.

Yorgi, at her side, voiced her exact feelings. "I wonder if we'll ever see them all together again."

CHAPTER FORTY

President Coburn and the Secret Service had made the decision not to relocate immediately to the White House or any secure bunker, but to safely address a select few decision makers whilst Kovalenko was still thought to be actively on the run.

So, although Kinimaka was now the acting head of SPEAR, and Drake was and always would be a gnarly Yorkshireman, it was still the ex-SAS soldier who was invited into the hastily assembled inner circle. Even Drake was surprised, but mitigating factors included the rationales of speed and Kinimaka's absence and the fact that Drake had been part of the team which helped saved Coburn's life—even fighting alongside him.

A government building on 23rd Street was taken over, swept, secured and prepped in under an hour. All lingering students were quickly relocated. Policy dictated that the President should not stay in the area, but all the military men and minds present applauded the decision whilst the dyed-in-the-wool politicians dithered and moaned.

As Coburn had said, "We now have need of a military leader, not a political figure. Only the future can truly judge my next actions, but I believe they should be powerful, swift and severe."

Drake waited amid a knot of executives, the majority present purely because they were *there*, on site and in charge at a moment of crisis. When the Secret Service ushered them into a windowless holding room one by one, Drake fell into line. He took a seat and watched while the meeting was hastily called to order.

"My friends, I don't have long," Coburn began, walking to

the front of the room. “We have the White House, the VP, and other leaders on teleconference call, and we have you. The terrorist Dmitry Kovalenko and his men are on the run, and I have to make a public address within the hour. I need options, gentlemen. What have you got?”

Drake kept an eye on his phone. Kinimaka would text when he arrived, indicating that Drake could present his proposal with the full backup and commitment of his team.

Reports came in thick and fast. The NSA were monitoring all signals and reporting that overall chatter was quiet. The CIA stated that all of its foreign assets were on full alert, but had so far learned nothing. At domestic level, the FBI had alerted every one of its agents and was out in force. Other agencies and forces gave more details, but actual suggestions remained thin on the ground.

The Chiefs of Staff soon stepped in through the teleconference call, all speaking at once. The FAA and NORAD took the opportunity and attested to the safety of the skies. The first person who actually stood up to be counted was the DC Chief of Police, who stated that although every available officer was being utilized in the search for Kovalenko and in scrutinizing the Metro stations and other egress points from the tunnels, it should be assumed that their quarry had already escaped by means of a carefully pre-planned route. Hundreds of thousands of square feet of abandoned tunnels ran beneath the city at varying points and, although some were monitored, it also had to be said that some were not.

“If his escape plan is as formidable as his plan of attack,” the Chief said. “Then he may have already left DC and its environs.”

Coburn didn’t bat an eye. He’d no doubt already been informed that might be the case. “One thing is clear cut,” the President said. “He will not be allowed to escape this country.”

The Director of the FBI spoke up. “Before any of you smart people think of tracking the rogue agent, Marnich, through the Special Agent Grid, let me tell you right now that it’s a dead end. The Grid has been compromised.”

Drake knew the Secret Service and several other agencies wore trackers which allowed a central command point to know their exact location at all times—most called it ‘the Grid’. He listened as the CIA Director explained that every single one of Kovalenko’s old contacts were being monitored and none had received any form of contact.

“He has money,” a man seated in front of Drake said. “This damned operation of his has been financed from somewhere. Can’t we follow that?”

The FBI Director took that one. “Without laboring the point, sir, we never did find all of Kovalenko’s accounts. And perhaps he has a new backer. We’ll start to follow the trail but it’s going to take some time.”

Drake thought he might as well start the ball rolling. “Have we retaken the prison yet?”

“Recently,” the Chief of Staff of the Army said. “The prison is now ours.”

Coburn looked directly at Drake. “Are you thinking he may have left something behind? Some kind of information?”

Drake pursed his lips. He really wanted to wait for Kinimaka, but his natural enthusiasm had risen and jumped the gun. There was no delaying the President.

“Kovalenko’s goal is the fulfillment of his ‘Blood Vendetta’,” he said. “For any of you who don’t know what that is—it’s the murder of anyone connected in any way to his original downfall. The President. The Secretary of Defense. The SPEAR team. I say we give him the chance to realize his dream.” He paused expectantly.

Kinimaka texted at last. Drake relaxed.

Coburn sat forward. “Tell me more.”

Drake left the meeting early, called Kinimaka’s cell, and let himself be guided to their position. When he saw the Hawaiian he felt a sudden urge to hug the big man.

“Thank God you made it through, Mano.”

“We were lucky.”

“And Hayden?”

“Still in surgery. There’s no word yet.”

Drake steeled his heart. He couldn’t show too much emotion right now. The stakes were still space station high. His gaze moved to Karin, and when her bottom lip started to tremble that decision went out the window.

“I’m so sorry about Ben,” he said. “And . . . and your . . . I’m so sorry.”

“I know.” Karin came forward and buried her head in his chest. “I know.”

Drake allowed a few moments of mourning. It was hard to believe but as he looked over his gathered colleagues, his team mates, and more than that – his new family – he saw pure iron resolve. There stood Alicia, battered and devastated; Kinimaka, mourning his mother’s loss; Smyth, trying not to show how deeply he had loved Romero; Karin, who had lost her entire family; Komodo, who would also have to deal with her losses for the rest of his life; and Dahl. The Swede’s family had remained mercifully untouched but Drake knew every single death would have driven spikes through the man’s heart and soul.

But the steel in their eyes was as resolute as the hardiest warship, as resilient as the strongest sword, and ready to be put to work. Drake nodded at Kinimaka.

“They’re still debating half a dozen other plans. But essentially they went for ours.”

Karin pulled away. Komodo put his beefy arms around her. She wiped her eyes. "So we're going to Death Valley? Now?"

Drake nodded.

"We getting any cover?" Smyth growled. "Not that I give a shit anyway."

"Area 51's close by," Drake said without inflection. "Whatever else that place may be, it's still a big military base. They're flying a fully equipped fuckin' army into there."

"So we're really doing this?" Kinimaka took a huge breath.

Drake nodded grimly. "The Blood King started a war. He's about to get one. It's game on, motherfucker."

CHAPTER FORTY ONE

The Blood King knelt inside the rear container of a large transport vehicle, thinking the roll and sway of the truck wasn't unlike the heave and swell of the ocean waves he had been used to for the best part of his life. They were rattling down a dark US highway somewhere in between Crapsville and Shittown, and the hard nucleus of his team lounged all around him. The inside of the container was fully insulated, wired, furnished, and contained everything Kovalenko's super-hacker required to achieve the tasks he had been set earlier that night. A mobile ops center was always much harder to track down than one that was fully grounded.

Kovalenko allowed the events of the night to pass through his mind, filtering the best parts for review. The President's face when the Blood King had stepped out to greet him. The disgust he had shown at Marnich's betrayal. As if it should come as a surprise. Betrayal was one of the better parts of human nature, and something men like him thrived on.

And all the rest. Particularly those moments when news of the vendetta's ongoing triumphs reached his ears. A member of his somewhat decimated German unit had sent him an admittedly scary picture of Alicia Myles's death-defying charge over in Germany. Someone who lived in York had facebooked about Ben Blake's dead girlfriend lying in the streets. Mordant had recounted details of the skirmish he'd had with several SPEAR members. Hayden Jaye lay in a hospital bed, almost dead but sadly out of his reach.

But this day, as they said, would live in infamy. *The night of the Blood King,* he thought, *Has a nice ring to it.* A wave of disappointment crashed through his mind, making the tips of his fingers itch and the edges of his teeth ache. Had it all been for nothing? Still the Blood Vendetta remained unfulfilled. What were the chances of him mounting this kind of detailed operation again? The Blood King peered around inside the truck, needing something to kill. At times like this only pure fresh red blood sated his outrageous desires.

"Sir." Mordant knew that expression. "Would you like us to stop at the next town?"

Kovalenko allowed a twisted grin to raise the edges of his thin lips. "Dah, my lieutenant. That is very good idea. Bring me anything, I do not care, so long as it is fresh meat."

Mordant radioed the driver, delivering the instructions. Kovalenko managed to relax a little, anticipating the pleasure soon to come. He watched as Mordant settled back, eyes reduced to thin slits. The man almost appeared to be asleep but Kovalenko knew that to be far from the case. Mordant saw and heard everything, and the laid-back sleeping pose was one of the ways he accomplished that. Gabriel, beside him, was quite the opposite, always grinning like a circus freak, always upbeat and nodding along to his own internal annoying beat. Right now he put a hand on his 'twin's' arm, grinning at something Kovalenko didn't want to know about.

"So," a voice interrupted his musing. "What happens next?"

The Blood King regarded Agent Marnich carefully. The traitor sat with both legs drawn up, worry etched across his face. Such body language spoke of insecurity and was a sign of weakness to the Russian.

"Stay sharp, stay useful, American," he said. "And you will live to see your payment."

Marnich nodded, lapsing into silence, but his question did have some merit.

What next?

Kovalenko entertained the notion of just waiting. It would

be fun to maybe set up some sort of shadowy surveillance and watch as his targets grew more anxious as the weeks and months passed, always looking over their shoulders. Occasionally, he could remind them of his presence, lift the shroud a little, to heighten their terror. Such amusement might even see him through happily to the end of his years.

But one thing rankled above all others. *Drake.*

He held a deep hatred for the ex-soldier. From his ridiculous accent to his pathetic humor. From his privileged training to his infuriating confidence. Drake was the only man who had ever really gotten under Kovalenko's thick skin.

"Vodka," he suddenly said, waving at Marnich.

The American passed him a bottle of Southern Cross, one of his own superior brands. Kovalenko twisted off the top and upended the bottle, letting the cold liquor pour straight down his throat. He listened hard as the truck's engine tone changed, feeling the vehicle start to slow.

Mordant reached out for the bottle. "He's leaving the highway for the town. It will be soon now."

"Good."

A squawk drew his attention to the front of the long container. It was there that the super-hacker sat on a chair bolted to the floor, facing a daunting arrangement of consoles, mini-TV monitors, keyboards and portable tablets. The man went by his nickname, Salami Bob—SaBo for short—and it was said he had once hacked the Pentagon, the NSA and NORAD in the same day. One of his past accomplishments had been to take down the security system of Fort Knox, but the ground team had made a mess of the infiltration, getting themselves caught. SaBo had been on the run ever since, until the Blood King's men had found him and offered a secure sanctuary with all the money and perks he could ever need. And even that was not enough. Salami Bob's skills were now required over in the UK for a forthcoming project, and once the Blood King's men were aware of the project leader's identity they had agreed to let him go by tonight.

Coyote. The name struck fear into the hearts of anyone who knew her history, or even a part of it. Even men like Mordant and Gabriel. The Blood King himself had contacted her recently, through a third party, offering a lucrative contract in the event of his death or disability. The future was not rosy for Drake and his team.

Kovalenko's humor turned at the thought of that smug little crew. They were good, to be sure, but to be the best you had to be a loner. Like the Blood King had always been. They were a family, and that was their ultimate weakness. Something both Kovalenko and the Coyote would turn against them. They already had. The Blood King enjoyed a moment of self-satisfied superiority.

The list of their current losses was a gratifying one. It would only get longer.

His faraway eyes finally focused on the piece of now useless material that lay in a shapeless, discarded lump to one side of the van. The nano-vest, the outstanding piece of work Mr. Tyler Webb had supplied him with, now seemed pointless, futile. Nano technology was the 'new thing', apparently, the manipulation of matter on an atomic and molecular scale, and Webb's multi-billion dollar company was at the leading edge of the new technology. A good thing in some hands, but not so much in Webb's. His research also extended to weapons and the fusion of nano-explosives and this clever vest was an experiment which should have been carried out on the President of the United States in the tunnels under DC. The final and most crushing blow. Unfortunately, Drake and his annoyingly enthusiastic play-friends had short-circuited that particular event. Webb wouldn't be best pleased. To him it was a major trial. But there were others planned, he knew. Kovalenko would have to deal with him, or maybe join the New Order to save some face. He snorted. Another bunch of megalomaniacs getting together in the wake of the Shadow Elite's demise. *But then they do have some major clout*, Kovalenko reflected, *and at least one highly placed official on their side. Perhaps they will succeed.*

But Pandora's Box? Really? Wasn't that just a myth, an ancient mystery made up to scare the kids?

Just like the ancient Gods.

The Box contains all the sins of the world . . .

The Blood King thought back to Hawaii and the Diamond Head mountain. Captain Cook's seven Hells underneath, so carefully catalogued. *I beat Cook, got further than the old explorer until . . .* again he cursed and slugged vodka.

His mind turned again, flicking across the drone and its procurer. All thanks to the *New Order.* Kovalenko snorted again and threw back more vodka.

Just then SaBo turned around, red face screwed up in ecstasy, a long strand of greasy hair stuck across his chin. "I think we got something. I really think we got something."

Kovalenko's voice, already rougher than a cheese grater, came out even harsher after the glugs of vodka. "What is it?"

SaBo blanched, probably thinking the Blood King was angry. "I believe you will like this, sir. I have been monitoring all channels as requested. Two of the most secure government comms channels just relayed the message that the SPEAR people are being sent to the facility at Death Valley to investigate your, um . . . breakout. They hope to find something you might have overlooked, clues as to who helped you and where you might go next."

"Secure channels?" Mordant questioned. "How secure?"

"One of them is linked to the Special Agent Grid I cracked.

They won't find my hack. It's too good. I can also say that both these channels have been transmitting genuinely throughout the night."

Kovalenko took a moment, but then felt his pulse start to race. "It is genuine? No trick?"

"It's genuine, sir. The SPEAR team are on their way to the Death Valley prison facility right now."

Kovalenko fought the urge to punch the air. "Call our Nevada compound! Prep the men. Send choppers to pick us up. I want to be there. How many men do we have left?"

Mordant frowned. "In total? Maybe a hundred or so."

"Send them all. Use any means possible. Do it."

"It's risky, sir. We have no plan." Mordant, despite his callous penchant for murder, was a careful man.

"For this, we do not need a plan. Just send everyone, you hear? *Send everyone!*"

CHAPTER FORTY TWO

During the flight to Death Valley, Drake gave Mai a call. It was early morning in Tokyo, but the Japanese woman didn't sound at all sleepy.

"It is not easy," Mai told him the opposite of what he wanted to hear, "But I have friends in Tokyo too. We will take down the Clan together."

"You called in some help?" Drake whistled softly. "Must be bad."

"The Clan are international murderers. Global assassins. They are formidable."

"Well," Drake murmured. "So long as it's not Dai Hibiki. I'd almost rather have you working with Smyth than that guy."

"Really?" Mai laughed lightly. "Are you so jealous of all my admirers, Matt?"

"No." Drake said it quickly and venomously, making her laugh out loud once more. Through the connection, Drake heard the sound of her text message tone and then another quieter laugh. He glanced suspiciously over at Smyth as the man's own very realistic gunshot text alert went off.

"Seriously, mate. Are you for real? You're texting my bird while I'm actually talking to her?"

Mai instantly quit laughing. "I am not your *bird.*"

"Sorry, love. It's just a saying."

Smyth scowled. "It's been a rough couple of days."

Drake relaxed. "That it has." He sighed. "That it has."

"And you have nothing to worry about where Hibiki is concerned," Mai went on. "He is dating my sister."

Guy's a player all right. Drake shook his head. *First Mai. Now Chika.* "What's his secret?"

"Do you really want to spend this call discussing Dai Hibiki's assets?"

Drake blinked. "Not when you put it like that, no. What's your timescale?"

"The Coscon is today. The plan is to go there first, seek out the Yakuza, and then head to the village. It should all be over by tonight."

Drake remembered the original Coscon and the now world-renowned events that had occurred there. He hoped today's episode would turn out far less dramatic but, knowing Mai, it was unlikely. He could spend an hour saying all the things he wanted to say to her but knew there were no words, not between soldiers such as they. The meaningful things went unsaid, but were no less heartfelt.

"I'll see you soon," he said.

"Aye, lad," Mai said in a terrible mock-Yorkshire accent. "That y'will."

He cut the connection. In more ways than one, Mai did not sound herself. He forced his attention back to the mission. Ahead, and soon to be below them, lay Death Valley, the lowest, hottest, driest area in North America, with the spectacular Panamint Mountains ranged along its western border. To his right, Dahl was just finishing up with his wife, Johanna. To his left, Kinimaka was talking softly to Kono, his sister. Karin leaned in to Komodo, whispering softly. Alicia fended off the calls from her biker gang, every member of which had wanted to accompany the SPEAR team on this desperate mission. If Death Valley had been closer to Washington, Drake knew they would have organized their own transport and found a way to help. But not this time.

They were heading into the Blood King's trap.

Kinimaka's cell chirped. He quickly checked the screen, blanched, and ended the call with Kono. His first words chilled every heart in the cabin.

"She's what?"

The Hawaiian's face fell even further, desperation never so plain on a man's features. When he ended the call he took a few minutes to collect himself.

No-one spoke.

Finally, Mano Kinimaka looked up. "She died. Hayden died and they managed to revive her. Another surgery. But she's failing. . ." his voice broke. "Failing bad."

The pilot's voice cut harshly through the grief. "Choppers are coming in hard from the left, folks. We're under attack!"

Dahl sniffed and whispered. "About bloody time."

Out of the searing light they came, three matt-black helicopters without munitions, but when doors had been torn off to allow groups of gun-toting, harnessed men to hang upright in the empty gaps, what need did they have of integral armament?

Drake hung on as their own chopper veered away. His view of the sky became a view of the ground: scorched desert and barren badlands, plus a brief glimpse of the small facility from which the Blood King had escaped a few days ago.

How did a man plan a campaign like this from prison?

With crucial aid, he thought, *with one or more key figures backing you.* Somebody had helped grease the wheels. Somebody had helped procure a drone which had turned out to be the main facilitator of Kovalenko's escape. And drones, Drake knew, didn't exactly come easy. Not even for a man like Dmitry Kovalenko.

He needed to consider the whole picture, including Jonathan Gates' death. Someone was benefiting immensely from all this. The SPEAR team just had to figure out who.

The chopper swooped nose first, almost sending Drake's stomach through his mouth. A wave of bullets flew through the space they had just vacated. Alicia swore as the ground rushed up to meet them, but then the pilot tugged on the collective, taking the chopper out of its dive. In another second he had jerked the machine sharply to the right, but even so the edge of a fresh wave of bullets clanged off the bodywork.

Alicia twisted and turned, trying to keep track of their enemy, cursing them with every breath. Dahl regarded her curiously.

"You okay, Al? You seem a little . . . jumpy. Not like yourself."

"I'm fine, Torsten. And did I say you can call me Al?" She blinked, then shook her head, realizing what she'd said.

Dahl smiled. "Got you. God, you're easy."

"So it's been said, but rarely to my face."

Drake stared at them as bullets peppered the chopper's body. "Wait. What's this? Something new?"

Dahl nodded, holding onto a strap with his right hand and swaying with the sharp movements of the chopper. "My idea. All you have to do is trick someone into speaking a song title."

"Where'd you learn that?" Drake poked. "Shiny-arse school?"

"It's a damn sight better than *Dinorock.*"

Drake didn't answer. Ben Blake had been his main Dinorock conspirator, Mai his second. Now one was dead and the other in the fight of her life. The open wounds were as raw as they were painful. Drake closed his eyes tight and whispered a silent prayer for Ben. He could barely imagine the lad's eyes without life; unseeing, all thoughts and memory and purpose, all his experiences, lost and forgotten forever. *Goodbye, my friend,* Drake said to himself. *I'll maybe see you soon.*

There was no worse a death than the end of hope. Throughout his life, Drake felt like he'd always fought an uphill struggle with hope. As a child, the battles with his dad had all been about 'becoming better', taking responsibility and striving to be the best. This was almost before he'd started school. Had he joined the army to please his father, or to get away from him? Drake didn't know for sure, but in his heart suspected it was the latter. It didn't matter now, of course. His father was long dead, his mother too. Later, his adversities had been with the army itself: fighting promotion, fighting shiny-arse rich boys for their privileges, fighting himself to overcome weakness and be the very best, fighting the enemy.

All his life.

More recently, the fight had become more personal. Since the Odin thing had happened, Drake had actually found himself able to take charge of the fight, instead of watching it happen to him. It felt good. But the line between personal battle and personal tragedy was a thin one and, it seemed, an unavoidable one.

The battle continued. He had the worst feeling that it would continue for the rest of his life. Would he ever find peace? Maybe . . . but Kovalenko and Coyote needed to be taken care of first. The road to Coyote had always been a dead end, but recently he had uncovered the slimmest of leads—Zoya, Zanko's crazy grandmother, had once been in contact with the world's greatest secret assassin. Nothing more. It was barely a straw, but one that needed to be clutched.

Soon . . .

Now Dahl smiled cheerfully as the chopper swooped lower and lower through its evasive strategies. Alicia whirled and spun, keeping her eyes firmly on the enemy. Komodo gripped a strap with one solid fist, the other arm held like a rod of iron across Karin's stomach to help keep her from falling around the cabin despite her belts. Smyth sat expressionless, like a man waiting to appear on stage and show off his outstanding skills. And Kinimaka . . . well, the huge Hawaiian conveyed a mixture of emotion. One expression displayed raw will and hatred—he wanted to finish this whole endless grisly battle with the Blood King and move on. The next radiated pure longing—he wanted to be with Hayden, sat by her side, holding her hand and never having to let go.

Drake wondered if it could ever be that way between him and Mai. *We're such specialist soldiers, can we ever let go?*

A chopper, matt black in color, suddenly dipped into their flight path ahead, weapons blasting. This time the strafe of bullets shattered the windshield and riddled the outer cockpit, making the pilot execute another emergency dive.

"Going down!" He screamed the words. "Brace for impact!"

The chopper dived hard and its occupants shouted, grunted, complained or set their faces to stoic; whichever method they used to gather their courage. Even Dahl put two hands to the straps, but the grin remained genuine. Screw Six Flags, this was his kind of ride. Three choppers dived after them, deadly birds of prey lunging through the skies, never once letting up their raking lines of fire. The pilot hauled up as the salt flats dramatically enlarged, the nose of the chopper and the stomachs of its occupants lifting a little, but the first impact was still a heavy one, its force shattering overstressed steel. The landing skids tore away. The nose cone crumpled. The chopper bounced and rose, leaving a deep cleft in the earth and a wide spray of white salt in its wake. Drake's head struck a metal strut and he cursed. Alicia mumbled something about the impact being unable to do much harm. The chopper bounced again, rending the tail boom and part of its rotor from the rest of the body. It began to slew, the front digging in, but thankfully by then its lessening speed meant it didn't start to roll over. It came to a shuddering halt, obscured by rising clouds of dust, salt and churned-up earth.

Smyth was first to react. "Don't know 'bout you guys, but I

ain't goin' out as no sittin' duck."

He kicked open the side door and swung himself out. Drake pounced next, eyes already scanning the surroundings as he jumped to the ground. Kovalenko's birds blasted overhead, full to the brim with mercs and commandoes and whatever other killers-for-hire his men had managed to purchase since Christmas. He ran forward, giving the rest room to escape and tracking the birds as they changed direction.

"Get ready," Smyth said, taking aim.

But the birds suddenly lost momentum, started to hover, then began to lose altitude. They were landing.

Smyth stared, letting his rifle hang loose. "Thought they'd at least have tried to take a few of us out." He looked at Drake. "Isn't that Kovalenko's way? Sacrifice the many to slaughter the few?"

"He's all about the spectacle," Drake said. "But I have to agree—"

"It's not about that," Dahl said as the rest of the team came up behind them. "Whilst we were playing Wall of Death in the back, our pilot here had full view of the rest of the valley. Tell 'em, Lewis."

The pilot nodded. "Coming along the road. Cars. Many armored vehicles. A truck or two. Heading along here." He pointed to the thin snake of road cutting through the flats. "Maybe five, six miles out."

"He has an army," Drake said. "Close to the prison. I guess that makes sense. There's any number of ghost towns and abandoned businesses out here, not to mention old ranches, Indian villages, gold and silver mines. Christ, you could easily hide a small militia outside the National Park."

"Been doing your homework?" Alicia leaned in.

"Always do. Kovalenko's men could have gathered the bulk of his weapons and intel systems there. I wonder if he controlled the drone from around here?"

Everyone turned to Karin. The girl with the genius level IQ shrugged. "How the hell should I know? I'm no weapons expert. I guess it's possible. Depends on the operating system."

"Look," Smyth growled. "Can we concentrate on what we can actually see for a minute? You think that's possible? We got three choppers full o' mercs comin' in and a mobile army as backup. What's the plan? This area ain't called a salt *flat* for fuckin nothin', you know."

Drake cast his eyes across the dusty white hexagonal salt crusts, dotted here and there with brush, and in the distance some gentle curves of desert sand leading to craggy, contoured and severe looking mountains. They could call in the cavalry at any time, but it would be all for nothing if Kovalenko wasn't around.

"What's that?"

Drake followed the line of Karin's finger along the blacktop, now spotting an irregular line of green trees at the top of a small rise and, beyond them, what looked like white walls and red roofs. "What *is* that?"

Lewis, the pilot, broke out a map of the area. "Yeah, it's Garner's Castle. I thought as much. Built in 1922 as a holiday home for the rich, now it stands as a tourist attraction, though closed throughout the winter season. Sometimes called the mansion, fortress or castle of the valley, it actually *does* resemble a castle, though I have no idea as to its functionality."

Alicia shoved him. "You go to college?"

"Leave him alone." Dahl pushed her out of the way. "It's a good hike. If we want to make it in time we should get going."

Drake surveyed the rest of their surroundings whilst Komodo and Kinimaka did the same. The arid plains were almost featureless and in keeping with the name of the region. Nearby Badwater Basin had the lowest elevation of any point in the northern USA; it was below sea level, whereas only eighty four miles to the northwest, Mount Whitney, the highest point, raised its jagged head. Other place names like Dante's View, Hell's Gate, Furnace Creek and the Devil's Golf Course confirmed the adverse nature of the area.

"Let's go. And don't forget, we need to look as though we've been ambushed."

Dahl sniffed at that. "I think we were."

With constant glances back to the newly grounded choppers and along the blacktop road, the team ran hard for Garner's Castle, the last outpost in their terrible battle with the Blood King.

CHAPTER FORTY THREE

Drake slowed only when they had passed the scrappy line of thin trees and were approaching the sprawling mansion, house or castle; or whatever the hell it was supposed to be. He could see now why it had been given the idiosyncratic title of *castle.* The entrance was a faux portcullis, the gate itself simply made of redwood. Small towers stood to both sides with the bulk of the structure stretching back from each tower with an inner courtyard in the middle. Red-tiled roofs covered the clutter of buildings, of which there were at least a dozen, each one seemingly attached as an afterthought to the last. The walls surrounding the whole place were built of solid stone and crenellated in the manner of a castle. Happily, they were also high enough to defend. Every door opening was a high archway, and every window was protected by a wooden shutter. Drake could see, rising from the back of the compound, what looked to be a tall castle keep, flag pole fluttering on top. Several black weather vanes topped the other roofs.

"So let's get t' fettlin' and feightin'," Drake said in his best Yorkshire accent. "It's too bloody mafting to hang around out 'ere anyway."

Dahl and Smyth shook their heads together. "Would you like to translate that to English?"

"I can see I'm gonna have to start giving out lessons," Drake said as they walked towards the entrance. "Skoil is school. Ginnel is an alleyway. Thine is yours. Make sense?"

Dahl couldn't hide a grin. "Do you ever?"

"So let's stop *callin'.*" Drake smirked back. "And make ready. 'Cause the enemy's right behind us."

Smyth facilitated their entry. The interior of the castle, past the sturdy gate, was indeed a long courtyard, sided by two rows of guest rooms. The front part of the courtyard also held the main reception and restaurant, the rear the manager's offices and storage units along with the castle keep. Drake motioned quickly.

"Spread out. We need intel on this place and fast. Places to hole up, places to defend. Where to get onto the roof. We need an escape route. A plan B. Nope, wait, I'll sort that out. Can they flank us? How long can we hold out?"

"Drake," Alicia said. "We know what to do. Now stop worrying about the sprite and get on with it. Besides—" her face took on a stony look. "We're all here for Kovalenko. Once he shows his face we're gonna rain down our piece of biblical hellfire. We have an army of our own on standby."

Drake winked. "Amen to that."

The team split up. Drake headed straight for the walls, taking the rugged stone steps two at a time and coming up onto a wide ledge. The rough crenellated wall stretched away from him to either side, and he stepped up to one of the gaps, looking over. Below him lay a scrappy concreted courtyard, and then the rising shale mounds which surrounded this place. The enemy would have to climb those mounds and then descend since the castle stood in a shallow dip. Bad luck for them.

Footsteps pounded behind him as Komodo, Karin and Kinimaka caught up. The Hawaiian caught Drake's eye.

"Smyth's in place."

"Good. Let's hope he stays there long enough to be useful."

"I still think we'd be better off using him in the defense," Komodo said. "But I guess the majority rules."

"I didn't hear you argue when Alicia proposed the plan."

"Shit." Komodo pulled a face. "That look she's got goin' on. It's pure fury, man. I wouldn't wanna argue with that."

"Well," Drake said. "Here come a few assholes who're hopefully gonna die trying."

The sound of shale being displaced heralded the appearance of most of the soldiers who'd occupied the helicopters. Over the top of the mounds they came; slipping, sliding, struggling to get their guns up and desperately trying to scramble to level ground. Komodo raised his HK.

"Let's bag us some ducks."

Drake made sure he was covered by the crenellated wall, then peeked out and opened fire. One quick burst and he dipped his head back inside and looked backwards across the jumbled castle roofs to where Dahl and Alicia lay on opposite sides, bodies flat. The disorganized dips of the various roofs easily concealed their figures. Drake fired again, matching Komodo and Kinimaka round for round. Their enemies tumbled down the mounds, unmoving, to be half-buried in shale slides and mostly hidden by the rising heat haze. Some of the mercs paused, knelt, and fired back. Bullets pockmarked the castle walls, taking chunks out of the old stone. Drake stole a glance. Some of the attackers had descended the mounds and were now running across the short courtyard. Drake angled his rifle, shooting among them, then ducked back as they tried to pick him off. Kinimaka was further down the wall and with a better angle. His short burst finished off the runners, but return fire came dangerously close to his bobbing skull.

More men crested the mounds.

Machine-gun fire stitched its way across the castle walls from one end to the other. Where bullets passed between the crenellations they flew on to impact against other buildings or the higher castle keep, or even further to the higher hills that bordered this place. Drake crouched behind the walls and peered across the line. Karin was closest to him, sitting with her back against the wall and staring over the castle roofs. The tech-girl was keeping in constant touch with the nearby base through walkie-talkie. Komodo was next over, never far from her side. Then Kinimaka, still in the dark as to Hayden's fate, dual expressions of rage and hurricane-like ferocity carved into his face.

"Here they come!" the Hawaiian shouted. "Keep 'em out!"

Drake sprayed the top of the mounds, then the courtyard below. Men screamed and fell. Others flinched, threw themselves prostrate, or dived for the walls. A bullet fizzed over his head, almost close enough for him to write down its flight path. He picked off a soldier who had been trying to get a bead on Komodo, then threw himself to the floor as one of the big black choppers suddenly thundered out of nowhere.

"Shit!"

The helicopter blasted up over the mounds and low over the castle walls, so low Drake could have reached up and touched the bottom of one of its skids. The noise assaulted his eardrums, but that wasn't the worst of it.

It was the half-dozen men leaning out of both sides, taking aim with high-powered weapons.

Drake scrambled along the wide ledge as a fusillade of lead smashed into the walls above his head. Some of the bullets shot through the crenels, hopefully maiming their own men in the courtyard below. Drake cursed as he dashed along. The distraction would give the attackers chance to cross the courtyard and gain the main gate.

Drake crawled fast, knowing the gate was strong but not wanting to leave anything to chance. Behind him, Komodo returned fire at the swaying chopper, sending two men bouncing brutally to the courtyard below. Kinimaka stayed on his mark, completely ignoring the threatening black bird. Drake reached the concrete steps, sensing Karin at his heels. He glanced back.

"What do the army say?"

"There's still no sign of Kovalenko. They're holding off but they aren't going to stay there for much longer!"

"Tell the bastards to hold their fuckin' horses. We're the ones with our bollocks on the chopping block. Not them!"

Karin winced as someone spoke in her ear. "Line goes straight through to the White House, Drake. President Coburn says he'll give us a few more minutes."

Despite the situation, Drake made a face. Diplomacy had never been his strong suit. He shrugged.

Fuck it.

Swinging his legs over the top of the steps, he instinctively ducked as another stream of bullets gushed from the chopper's open doors. He fell backwards over Karin, his body covering hers. One of the bullets actually glanced off his vest and skimmed on over the wall.

"We're gonna get shot to bits up here."

Then he raised his head, astonished. If he had been religious he might have started praying. As it was, he did stop breathing.

Karin looked stunned. "Oh my God."

Creeping across the roofs on their bellies, Dahl and Alicia came below the swaying chopper. In one fluid lunge they jumped up and grasped hold of a skid on separate sides, then boosted themselves until they were sat astride them. Alicia aimed her weapon upward and smiled. Drake couldn't tell what she said, but imagined it wouldn't be entirely pretty. Dahl just fired.

Bullets hammered up through the chopper's floor, decimating the strapped-in men and blowing holes through the roof. The prop shaft and rotor took direct hits. When the chopper jerked sharply, Dahl and Alicia jumped off, hitting the castle's red roof tiles and rolling clear. With a fractured roar the big machine tilted at an angle, leaning over like a foundering ship in rolling seas, then fell with a shriek into the courtyard below. Metal ground and screeched on impact. Glass shattered. The rotor blades tore off and whickered away at high speed like king-size knives thrown by a titan. The building beside the explosion crumbled under force of the collision; walls crumpling, roof tiles slipping and sliding down in three separate red streams. A fireball boomed skyward, black smoke billowing and obscuring the crash site, but the intensity of the flames assured Drake no one had survived.

He cheered. Alicia saluted. Dahl dropped to a prone position and fired at something directly below Drake, most likely the castle gates. He spun toward Kinimaka.

"How we doing?"

"Five at the gates. Now four, thanks to Dahl. Two in the courtyard. Four on the hill . . ." He fired expectantly as he finished speaking, then looked a bit sheepish. "Shit," he said. "Still four."

The next noise was almost as loud and menacing as the approaching chopper had been. Drake knew the sound, but couldn't believe it. "Is that . . .? No way."

He spun to the nearest crenel, looking out. His mouth dropped open as a large truck topped one of the mounds, then came jouncing down the other side. An entire row of black-clad men stood atop the hills, staring across the gap, rifles held high.

A battle cry went up.

The men charged.

CHAPTER FORTY FOUR

Amidst the battle cries and the bedlam, Drake heard the revving engines of arriving cars. The Blood King's main force was already here. His heart thudded. *Just one sighting, just one!* That was all they needed to call in the cavalry.

A fitting analogy, he thought. *Out here, in these dry, desolate badlands—more than fitting.*

The big truck hit level ground and bounced and clattered its way across the courtyard, revving and swerving as if James Hunt was trying to shunt his way past on the inside. Komodo and Kinimaka came sliding up to Drake.

"Sure must seem like we're trapped here," the Hawaiian grunted. "So where's Kovalenko?"

"Kovalenko has a source in the government," Drake pointed out. "If we needed any proof, the drone confirmed it. Now that source will either throw him to the dogs—that's us," he clarified unnecessarily. "Or warn him off."

"He's here," Kinimaka growled. "I can smell evil a mile off."

Drake regarded him. "Is that a Polynesian thing?"

"CIA training."

Drake laughed. "Must be the advanced part of the course, eh?" Without pause he rose and sprayed the courtyard with bullets. The huge truck barreled on through. A wave of men came behind it and a second wave behind them. A foul chorus of vile intent rose from their ranks. Drake fired, Kinimaka and Komodo standing alongside him, and several of the running men fell, but the rest charged on. The ground passed swiftly beneath their feet as they hurdled the fallen. Drake dropped more, shooting indiscriminately. The truck roared past his eyeline and smashed into the gate, making the castle walls shudder with the impact. Its front end blasted inside the castle, but its canvas-covered bed got stuck in the gap half way through and ground to a vibrating halt.

Drake pulled out a military-issue knife. “They all die.”

With that he jumped right off the castle walls, sailing into space and landing atop the canvas cover. He held his balance, feeling the cover belly out beneath him, then fell to his knees and slashed hard with the knife. Komodo and Kinimaka, coming five seconds after him, fell right through the gap into the bed of the truck below, and Drake followed a split second after them.

Hard-looking men started in shock. Komodo was amongst them before they could react, slashing a throat; a cheek; a chest. Kinimaka had held on to his Glock and whipped it out now, three single shots signaling the deaths of three dull-witted men. Drake jabbed one man in the throat with his knife, then another across the forehead. The last was too far away to touch . . .

. . . and already held a pistol leveled precisely between the Englishman’s eyes.

“G’night fu—”

Drake threw his knife end over end. It embedded to the hilt in the man’s throat. The reflex shot went high, skimming up into the roof. Komodo was already jumping through the gaps in the side-canvas, hitting the ground before turning to finish the driver. Drake leapt through the other side, taking the passenger down into the dirt with a chokehold.

“Where’s Kovalenko?” he whispered into the man’s ear. “Did he send you to die alone?”

The man struggled but couldn’t break Drake’s hold. The Englishman tightened it a notch. “Tell me.”

“He’s out there. With his lieutenants. Don’t worry. He’s

coming for you."

Drake choked the man out and rose to his feet. The truck now effectively blocked the gap where the gate had been, but men were already tearing the remainder of the gate apart. They would be through in minutes. Plus Drake could now see them atop the walls, having gained access by jumping from the mounds that passed close to either side.

"Time to fall back," he said, but then Dahl's voice rang out.

"The walls!" he cried. *"Go to the walls!"*

If it had been anyone else, Drake would have paused and questioned it, but knowing Torsten Dahl as he did there was no choice. He pounded hard at the steps and found Karin standing at the top, isolated, staring out over the walls as enemy commandoes came at her from both sides.

"He's out there," Karin said softly, oblivious to her danger. "That bastard is right there, watching us."

Drake smashed into a commando running at him full pelt, slightly dipping his shoulder and letting his momentum send the guy flying off the walls. The second he met with a palm to the face, breaking his nose and letting his own tear ducts destroy his vision. He sensed Komodo at his back, meeting the attackers who charged in from the other side. The two men fought hard on the castle walls with Karin between them, hand-to-hand combat being more practical in the enclosed conditions. Komodo threw a man over the walls to the concrete below, blocked knife strikes, and used the enemies' own force of numbers against them, employing them as shields and foils, toppling them like dominoes. The heights of the castle rang with clanging steel and dying screams. Drake did take a bullet, but it only drove into his vest and knocked him back less than a step. Without missing a stride, he broke the shooter's wrist and twisted the weapon away from him, using its full magazine to thin the herd.

In a moment's respite, he turned to Karin. "Show me."

She held out a hand. Drake followed her pointing finger and there, atop the highest mound and flanked by Mordant and Gabriel, stood the Blood King. The Russian regarded the scene for a moment before starting forward.

"He's coming in," Karin yelled, and then remembered the walkie-talkie in her hand. "I have to—"

"No time." Drake grabbed her and almost threw her down the steps. "Go!" Both he and Komodo followed her down to the courtyard, dodging bullets as they ran. The truck lay idling away down there, and beyond it the helicopter burned like a furious beacon. Dahl and Alicia stood close to the truck, watching the castle gates finally fall.

"Low on ammo," Alicia said. "We gotta conserve."

"Kovalenko will be inside within minutes." Drake said. They ran as a group, heading past the chopper's blazing wreckage. The heat was a furnace blast in Drake's face as he skirted it, raising the temperature of Death Valley to an even more deadly notch. They used the arched doorways as cover when Kovalenko's men broke through, hiding and firing in pairs, leap-frogging each other to reach a safer place.

And, finally, Drake gave Karin the nod. "Make the call."

Karin's eyes blazed with pure hatred as she ducked a hail of gunfire, rose amidst the smoke of pulverized stone and charred metal, and spoke into the receiver.

"Bring the fire!" she cried, looking up to the burning skies. *"Bring the fires of hell down on this motherfucker!"*

CHAPTER FORTY FIVE

At the same time, Smyth burst out of his hiding place, rushing forward in full assault mode. The team had all agreed that leaving a man behind was actually a good idea on this occasion. It had been Alicia's plan. Smyth had listened to it and allowed an evil little grin to spread across his face.

"I'll do it," he snarled. "I'd love to waste all these bastards. It'll be my personal revenge for Romero."

The Delta man had carefully dug deep into a mound of loose shale on the far side of the courtyard so that now, as he burst into sight, he was behind them. His machine gun was turned to full auto, spitting and coughing in his hands, spraying the field, and the fact that he shot many a mercenary in the back did not faze him at all.

They had butchered and terrorized, had this group. They had murdered without remorse. They had massacred and, not only that, they had done it all without the slightest care for civilian welfare. The innocent were no more than obstacles to be smashed aside in their eyes.

Let them die badly then.

A cluster of men by the gates went down, never understanding what hit them. The last of them tried to twist around but lost his head in Smyth's next burst. As he ran, the concrete base around him kicked up dust and chips. Bullets pecked around his own feet. He chanced a look to the rear and saw Kovalenko and his two lieutenants surrounded by many men, some of whom were firing at him.

Damn. If I had waited . . .

But that was not the plan. The nearby American base would be sending the hand of God to fall upon this place very soon. If he wanted any hope of surviving the strike, he had to be with the team. Smyth's feet fairly danced amid the bullets, each step taking him nearer the shattered gates. In another second he was through and let the machine gun rattle once more, taking out another three targets.

Head down, he ran on, hoping to God one of the SPEAR team was keeping their eyes on him.

CHAPTER FORTY SIX

At around the same time, Mai Kitano met Dai Hibiki on the steps outside the Tokyo Game Show. Her old partner stopped dead when he saw her, raising both eyebrows so far they practically disappeared into his hairline.

"Wow. Who are you?"

"It's Mai, you idiot," she said, thinking he hadn't recognized her, then understood. "Oh. What do you think?"

She spun slowly, posing with her hands on her hips, conscious that every eye of every man and woman outside the Game Show was fixed upon her. The sensual feel of soft leather on her bare skin was more than invigorating.

"I don't know, but if that ass wants to lead, I'll follow it anywhere."

Mai ignored his bravado. Maybe she would recount his words later to Chika and make him pay. Maybe she would just see if he realized his error and let him make it up to her. "I'm Maggie Q. Do you know her?"

"I know *of* her. Nikita, yes? She's got nothing on you, Mai."

"That's better. Now, are you ready?"

"As I'll ever be. The rest of my guys—your old friends from the agency—are in place too. Are you sure about going all the way with this?"

"I have no choice. The Clan brought this down upon themselves, not me."

Hibiki started up the steps. "Then let's end them."

"Even better." Mai climbed after him.

"I have to ask, though." Hibiki peered at her out of the corner of his eye. "Why Maggie Q?"

Mai smiled secretly. "A surprise for a good friend," she said.

"And a reminder to my boyfriend that he's not the only one interested in me."

Hibiki shook his head. "I think Drake already knows you can never be tamed, Mai."

"Sure he does, but a gentle reminder never hurts."

Inside the Game Show the exhibition space was split into several large areas. Far over to the right stood the over eighteens area, enclosed by a wall of eight-by-eight-foot panels. Closer by, and laid out in seemingly endless parallel lines, were rows and rows of game stations, each one showcasing a brand new version of a popular video game. The area was already jam-packed with onlookers, every seat taken by an enthusiastic gamer whilst, behind each one, several more waited in line or watched. The in-game noise effects and the sound of excited chatter were almost overwhelming. Crowds wandered between the rows. Over to the left stood even more stations, some reserved for dancing games, others for RPGs or retro-gaming. Still more areas offered the chance for competitions. The show itself was every gamer's wet dream, not to mention the cosplay side of it. The sides of the exhibition hall were lined with stalls, shops and eateries, each one doing a brisk business.

"I forgot how busy this place gets." Mai posed for a picture with two young guys, never losing a beat.

"Stop enjoying yourself," Hibiki said. "We've a job to do."

Mai smiled sweetly and offered Hibiki her phone. "Here, take a picture so I can send it to the boys when I leave."

The agent sniffed and shook his head, but did as Mai asked. They began to thread their way among the rows, moving ever closer to the over eighteens area. Once there, they went through a security checkpoint where Mai again was asked to pose for pictures.

"Good job we aren't in a hurry," Hibiki muttered as they crossed into the restricted area. Here were situated the more violent games—the Call of Dutys and GTAs—and the lines to play them doubled back on themselves at least four times.

"There's the bar." Hibiki nodded ahead.

Mai had already spotted it. This was the only place a person could buy alcohol at the Game Show and thus primarily attracted a certain sort. If it seemed odd that an organization like the Yakuza would frequent a video games show, Mai knew it was not. The younger gang element played video games just like any other young Japanese. The older element liked to peruse and safeguard their investment—the fact that they owned one of the biggest video game developers in Japan was a badly kept secret.

Since its early days, the Game Show had become a tradition for most people. Once a year they made the pilgrimage. Once a year they met gamer friends and talked over the last three hundred and sixty five days. Once a year they became consummate geeks, lost in the herd.

Mai spotted the man she was looking for straight away. He was thin and rangy, hard-faced, and wearing dark clothing which covered every one of his gang tattoos. He sat toward the back of the bar, among a group of fellow gang members, giving death glares to any unfortunate soul who passed close by. The Yakuza might enjoy the Game Show to a point, but they did not want to make friends here.

Mai took a breath. "Tokyo Coscon part two," she breathed. "Here I go again."

Hibiki melted away, choosing a clever vantage point whilst pretending to watch some super-geek playing the new Final Fantasy installment. Mai headed for the bar, taking a slow walk, making sure every gang member noticed her. Truth be told, it wasn't a tough job. A blind man in a snowstorm would have sat himself down just to watch her walk.

She leaned over the bar to be sure their attention was properly focused. “Got any milk?”

The bartender put down his towel. “Baby-changing station’s back by the entrance doors.”

“Oh. How about a pint then?”

“Got a preference?”

“Not really. Surprise me.”

“I’d love to.” The man turned away from her stare and pulled down a glass. By the time it was full she sensed she was no longer alone.

Without turning around she took a sip. “Can I help you?”

“Me and the boys have a bet goin’. Which one of us gets to peel those tight leather pants off tonight.”

Mai spun in place, leaning back with her elbows on the bar. “Well, you’re certainly going the right way about doing that.”

It wasn’t her target, just one of his minions. She nodded over at his table. “A bet, eh? And just for taking my pants off. What’s the take?”

“So far? About a thousand. Why? You interested in taking a cut?”

Mai didn’t answer, just made a show of looking the gang over. “If all you wanna do is take my pants off . . . doesn’t seem worth my time.”

The minion laughed. “There’s more than that laid out on the table. Much more.”

“Mmm, sounds good. But it’s not quite fair. There’s only six of you.”

The minion almost choked. “Hey lady, you should be a little more—”

“Careful?” Mai smiled wickedly. “Careful’s for the weak and the powerless. And believe me, I’m neither.”

By now her target was taking more of an interest, clearly

wondering what was being said. He stood up and beckoned her over. Mai thought about her parents, about Gyuki, about Hibiki and Chika. She thought about the clan master and all the dreadful things she had witnessed as a child growing up in his community. There really was no option here.

Her target, a man called Hikaru, called to her. "Are you a cosplay girl? I thought I knew them all. Are you new to the circuit?"

Mai felt six pairs of eyes watching her as she walked up to him. "Freelancer. Thought I would give it a try this year."

"Are you alone? You look a little familiar."

"Don't you recognize me? I'm a movie star." Mai let out a little giggle. "And no—my boyfriend's around somewhere playing his *games.*" She rolled her eyes on the last word, showing her distaste.

"Ah I see. So you were dragged to the show were you? And you want to what . . . teach him a lesson by playing a little game of your own on the side?"

Mai shrugged. "Why not? I've already decided this is going to be my year of firsts."

Hikaru grinned. "I could think of a few 'firsts' right now."

Mai let the giggle out again. "How would you know?"

"There's a restroom just over there. I'm guessing that'd be your first 'first'. Wanna try?"

"Only if you have a little stamina. I'm sick and tired of the nightly five-minute desperate Hail Mary passes."

Hikaru exhaled. "Jesus, you're fuckin' hot. C'mon. Ichiro, Kyo, watch the doors. No one gets in, you hear me? *No one.* Hey, girl, what's your name?"

"Maggie." She giggled and took his hand, giving him the full fantasy. The look in his eyes told her he had totally bought it, as had every one of his cohorts. *Were guys really so easy?* she wondered. *A pair of leather pants, a giggle, and a bit of sex-talk. Was* Drake *that easy?*

Or was it just the bad guys and their raging, repressed hormones?

Hikaru led her toward the restroom, crossing a short length of blue carpet. The orange symbol for the gents glowed above the door. Mai slowed and looked around, feigning sudden doubt, but actually scouting the area. Hikaru pulled her hand hard, leaving no doubt as to his intentions and chivalry, and she let herself be dragged through the door. Inside, everything was stark white, bright and relatively clean. Hikaru turned her around and forced her against the wall, hands first.

"Stick your ass out, Maggie. You're gonna experience a first your geek boyfriend wouldn't dare ask you for."

Mai wiggled. "Do it. I'm nothin' if I'm not a dirty freak."

"And when you're snuggling up to him tonight." Hikaru shifted his pants down. "Remember this!"

It was the moment she had been waiting for. In her past experience as an undercover agent for the Japanese agency, she had learned that a man never fought the same with his tackle hanging out. She whirled, slamming an elbow into his ear. Before he could utter a screech, her hand gripped his voice box so hard his face instantly turned white.

Mai grabbed the only thing about him that wasn't hanging as limp as a wet rag and pulled him close. She whispered in his ear. "Little Hikaru," she said. "That was so easy. I have been sent to kill you. Do you know me now, I wonder?"

Pure terror suddenly lit the Yakuza boss's eyes. He knew. At last, the old legends were starting to come back to him. The searing humiliation, the outrageous memories.

"Mai Kitano," she said. "A name that's whispered with some reverence around these parts, or so I'm told."

The man didn't move a muscle. He was hers to control. "So," she whispered into his bleeding ear. "Still think I'm hot?"

Despite the situation, Hikaru nodded.

Mai stepped away. "Well, I guess I am pretty." She laughed. "One squeak, Hikaru. One squeak and I'll end you."

The Yakuza boss motioned at his pants.

"Oh, put it away, Hikaru. I couldn't even scratch my nose with that thing."

Mai pulled him to the far wall. "Now listen. Like I said, I have been sent to kill you. The Tsugarai sent me. I'm willing to give you a pass this time . . . but I need your help in return."

"What?" Now that Hikaru was fully clothed again, part of the swagger had returned. "What could I do for you?"

"Pretend to be dead," Mai said. "For about three hours."

"Pretend . . ." Hikaru shook his head in disbelief. "How would I do that?"

"The Yakuza are a close-knit gang," Mai said. "It's possible and believable that they would not want your death broadcast around immediately. Just *disappear,* Hikaru. For a little while."

"And if I don't?"

"I'll come back for you one night. And that twig dick will be the least of your worries."

Hikaru remained silent as he weighed his options. His next words proved there was at least a little intelligence behind the ever-present red haze of lust and brutality. "The Tsugarai. I know they own you. This is your homecoming, yes?"

"They do not *own* me," Mai hissed. *"Nobody* owns me."

"I'm just saying . . . we don't exactly love the Tsugarai either."

Mai stared. "You're offering to help?" The idea hadn't occurred to her.

"Rock 'n' roll." Hikaru grinned.

"I have all the help I need," Mai told him. "But one day . . . maybe one day. Another time."

"Just come around wearin' those pants and I'll know you need me." Hikaru touched his finger to his nose like a conspirator. "I'll know."

Mai nodded. "Agreed. But Hikaru, listen. Don't fuck me on this. You will regret it."

"When you say it like that," the Yakuza boss said. "I'm just putty in your hands."

"More like a pussy in my hands." Mai doubled him over with a hard blow to the solar plexus. "That's for being a gang-rat piece of shit. Now, stay here and do as you're told."

She exited the restroom swiftly, inviting both of Hikaru's guards over with a saucy little wink and closing the outer door after them.

"We voted," one said haughtily. "I'm first."

Mai smiled. "Oh, alright then."

His scream followed her all the way back to the game stations, but she barely heard. She was trying to force an ominous new thought from her mind—the one whispering on eldritch wings that whilst she had killed the mostly innocent money launderer, she had spared the totally guilty Yakuza boss's life. A worrying reflection, but not one she could allow to confuse her now. This was the hour she had been waiting for. Everything had led to this. It was time. All her life she had been waiting, training and fighting toward this very moment.

It was time.

CHAPTER FORTY SEVEN

Drake saw Smyth overcome a ragged bunch of mercenaries below and silently thanked Alicia for her ingenious foresight. Thanks to her, they now had only half as many enemies to deal with. He lingered by the back of the burning chopper, easing the Delta man's passage with a few well-placed shots. Men twisted and fell before him. The raging fire licked at the buildings all the way up to the roof. The scream of officers giving orders and men shouting in agony sounded little different in the chaos. When Smyth barreled past Drake and rejoined the group, Alicia grabbed him and planted her lips on his.

"Beautiful one," she shouted. "Very well done, Smythy, ya mad, angry, little bastard."

Smyth backed away. "Ah, thanks."

Drake swore. "Look lively, guys. This ain't gonna be pretty."

A knot of Kovalenko's men, temporarily cut off from their comrades by the inferno, charged at them. At the precise instant when their weapons coughed, Drake's team flung themselves every which way but loose. Drake hit the dirt, landing prone on his back, shooting between his own feet. Dahl threw Karin into a doorway, took a bullet in the vest, and returned fire without missing a beat. Alicia and Smyth ducked and sprinted to the right. Komodo slipped behind the chopper, his face lit by the flames.

The first runners collapsed at Drake's feet, and he had to roll to keep his legs free. Sand and grit turned into a red mush of spilled blood. A man launched himself headlong, coming down on Drake's stomach. A knife slashed. Drake watched the blade pass between his armpits. When the blade struck dirt, he fired into the man's abdomen, making him twitch. Cognizance soon vanished from his eyes.

A merc stamped past. Drake reached out and tripped him. He scrambled until his back was against the wall. The merc came at him with a knife and pistol. Drake kicked the pistol aside as it fired, sending the shot skyward, and danced along with the thrust of the knife. In the first eight seconds the merc didn't make a mistake, staying sharp and lethal. Two seconds later, he had lunged a few inches too far and paid the ultimate price.

Alicia and Smyth joined Komodo in finishing off the last of the attackers but, by then, another sizable group were negotiating the flames.

"Fall back," Drake shouted. "Ammo's low."

"You hear that?" a voice suddenly screamed. "Did you? They're almost dry. Take them! *Take them now!*"

Drake met the eyes of the others. There was no mistaking the gravelly voice of Dmitry Kovalenko, no matter how perversely excited it sounded. Drake looked at his colleagues, searching hard for their inner resolve, and found pure fire and steel and a will tough enough to withstand hurricanes.

"This battle just became worth every fucking cut and bruise," Kinimaka grunted. "Everyone here owes this bastard the harshest death."

"Be careful of his bodyguards," Karin said. "Mordant and Gabriel. I read about them. They're said to be the hardest, most dangerous men the penal system has ever seen."

Kinimaka grunted. "I can second that."

Drake readied his weapon and turned to face the roaring flames. "The cavalry can't be far away," he said. "But this battle ends here and now. We stand."

Dahl stepped to his right shoulder, Alicia to his left.

Komodo, Kinimaka and Smyth ranged out behind him. Karin Blake moved to her boyfriend's side.

"We stand."

CHAPTER FORTY EIGHT

Through flames of light and shadow they came, the last of the Blood King's army; faces cast in flickering fire; eyes blackened into demonic pits by the lowering dark; teeth bared and mouths spread wide as if all they wanted was to devour their enemy.

Initially there were a dozen of them. They were followed by Kovalenko himself, flanked by Gabriel and Mordant, The Twins grinning fiercely. This was their arena, their element. This was where they would shine.

The two forces paused for a beat, every man and woman there recognizing the significance of the moment. Who would win and who would die? This place, right here and now, was where the real warriors would prove themselves. Courage was everything. Those who turned away, those who ran, would keep running forever.

"Live or die this day," Dahl whispered amongst his own. "Live or die."

Drake turned to them all. "If this is the last and best fight of my life I could not have stood among worthier friends. Thank you."

Then the ranks broke and the screams went up. The charge was on. Dahl smashed into one well-built merc so hard he actually sent the man tumbling back into the flaming chopper. The mad Swede didn't even break stride. He barged aside another man, breaking the guy's shoulder in the process, leaving him on his knees and heaving with pain. Drake hit a third head on, using his forehead harder than at any other time in his life. Fresh blood spattered his face, and he ran right over the collapsing man. Alicia broke a man's windpipe without losing a beat.

All eyes were on the Blood King.

If this is the last and best fight of my life . . .

The Blood Vendetta would end today. No more innocents would die. They carved through the Blood King's ranks; a deadly, unstoppable phalanx of invincible purpose, and it was Dahl, Drake and Alicia who suddenly found themselves facing off with Mordant, Gabriel and Kovalenko.

Time stood still. For them, the whole world might as well have stopped turning. Violent flames lit the scene, flaring, bursting and wreathing between metal, stone and shadow. Kovalenko gave them his most smug grin.

"You cannot beat these men, dah? I am glad it has come to this—to us. A much more fitting end. I could not have written it so well."

"This madness is finished," Dahl said. "You are finished."

"Ah, the great Torsten Dahl. The hero himself. What is it they call you? The Mad Swede? Your family were moments away from good Russian execution, my friend. Moments. They will not survive next time."

Drake took a step forward. "You killed my friends. You killed Ben and his parents." He counted each atrocity off on his fingers. "You murdered my team's families. You might have killed Hayden. Mai. Chika. Jonathan. You kidnapped the bloody President and launched a drone strike on Washington DC. What kind of demon are you, Kovalenko? Is there even a name for the part of Hell you come from?"

"Meh." Kovalenko flicked it all away with a shrug. "A man born in blood aspires to be serial killer. A man born of evil father aspires to become good marine. But a man born in war aspires to war." He shrugged. "It is the way of the world."

With that, Gabriel and Mordant lunged as one, the pair seeming to share some kind of psychic link. Dahl blocked a strike from Mordant, backing up. Drake met Gabriel head on, and felt the power and fury of the man's blows immediately through every bone in his body. Christ, this guy hit hard. The manic grin never left the dark-skinned face and the body almost seemed to jive to an inner beat. But the blows were relentless, precise and debilitating. An arm that blocks ten severe strikes is not the arm it once was. Drake strove to get on the offensive, but Gabriel never gave him a chance.

In front of the Yorkshireman, Alicia lashed out at the Blood King. Kovalenko was tough, strong and trained, but he was no match for either the Englishwoman's skill or her fury. He staggered almost immediately, caught himself, then found he was being driven toward the flames.

"Bitch," he spat. "I am King. I will end your days."

"Those men who hang around me and have a God complex," Alicia said. "Those men who fuck with my friends and family often find their balls being kicked so hard they end up with three Adam's apples. Here, let me demonstrate."

Alicia feinted and waded in, jabbing Kovalenko's throat so that his hand went up, then she put her entire weight behind a knee to his groin. Eyes bulging, the Blood King tried to fall to the ground. Alicia didn't let him. By digging her fingers into the meat of his throat, she ensured he would stay upright.

"Time for *my* blood vengeance," she said, then paused when she heard Drake's cry.

Kinimaka went down on one knee, using his Glock to pick off the slow and the careless. But he knew he couldn't stay in one position too long for risk of becoming a sitting duck. Not that anyone had ever compared him to a duck, he knew. In the bird comparisons, he'd have to be an albatross. He slipped over to the wall, noting that six mercs remained on this side of the battle. He met a challenge head on, arresting the guy's swing and literally hurling him off his feet and against the wall. The man connected hard, then fell back, lifeless.

Kinimaka whirled to see Smyth beset by two adversaries, but before he could even begin to race over to help, Karin had stepped up. Without regard for her own safety, she used long-ago learned martial arts skills to get the attention of one of the men. Karin wasn't stupid, and would know that local dojo learned skills were no match for military training, but she waded in anyway, limbs kicking and punching. The man facing her looked bemused, as if he couldn't figure out if he was actually being toyed with, but his lollygagging cost him dearly. Smyth dispatched his own opponent, then turned to disable Karin's, finishing the man with a kick to the nose. Lights out never came so fast.

Komodo smashed both arms down onto a merc's shoulders. The man staggered under the hefty blow, falling heavily to his knees. Flames lit Komodo's face as he lifted the man by his own jacket before throwing him into the inferno.

Kinimaka almost cheered. The odds were now four good guys against two bad. His heart soared, but then two new sounds reached his ears; one uplifting, the other terrible. First he heard the sound of raucous American voices, marines coming to their aid. But on the heels of that came the roar of two ascending choppers—the Blood King's choppers coming to strafe the battlefield.

Drake cried out as Gabriel snapped a quick kick to his right knee, almost breaking it in half. The pain shot through his body like a barbed arrow as he fought to stay upright. Gabriel sought to press his advantage. Drake let the momentum take him, folded, let Gabriel's flurry strike nothing but thin air, then came up on the other side.

"Not so easy, pal."

"You fight like a fairy, mon. Tinkerbell. Tinkerbell Drake!

Haha."

Drake was getting pissed off with all the recent aspersions on his good name. First that hairy bastard, Zanko, and now Gabriel. But then Zanko did end up taking a head dive down the deepest, darkest pit on Earth.

"Like the fairies, do ya? I heard jail will do that to a man."

Gabriel fumed and lunged. Drake danced around the swipe and dealt him a crushing blow to the temple. He had found Gabriel's first flaw but how could he exploit it? Past the dark man he saw Dahl engaged with Mordant. The albino looked like a ghoul in this vivid half-light: monstrous, a legendary apparition. But this was an apparition made of solid flesh and bone, and one that could fight well. He held Dahl in a bear hug, exerting every ounce of pressure on the Swede. Neither man uttered a word or sound, but the silent struggle was immense. Mordant's face was set in a demonic rictus, a snarl of exertion.

Drake caught several blows on his elbows, more strikes with his thighs and knees. He stopped bone-breaking jabs with deft flicks of his wrist, glancing them away. But he couldn't get close to Gabriel, couldn't break down the man's defenses. Every new thing he tried, Gabriel countered. The two men were evenly matched.

It was only when Drake heard the arrival of the Americans that his spirits lifted. A wide grin stretched across his face in direct contrast to the crestfallen look that transformed Gabriel's. A moment later, the sound of ascending choppers turned the tables again. This place was about to go ballistic.

Fuck me, he thought. *Our arses are about to be lit up like Times Square and we've nowhere to bloody go.*

Dahl matched Mordant muscle to muscle, sinew to sinew. The battle of pure strength strained him to breaking point, but he was rewarded by the sight of the albino's ugly face stretched with agony, the red of his gums and eye sockets standing out like bright-red wounds.

"When you cringe like that," Dahl whispered. "Your face looks like it's turned inside out."

"Fuck." The albino crushed harder. "You."

"No," Dahl growled. "You killed Romero and maybe Hayden. *So fuck you!"*

With a bellow and an effort that almost burst his heart, Dahl somehow managed to lift Mordant off his feet. The albino gaped around, at a loss for the first time in his life, but even Dahl couldn't hold him for long. The Swede threw him to the ground and followed up with a colossal blow that would have broken some men in half. The albino gasped, but still managed to roll away. As Dahl lunged after him he spun back, swinging an arm, catching Dahl across the face. Blood poured from a fresh cut over his eyebrow.

"First bloo—" the albino started to say.

Dahl punched him in the mouth. Teeth flew and blood exploded. "You were saying?"

The albino struck again. Dahl took it squarely on the forehead, using the precious seconds to get up close to his enemy.

"Jesus fuck," the man gasped at him. "You are one mean mother."

Dahl jabbed him twice, following it up with a punch to the ribs. A sharp crack made him smile tightly. "Stop talking," he said. "You aren't good enough."

Mordant jackknifed his body, squirming far enough away to make a gap. Dahl followed relentlessly. When the albino feinted and suddenly came in close, Dahl knew what was coming. Many prisoners used the forehead to get ahead. When Mordant's forehead dipped, Dahl's elbow came up simultaneously, purposely positioned slightly lower.

Mordant's nose exploded against his sharp bone.

"Aaahhh!"

Dahl sat back. His body was exhausted, screaming for a moment's respite, which he was smart enough to allow. When Mordant also sat back, the two enemies faced each other in the heat of battle, their own blood and sweat coating the ground between them, and the prison fighter inclined his head.

"Not bad for an Englishman."

Dahl roared, "I'm not bloody English," sprang to his feet and leaped forward. His huge hands grabbed hold of Mordant's jacket and shoved him hard down to the floor. Dahl heaved his tired body on top, pushing his knee against Mordant's throat and bringing all his weight to bear. The albino struggled weakly, unable to breathe.

When it was over, Dahl cast around. "All right. Who wants to go next?"

Drake pushed Gabriel away and threw himself against a wall as the first chopper thundered overhead. A double line of shells strafed the ground. The bullets passed through the approaching American forces, the castle walls, the burning helicopter, and the Blood King's own men, but didn't strike a soul. Kovalenko was on his knees, cowering before Alicia, and, though it was a simple sight, Drake's soul soared.

"Your boss," Drake panted. "Is beaten."

Gabriel shrugged. "Never trust a fookin' Russkie, mon. Never trust anyone. There ain't no good men left no more."

Drake smiled as he felt familiar presences at his back. "I wouldn't say that," he said. "You just have to belong to the right family."

Kinimaka struck from the left, Komodo from the right. Drake took a breath and allowed Smyth to skip by him and assault Gabriel head on. The wiry African traded the three men blow for blow; he drew blood from Komodo's nose and Kinimaka's cheek, but was always on the back foot, always wilting. In minutes he was on his knees, still fighting hard, taking crushing blows and coming back for more. He fell at last when Kovalenko's second chopper blasted overhead, the stream of bullets actually passing through the middle of his body.

"Shit." Smyth jumped away. "Thought the bastard was never going down."

Drake regarded the twitching body with respect. "Truth be told, I don't think he was. Bloody hell, I feel like one gigantic bruise."

Smyth squinted at him. "Your lip is puffing up a bit."

Drake jerked his head back in shock. "Was that a *joke?* Whoa, Smyth, watch it. We're gonna start thinking the Koreans replaced you with a robot, mate."

There was no time for a rejoinder as the choppers swooped back around. Then several things happened all at once. The American marine commander appeared through the black smoke, screaming at Drake's team to take cover. Something big was coming. The Blood King's helicopter team opened fire again; bullets thwacked off stone and dirt, and whickered through the heavy, menacing air. Kovalenko rose like an avenging demon, using the last of his strength to push Alicia aside and make a beeline toward Drake.

The supersonic roar of a jet-fighter, a Raptor, boomed like God's own thunder across the valley, shaking the very mountains. With a whoosh like an ocean boiling, the first missile was loosed, scoring a direct hit on the first chopper, causing a mid-air explosion. The second missile destroyed the second chopper a moment later; fire, machinery, flesh and bone thrown skyward and straight down to the ground.

Drake suddenly found himself in a hellfire battle. Charred

bodies and burning chunks of metal rained down all around him and his team. Boulder-sized chunks of jagged metal delved into the earth. A huge intact rotor blade slammed against the tiled roof directly above them and started to slide down, still spinning faster than the eye could follow.

"Move!"

Drake hurled his battered body from under the roof, dragging Komodo with him. Alicia and Dahl hurtled clear. The Blood King slipped and fell, directly in the path of the onrushing rotor blade.

At the last second, Smyth audibly cursed, reached down and scooped Kovalenko up; the Delta man running and dodging deadly debris, all but dragging the Blood King with him. The rotor smashed into the ground, crunching its blades. Deadly shards sheared away in the collision. Drake heard the sonic boom of the Raptors coming around and the shouts of the American commander to say all was well on the ground.

All's well? Are you fucking kidding me?

Drake looked up, still dodging and ducking as death rained from the skies. The bulk of both choppers now crashed down into the courtyard with an almighty noise, not exploding but sending out another wave of compressed machine and body parts.

Drake staggered as the shockwave struck, shielding his face with his arm and turning away. Something hard glanced off his Kevlar vest, leaving yet another bruise; something soft and wet collided with his leg. He didn't look down. A spray of tiny objects spattered past, at last leaving a vacuum in their wake.

Only a burning hell remained, but it was now a safer hell. Drake turned to see where Smyth and the Blood King had landed.

"Looks like you got to the gates of Hell twice, Kovalenko."

The Blood King grinned back at him.

"Which one of you assholes dies first, hey?"

CHAPTER FORTY NINE

Drake goggled and listened to the rest of the team's simultaneous curses. Somehow the Blood King had wrenched away from Smyth, found a pistol, and was now holding it against the soldier's head. His body was almost entirely concealed by Smyth's bulk and he had positioned his back against a soot-smeared, half-crumbled wall.

Drake let out a long breath. "Jesus Christ, Kovalenko, don't you know when you should just *die?"*

"Death does not scare me."

Alicia came to stand beside Drake. "It's over," she said with an uncharacteristic softness in her voice. "You are well and truly done."

"Perhaps. But my Vendetta will live on. I take as many of you with me as I can, and then *she* will—"

The Raptor boomed overhead for the last time, drowning out Kovalenko's next words.

Drake met Smyth's eyes. The soldier was ready for any instruction, letting his body stay relaxed and loose. The gun barrel wavered not an inch from his right eye. It was going to be almost impossible to save Smyth's life.

Kinimaka whispered from the rear. "I have the bastard in my sights."

The approaching army ground to a stop as its commander saw the situation. The man crouched and waved some of his men forward. Each one took careful aim. The commander spoke quietly into his comms.

The crackling of many fires, the groans of injured men, and the soft warping of overheated metal were the only sounds. The castle was lit by a silvery moon and savage flame. Once more, time stood still.

Drake took a step forward.

"You have done enough damage. Kovalenko, your name will become the staple word for dishonor. For infamy. Your fame? It will be meaningless."

"You think I did it all for fame?"

"Course you did," Alicia said. "You're a damn psycho bird."

"And I had plan for you, Myles. A great one. You were to be my masterpiece. I would take you and break you. Lock you away in dark place for many years. And when hardships of my life got me down, I would look at what you once were, and what you had become. A broken shell. You would have been my object lesson, the example for any future potential traitors."

Alicia looked sideways at Drake. "He really has to die."

"Wow, I'd almost forgotten you used to work for this freak. You didn't . . .?" Drake raised an eyebrow suggestively.

"I worked for him for a couple of hours." Alicia sniffed. "Doesn't really count. And *no!* I don't shag everyone I work for, you know."

Drake grunted. "I bloody well hope not. We're working for the President right now."

All the while the two were drifting closer.

"Stop!" Kovalenko cried. "Stop with that moving right now! You think I am stupid? Eh?"

Alicia was in the middle of a dirty laugh. "C'mon BK. I'm in the middle of a fantasy about the Oval Office here."

Then Drake suddenly did stop. A thought had occurred to him, one both the SPEAR team and the American government really needed an answer to.

"Someone helped you secure that drone, Kovalenko. Give us a clue."

The Blood King took a moment to decipher Drake's accent,

then smiled slyly. "A new player has entered the game. And with a plan even I found intriguing. Unfortunately though," he grunted, "I can't join the New Order or the quest for Pandora."

Drake thought about that as his feet inched forward again.

Kovalenko ground the barrel of the gun into Smyth's temple. When blood began to flow, both Drake and Alicia stopped. They had drawn their guns and were mere feet away.

"Who dies?" Drake whispered hotly. "Live or die, Kovalenko. Who lives or dies today?"

The Blood King sneered. His finger tightened on the trigger. Drake felt his own finger pulling back. Smyth closed his eyes.

The world paused.

The gunshot, when it came, startled everyone. The noise was a harsh explosion that destroyed the menacing silence. Karin screamed. The marine commander let out a loud curse. Kinimaka fell to his knees in exhausted acceptance.

"Oh no."

Smyth slumped to the side. Drake reacted instantly, shouting abuse at the Blood King. His finger was a hair's breadth from discharging the bullet.

The Blood King stared back at him stupidly, shocked. No bullet his come from his gun.

Drake felt shock hit him like a blazing RPG. *The shot hadn't come from Kovalenko's gun!*

In fact, it hadn't come at all. Smyth's eyes suddenly flew open, his face twisting into a stupid grin. In that instant Drake knew the noise had come from Smyth's authentic sounding gunshot message tone, and he absolutely knew who the sender was.

Mai! She had saved Smyth's life and served the Blood King up on a platter all the way from Tokyo.

Now *that* was legendary.

Drake fired, shooting the gun out of Kovalenko's hand.

Alicia sent the next one through his collarbone. Two more came from the marines, the first blasting half his thigh away, the next hitting below the hip. The man slumped. Smyth scrambled away. Drake stooped and hauled Kovalenko up as blood fountained high from the major artery in his thigh, a fitting spectacle for a man with so much red on his hands.

Kinimaka rose to his feet. "Fuck this shit, I'm calling the hospital."

"That message?" Drake nodded to Smyth. "You should friggin' frame it. Saved your life."

"I know."

Drake crouched down and took hold of the Blood King's heavy jacket. "God, I hope you're not dead yet," he said.

Consciousness still swam in the Blood King's eyes. That, and a little bit of disbelief, a ton of hatred and hostility, and beneath it all—still a terrible unyielding purpose.

"Just this once," Drake said point-blank into his face. "I hope there is a hell and the Devil makes you his bitch."

"Not . . . over." Kovalenko faltered. "On my . . . death. *She* alone finishes the Vendetta."

Drake pulled back. "What?"

"Goodbye. I will see you in Hell soon enough."

Drake shook the man hard. Kovalenko's eyes closed as his blood gushed into the sand. Drake cursed and shook him again, slapped his face. He couldn't believe that *now* he was trying to keep the Blood King alive.

Alicia placed a hand on his shoulder. "He's gone. Thank God."

"No," Drake said. He slapped Kovalenko again. "You didn't hear—"

The Blood King's eyes opened wide. He took a deep rasping breath. "If I see any of your dead friends on my travels," he rasped. "I'll be sure to fuck them up."

Drake's jaw locked. He couldn't speak. How could so much hatred and enmity come from one mind? Even in death.

"She will come for you," Kovalenko said quite clearly. "You see, Zoya gave me her details. Now Coyote will fulfill the Vendetta."

Drake didn't know whether to be happy or sad. There were many pros and cons swirling around any new contact with the Coyote. "We will stand together," he said. "She is but one person. We are a family."

"Not with the plan she made." The Blood King let out a final death rattle. "The Kitano woman. Myles. The Swede. And you, Drake. You four will have to kill *each other.*"

Then he died.

CHAPTER FIFTY

Mai caught up with Hibiki near the bright sprawling Sony stand. There the sheer volume of people would make it very difficult for anyone to keep track of her. The charade with Hikaru would give her a few hours grace, no more. Hopefully the Clan were still egotistical enough to assume she would carry out their every order. If they weren't, and they were here, she had a plan B for that too.

Mai pushed her way into the crowd. Hibiki was leaning over a PS4. "Did you get what you needed?"

Mai gave him a look.

"Sorry. Of course you did. Silly of me to ask. So it's time to light the fire?"

Mai dragged him away from the new console and toward the exit door. "Light the fire. Call the boys. Ready the men, we'll be going in hard, dirty and hot."

"Sometimes I forget how much fun working with you can be."

Mai paused as they entered the Tokyo sunshine. She dug out her phone and sent a quick text off to Gyuki.

It's done. I will wait to hear from you.

As she started to walk away, she remembered the picture Hibiki had taken earlier, the one she wanted to tease Smyth with. She lined the message up. With her finger on the send button she suddenly paused.

Tease? Really?

No, not really. She just wanted to make his day. She felt sorry for the hot-tempered soldier and even more so now that his pal, Romero, was dead. She didn't love Drake any less, but she was still her own woman and would do some things as she fancied.

Decision made, she hit the send button.

Job done. Hope it helps.

Hibiki walked away from her. Mai flagged down a taxi and gave the driver an area outside Tokyo to start with. Once there, she would refine the directions. Hibiki and her old friends—the guys from the agency who still cared for her and wanted to see this thing through to the very end—would be following.

Mai relaxed as the taxi negotiated the strangled roads of central Tokyo. It took over an hour to gain the countryside, and by that time she had switched off her phone and was able to immerse herself in a clear stream of thoughts, all the way down to her core.

A bitter homecoming to be sure. The fight of her life, and something she had to see through if she was ever going to break free of her bonds, both mental and physical. Memories of that far gone day still came at her like killers ambushing her in a thick jungle. Hellish memories.

The old man smiles as he comes to take me away. The generous benefactor. The predator.

I whirl, turn back to my mother and see the tears washing down from her eyes.

The old man peels me away, hands like sandpaper. I strain every ounce of my body towards my parents as I'm dragged away.

The emptiness. The longing. The new broken thing that aches inside my body. And then . . .

. . . and then—the forgetting.

The old man, Bishamon, and Gyuki in particular had to pay for the atrocities they had committed in this country, at the clan home and around the world. The innocent victims, those still living and those long dead, needed some kind of recompense.

Mai paid the taxi driver and sent him on his way. By her

judgment, she was about two miles away from the village. The woods looked inviting, and Mai followed the gentle curve of a trickling brook, enjoying the dappling of sunlight on her face and the fresh scented breeze. Without dawdling, she used the journey to still the center of her being and to cleanse her soul. Her passage disturbed several animals, rabbits, mice, rats. She saw them all. Her concentration levels had never been higher.

The tree line ended up against a rough wooden fence. Beyond that, Mai saw the village as she had seen it recently, and long ago. It had barely changed, the only additions being the extra billet and the jail. She could hear the sound of chanting and assumed most of the 'students' were sitting around the fighting arena, watching bouts and demonstrations given by the masters. Mai touched the crude fence and pulled some stakes from the ground. She ducked through the gap, feeling the soft forest loam give beneath her shoes. She took a last look up at the clear blue skies.

This could be the last time she breathed freely. Or breathed at all. She had enjoyed the operation at the Game Show. She had enjoyed the attention. She loved the attention that Smyth gave her, and especially Drake.

Because it made her feel alive. And free.

Free. And if I lose my freedom I will find a way to die. Today.

Mai crossed the open grassland, stopping only when she came up against the second long billet. She risked a peek through a nearby window. The long hall was empty, the beds neatly made, the floors swept and washed. She could use this wall to mask her progress to the top end of the village. It might be useful to let Hibiki know her plan, but she had turned her phone off.

Never mind. He's clever enough to figure it out. She hoped so. If not for her sake or for his, then for Chika's.

Mai raced ahead. She reached the top end of the billet in seconds and peered around its ragged edge. The logs it was made of smelled earthy and damp. Across the way stood the small dwellings of the clan chiefs, and past them the low prison building. Almost directly ahead stood the ornate temple, Bishamon's lair, but standing before it now was something completely new.

A thick pole, dug and hammered into the ground, and tied to it a figure wrapped in a ragged assortment of dirty clothes, head hanging and seemingly left to rot.

Mai felt a jolt of dreadful memory strike her. It was as if the clock had turned back two decades and more. The person tied to the pole could have been her, many years ago. That person, she knew from experience, had somehow insulted the Clan. Maybe they had refused orders or struck a colleague out of turn. Maybe they had not listened hard enough. Maybe, if it was a girl, they had refused Gyuki's nightmare offer.

I will fight you for your body. Winner takes all.

Now Mai felt rage rise like molten magma. The eruption was about to hit, and it would raze this village to the ground.

She launched herself forward, taking no chances and ignoring the tied body for now. Her timing was perfect. Shouts sprang up from the fighting square, shouts which signified Hibiki's arrival. Mai cleared the temple steps in a single bound and yanked down on the heavy door handle. She pushed and a wedge of darkness was revealed, a path to the inner demon. Mai took the invite and stepped inside, letting her eyes grow accustomed to the gloom. The wooden floor was highly polished and bordered by a square of flickering candles.

Bishamon's voice rang out hard and cold. "Remove your shoes before entering the temple of the Tsugarai."

"I am here for my parents. And for you too. If you want my shoes . . . you come and take them."

Bishamon rose to his feet, now an old man with long straggling hair and brown wrinkled skin. Mai saw no change in his physical appearance. It was his attitude toward her that was now out in the open. Before, he had always been the kindly granddad, the accommodating benefactor.

"Then you will die today, Mai Kitano."

"Oh, how you have changed. Oh, how my clear understanding now makes your true colors shine through. The deeds you do are steeped in evil, old Master. The Devil will judge *you.*"

"How dare you?" Bishamon spluttered, coming across the candlelit square. As he walked, his robes flapped around his bare scrawny ankles, and white spittle flew from his chapped lips. "History has already judged me. I am seventy years old. Did God strike me down? No. Did the Devil send his Grim Reaper? No. My boot heels grind bone when they pass through forest and dojo and city street, Mai Kitano. That is the way of masters."

"You are no God, Bishamon. Just a pitiless, loveless, bitter old man. The world will not miss you nor ever remember you."

"Be as it may," Bishamon whispered. "I will have your shoes. One way . . . or another."

Mai had known she would be wasting her time, but she had to try. She would not hurt this man without an offer of repentance, no matter the suffering he had sanctioned. But now that offer was past its expiration date.

"For what you did to me. For what you made me. For the childhood you stole from an eight-year-old girl. For the love you ripped from my arms forever. I give you . . . this."

And she leaped like a lion, a tiger, a vengeful warrior of legend; faster than even the old master's eye could follow. Her flying kick took her across the flickering candles, across the polished square, finishing when the toe of her lead foot smashed Bishamon's windpipe into pulp. The old master's hands flew up, but he was already falling, already choking, already dead.

Mai spat on his cooling corpse.

"For all the innocence you have ever destroyed. For all the pure children you have corrupted. You will never get the chance again."

And then she turned away, tears falling like rain from her eyes. Vengeance was never pretty, and it was hardly ever fulfilling. It never achieved its purpose, never reclaimed the things you had lost. But it was all she could take, and this entire mission had been about achieving it.

She kicked over all the candles and watched the floor set alight. She turned as if in a dream and walked over to the doors. She left the temple behind, a bad memory, her past finally overcome, avenged and erased.

Outside, the scene had changed. The body was still tied to the pole, but beyond it the village arena was in uproar. Hibiki had brought the boys all right, and every one of them was tooled up to the max, fully-vested even as far as face masks, and all were aware that even one of these tricky little Ninja warriors could take out a dozen men. Guns were trained on the students and their chiefs with unwavering dedication, primed to fire, and the highly trained professionalism of the Japanese special agency shone through.

Off the books mission, my ass, Mai thought. Seeing this, it was clear that Hibiki had offered the big dogs the Tsugarai, and they had chomped off not only his hand but his entire arm. But they still couldn't have done it without her.

Or the sad death of a father and money launderer called Hayami.

Mai's attention receded as the body tied to the pole struggled. It was time now for Mai to confront the younger version of herself and hope this person had not been corrupted beyond saving. She moved around the pole.

"Hi. You're safe now. It's over."

The face came up, clearly Japanese and covered in dirt, blood and streaks of sweat. The black hair was matted, clumpy and stuck to the sides of her face. She looked to be young, maybe eighteen or nineteen, and the look of hope which totally transformed her face lifted the shackles from Mai's heavy heart.

"What's your name, pretty one?"

"I am Grace. It's Grace. But—"

Mai had questions, but didn't want to ask them here. The sooner they got the victims away from this place, the sooner they could start to heal. "We'll talk," she said. "Later."

"Look out!"

The shriek saved her life, but it wasn't just the scream, it was the raw, unadulterated terror behind it. The hammered-in mortal fear that the attacker inspired.

Gyuki came at Mai with everything he had: punching, kicking, spinning and leg-sweeping. Mai took two heavy blows in the first four seconds and found herself reaching for that calm spring inside which focused her being. What she needed was something to give Gyuki pause, to make him doubt. He truly believed, possibly correctly, that he was the world's greatest warrior. A man like that could win with brash confidence alone, but he could be shattered to a shadow of himself if he was made to sense doubt.

Mai spun away. "Bishamon is dead," she breathed. "What will you do now?"

Gyuki flicked a glance at the burning temple. "I will survive."

"The outside world will not accept a man like you."

"It will have to."

Gyuki sprang, executing a double front-kick. Mai caught both strikes on the palms of her hands and skipped back. Gyuki came in low, spinning and sweeping, but Mai hopped over the extended leg and came down hard as it flashed by.

The sole of her boot smashed his knee, drawing out a grimace of pain. Mai grinned. "I am better than you now. The best. Haven't you heard?"

Gyuki suddenly stopped in his tracks, surprising her. "So you have accepted the invite?"

Mai narrowed her eyes in utter confused. "What?"

"You have accepted?"

"I don't know what you're talking about."

"This proposed tournament in the UK. It is all everyone talks about. Even the Clan received an invite. For me, of course. I will go. Some of the greatest warriors, fighters and military people on the planet are taking part. Others," he eyed Mai speculatively, "Are not being given any choice."

Mai shook her head in bemusement. "Assembled by who?"

"A woman." Gyuki put two fingers to his lips and blew a kiss. "Sugary sweet, with a voice I'd like to fuck. That is all I know."

A shot rang out in the square behind Mai. Her attention was diverted, now fearing for Hibiki and his men. Gyuki used the distraction to fly at her. She dodged, spinning twice, but missed with her follow-up. Gyuki crouched with one hand on the ground, a black viper sizing her up and waiting to strike.

Mai advanced. The roped girl, Grace, moaned as Gyuki's eyes passed over her. It was only now that Mai noticed her bare legs and midriff. She shuddered, hoping she had made it in time.

"What do you say, Mai?" Gyuki hissed. "I'll fight you for your body, and hers. Winner takes all."

"This time I will take your body. And neither your bitch of a mother nor your closest cohorts will recognize its remains."

Gyuki struck out. Mai ducked, weaved, and hit hard. She caught a nasty blow on the ear, another to the ribs. Gyuki moved in and tried to grab her waist for a throw, but his hand slipped down the seat of her leather trousers.

Unbalanced, he staggered.

Mai pounced instantly, recognizing his mistake, the only one he was ever likely to make. Four lightning-fast blows in less than a second smashed his windpipe, his right eardrum, his left eye and at least one testicle. Gyuki was out of the fight before his head hit the dirt.

The girl, Grace, goggled at Mai. "Oh God, you're my hero. My true hero! I love you."

"Even more than Miley?" Mai winked. She kept up with the times.

"Are you kidding? Twerking's way out of style."

"Or is it the camel tongue hanging down the side of her face?"

Grace laughed with high-pitched enthusiasm. "That's it! The camel tongue!"

Mai lost her smile. "You have been abducted recently? Yes?"

"I think so." Grace looked around at the heavy ropes entwining her body. "Can you get me down from here?"

"Sorry. Of course." Mai pulled at the knots, wondering if the Clan had recently taken to kidnap and coercion. Branching out. That was probably the reason for the second billet. More assassins meant more money. After a moment, Grace was free and standing over Gyuki's broken body.

"Can I kill him?"

Mai studied the girl's eyes. "Do you want to?"

"I think so." Grace turned to Mai, anguish in her face. "That's wrong isn't it? I didn't use to have those feelings. Not before I came here."

"How about this," Mai spoke softly. *"Could* you kill him?"

Grace returned her gaze to the fallen assassin. "Yes. I could break his neck with my boot. Stab out his eyes with my fingers. Choke him up close. Strangle him with the rope he used on me. Force its knotted end down his throat until . . ."

"That's enough." Mai pulled her away. "He won't harm anyone again. Come with me."

With a brief check to reassure herself that Hibiki had the situation in hand, Mai led Grace over to the small wooden house where the Clan had practically imprisoned her parents.

"Sometimes things do have a happy ending," she said with her hand on the door. "Even if it does take twenty years."

For Mai, this homecoming had become very sweet. The things she had said to Bishamon, the words that had torn apart her heart, the undying knowledge that her innocent childhood and all the love shared between a young girl and her parents had been torn to shreds, dissipated a little now.

And, for the first time she could remember, it totally vanished as she stepped through the door and into the open, loving arms of her parents.

CHAPTER FIFTY ONE

Days later, and the entire SPEAR team, or what remained of it, were finally back together.

Drake perched on the wide lip of a windowsill in the Presidential Suite of the Hotel Dillion, at the heart of what was now a slowly recovering city. The view of the White House behind him was spectacular, but he didn't have the energy to even register it, let alone turn around and endure the jabbing pains of a thousand new bruises just to look at it.

Kovalenko was dead, at last. So were his horrifying lieutenants, Mordant and Gabriel. The world had shifted again, back into the safe zone, at least for now. The only two members of the Blood King's team who hadn't been picked up were the rogue Secret Service agent, Marnich, and the cyber-geek, SaBo. It was assumed Kovalenko had paid the men off long before arriving at Death Valley. The hunt for Marnich and SaBo would be intensive to say the least.

Drake's friends, his co-workers, but most important of all—his family—were spread out all around him. They were picking and grazing at the spread that all but covered an immense table and even part of the floor. They were knocking back shots, mixing cocktails, brewing coffee. A crate of Mountain Dew sat near the door, a sight that somehow sadly brought the murder of Ben Blake nearer to the center point of Drake's mind. The entire group was convalescing, recovering, grieving, readjusting. If there was laughter it was subdued.

President Coburn had called personally to assure them that the SPEAR agency would not be axed; that it would remain safe for now at least until the next Secretary of Defense took up his post, and even then the President vowed to 'strongly recommend' that it stayed. Their track record was exemplary, and without peer, even before they had saved the President's life.

But it would never be the same.

Alicia caught Drake's eye first. Considering all she'd been through, she looked fresh and clean. But no soap or fountain of water, no cleansing of the soul, would ever take away the horror of what had been done to her and her new friends. Laid-Back Lex complained about the freshness of a peach, Dirty Sarah and Whipper whispered about splitting the fruit in half with the latter's weapon of choice—the closer to Lex's mouth the better. Trace, Ribeye and Knuckler tucked into a hearty liquid lunch. Alicia sat among them, watching them and watching Drake. *Will I ever be able to move on? It seems the scars of my life will hound and restrain me forever.*

Komodo and Karin held on to each other as if this was their last night on earth. Karin would have to return to the UK soon for her family's funerals, but had insisted that she would return on the first flight. Her family was here now. It was Komodo, and it was SPEAR.

Dahl's family were on their way to the States. Drake was looking forward to meeting them, and perhaps ribbing Dahl a little about his wife. Smyth was little different, but had proved himself an invaluable member of the team. He missed his buddy Romero every single day.

Next Drake's eye switched to Mano Kinimaka. The big Hawaiian had lost so much in the last few days, sacrificed a great deal of what he loved to the Blood King's insanity. The road back would be a long and dark one for him, but he was a strong man, a strong personality, and about as big as Mount Whitney. He met Drake's gaze, sad, melancholy . . .

. . . hopeful.

Hayden lay beside him on the sofa, using it as a makeshift

hospital bed, alive and recovering from her wounds and recent surgeries. It would take a while, but the boss of the SPEAR team was expected to make a full recovery. Drake's heart had lifted on wings of eagles when he had heard. It was like seeing the light at the end of the tunnel, and a kind of vindication that all they had done was justified.

Also beside Mano, and keeping to themselves for now, were Lauren Fox, Yorgi and Sarah Moxley. Their parts were yet to come, it seemed, but there was no doubt they would be called upon. And on that day they would earn their wings or they would flee; or die.

And finally, there was Mai. Seated beside the bruised and battered woman was a figure who could easily have been a younger version of herself. Mai had said her name was Grace, and that she needed help. That was all for now. And it was enough. The rest would come later.

Drake had already heard part of the story about the Tokyo Game Show and the Coscon. He had read part of what had happened on the Internet. The Yakuza boss had first been seduced, tricked, and then persuaded to fake his own death. And all for a pretty face and a lethal high-kick. Already another legend in the making.

He hugged her close and buried his face in her neck. The scent of her was breathtaking. "No matter what," he murmured for her ears alone. "No matter what happens tomorrow, or next week, or next year. I will always love you. I always have."

"So you two are together?" Grace blurted. "That's awesome! Sorry, I wasn't really listening. It's just my ears. They were trained by *ninjas!*" She burst out laughing and threw her head back, showing teeth.

Drake made a face at Mai. "Can we handle her?"

"Ach. Just imagine it's Alicia without the sluttiness."

Drake laughed.

Alicia poked her head above shoulder level. "I heard that, little Sprite."

"Oh, I know. *Taz!*"

Alicia was up on her feet in an instant. "Who told you about that?" She glared hard at the bikers. "C'mon, which one of you leatherheads is gonna take a beating?"

Trace, the youngest, gave her a sad smile. "I think it was Lomas."

Alicia deflated immediately. Drake took in the mood of the group and followed his heart. He stood up, lifting a half-full can of soda.

"A salute," he said. "Let's raise a glass to those we will always miss. Let's honor their deeds by drinking to their memory. And let's keep their memories because they can't. To our family, gone but never forgotten."

"To Jonathan." Hayden lifted her arm.

"To my mother." Kinimaka wiped the tears away.

"To Ben," Karin said. "And my mum and dad."

"To Romero." Smyth licked his lips.

"To Lomas," Alicia whispered, and the rest of the bikers named the others who had died.

"To Sam and Jo," Drake said, and drank deeply.

Throughout the silence that followed, the fallen were remembered and celebrated. Those that remained lived on for the dead, carrying their deeds, hopes and dreams with them; a shining talisman, because in our hearts and memories our departed loved ones live forever.

THE END

<u>Please read on for more information about the future of the Matt Drake series and a FREE and exclusive Matt Drake short story:</u>

Well, I raised a glass to those we will never see again. I hope you join the team and me, and do the same. It probably goes without saying, but this was a hard book to write. Several times I found myself having to stop writing and walk away to detach myself from the emotion of it all. Many times, I almost changed some of the events. At least once, I did. I hope you enjoyed the finished product. It is all part of the constantly evolving world of Matt Drake and the SPEAR team.

Matt Drake 8—Last Man Standing will bring to a climax the story surrounding Drake and the Coyote. Hopefully available around June/July 2014, but all the up-to-date information can be found on my website. If anything changes, and for all future updates, check it out. After Drake 8 a brand new phase will begin.

LAST MAN STANDING

'Dragged into a terrible war game, Matt Drake, Mai Kitano, Alicia Myles and Torsten Dahl must take on the world's greatest warriors, and then the master assassin, Coyote, in their deadliest battle yet.

A momentous tournament has been arranged, a sleepy town chosen as its unwitting venue. The competitors are armed to the teeth, out to kill, and fighting for the biggest prize of their lives.'

And now, to my loyal readers (I figure you have to be loyal if you've stayed with me this far!) I would like to offer a ***FREE*** Matt Drake short story. It's the action-packed tale of how Drake met Alicia all those years ago whilst fighting off a militant army in Africa, and is called *THE NINTH DIVISION*. Within its pages, and if read in conjunction with Blood Vengeance, you may learn the identity of Coyote before anyone else . . .

To download the short story for your Kindle simply e-mail me at davidleadbeater2011@hotmail.co.uk
I will send you the story as an attachment and instructions on how to download it to your Kindle. The e-mail address is also posted on my website:
www.davidleadbeater.com

Printed in Great Britain
by Amazon